MW01127588

Wrapped
in
LVE

Wrapped in LOVE

Evelyn,
Sometimes wishes
do come true!
XOXO,

New York Times Bestselling Author
LEXI RYAN

Lexi Ryan

Wrapped in Love © 2018 by Lexi Ryan

All rights reserved. This copy is intended for the original purchaser of this book. No part of this book may be reproduced, scanned, or distributed in any printed or electronic form without prior written permission from the author except by reviewers, who may quote brief excerpts in connection with a review. Please do not participate in or encourage piracy of copyrighted materials in violation of the author's rights. Purchase only authorized editions.

This book is a work of fiction. Any resemblance to institutions or persons, living or dead, is used fictitiously or purely coincidental.

Cover and cover image © 2018 by Sara Eirew
Interior designed and formatted by

emtippettsbookdesigns.com

Other Books by
LEXI RYAN

The Boys of Jackson Harbor
The Wrong Kind of Love (Ethan's story)
Straight Up Love (Jake's story)
Dirty, Reckless Love (Levi's story)
Wrapped in Love (Brayden's story)
Crazy for Your Love (Carter's story) – *coming spring 2019*
If It's Only Love (Shay's story) – *coming summer 2019*

The Blackhawk Boys
Spinning Out (Arrow's story)
Rushing In (Chris's story)
Going Under (Sebastian's story)
Falling Hard (Keegan's story)
In Too Deep (Mason's story)

LOVE UNBOUND: Four series, one small town, lots of happy endings

Splintered Hearts (A Love Unbound Series)
Unbreak Me (Maggie's story)
Stolen Wishes: A Wish I May Prequel Novella (Will and Cally's prequel)
Wish I May (Will and Cally's novel)
Or read them together in the omnibus edition, *Splintered Hearts: The New Hope Trilogy*

Here and Now (A Love Unbound Series)
Lost in Me (Hanna's story begins)
Fall to You (Hanna's story continues)
All for This (Hanna's story concludes)
Or read them together in the omnibus edition, *Here and Now: The Complete Series*

Reckless and Real (A Love Unbound Series)
Something Wild (Liz and Sam's story begins)
Something Reckless (Liz and Sam's story continues)
Something Real (Liz and Sam's story concludes)
Or read them together in the omnibus edition, *Reckless and Real: The Complete Series*

Mended Hearts (A Love Unbound Series)
Playing with Fire (Nix's story)
Holding Her Close (Janelle and Cade's story)

OTHER TITLES

Hot Contemporary Romance
Text Appeal
Accidental Sex Goddess

Decadence Creek (Short and Sexy Romance)
Just One Night
Just the Way You Are

ABOUT
Wrapped in LOVE

A one-night stand with the boss was never in her plans. Neither was falling in love . . .

The rumors are true. I'm a hot mess with an awful track record at love. Single mom. Down on her luck. Yeah, I'm bad news.

If the hardest part of moving back home to Jackson Harbor was going to be people talking, I'd be fine. I've kept my chin up through worse than their decade-old gossip.

I was wrong. The hardest part is resisting my boss. Brayden Jackson is the very picture of tall, dark, and handsome. And thanks to an ill-advised one-night stand we had seven months ago, I know exactly what I'm missing when I turn him down. Every. Single. Delicious. Inch.

But I have my son to care for and my job to keep, so I'll keep on saying no.

Until my string of bad luck continues, and suddenly my precious four-year-old and I find ourselves with nowhere to live. At Christmas, no less. It's for my son that I accept Brayden's offer to stay at his place. One by one, my defenses are falling, as fast as

I am. If Brayden was smart, he'd run, because it's only a matter of time before he realizes he deserves better than what a girl like me can offer.

Unless, for once, my bad luck is leading me exactly where I need to be.

For Miss Mary. To the moon and back, baby girl.

prologue

MOLLY

I open my eyes and find myself in a warm tangle of limbs and sheets.

When can I see you again?

He asked the question as I was falling into a deep sleep. In my state of postcoital bliss, the words made me smile. I hummed a non-answer and let him hold me in his arms as sleep pulled me under.

I feel so secure and comforted by the heat of him wrapped around me. I don't want to move, but I can't stay. Those words echo in my head. *When can I see you again?*

Now that I'm no longer drunk on pleasure or delirious from multiple orgasms, the question thrills and terrifies me. I wish I were someone else. I wish I could make promises and take chances. But I'm not. I have secrets and priorities that have

1

everything to do with the little boy sleeping at my best friend's house. Brayden can't know about Noah. No one can. But that doesn't change the fact that I don't want this night to end. Not yet.

The light slanting out from the bathroom door casts the hotel room in a warm glow just bright enough to allow me to see his face—the shadow of his thick stubble, the slight parting of his soft lips. His muscled arm is wrapped around me, his calloused hand on my hip, and the feel of his breath on my neck is so sweet that I want to close my eyes and savor this moment. But I can't. Because last night was a mistake. A terrible, rash, foolish, *delicious* mistake that I'll be thinking about for many lonely nights to come.

I slip out of his embrace and out of the king-size bed that sits in the middle of his swanky New York hotel room. My hands shake as I snatch my bra from the floor and slide it back on.

Slowly, cautiously, I turn to look at him one more time. His face is so soft—as if sleep vanquished the typical hard lines and stern face I always associate with Brayden Jackson. His cold demeanor never made an appearance tonight. We did a little official business, made a few of the introductions he came to make. But then we started drinking, and I caught him looking at my mouth. Suddenly, all-business Brayden was a thing of the past, a memory of a man I could have easily resisted as too serious, too uptight. But this sleeping Brayden? And the two-beers-in Brayden, whose mouth crooked into a lopsided smile when the bartender thought we were a couple? This Brayden Jackson would have taken a will of steel to resist—a will I hadn't known I'd need.

Tearing my eyes away from him, I scan the floor for my panties.

I swipe my foot along the side of the bed to see if I can feel them hiding under there. Where did I take them off? Images slam into me. *His thumbs hooking into the black lace. His hands dragging them down my hips. His mouth . . .*

I squeeze my eyes shut and turn toward the door, toward where I know I took off my dress. I slink into it and zip it without allowing myself to turn back. I need to walk out that door. If I look at his sculpted chest or the strong legs outlined under the sheets, I'm not sure I will. I know the delicious weight of that body on mine, how the faint stubble on his cheeks felt scraping against my neck, my breasts . . . *lower*. I know how those dark eyes made me melt a little inside.

I find my purse by the minibar and sling it over my shoulder. Pausing a beat with my hand on the doorknob, I pray he'll forgive me, pray he'll understand that I need this job and that last night was a mistake. As quietly as possible, I open the door, duck out into the hallway, and quickly walk away from my new boss and the hottest night of my life.

BRAYDEN

I reach for her in my sleep and find the bed empty beside me. I sit up. "Molly?" I click on the bedside light and scan the room. Her clothes are gone. So is her purse.

I rub my eyes. *Fuck, fuck, fuck.*

Snatching my jeans from the floor, I search the pockets for my phone. She's sent me a text.

> Molly: *Thank you for last night. You're a nice guy, but I want this job. I NEED this job. And that means it can't happen again.*

The clock by the bed says it's two a.m., but I text her back anyway.

> Me: *Your job is safe, whatever you decide. Last night doesn't have to mean anything you don't want it to mean.*

Putting the phone down, I drag a hand over my face and climb back into bed. *Shit.* I can't believe I didn't hear her leave. Did I say something to scare her off? Does she really think I'll fire her because of what happened?

My phone buzzes, and I lunge for it.

> Molly: *It was a mistake. I'm so sorry.*

I put my phone down and sit on the side of the bed, cradling my head in my hands. A mistake. If she was a mistake, she's the only mistake I've ever wanted to make.

One

MOLLY

Seven months later . . .

Top Three Reasons Not to Sleep with Your Boss:

Reason 1: Because no matter how good he looks in his business suit, you will always—*always*—be thinking about how good he looked sprawled out in the middle of that massive bed in his fancy hotel, one strong leg tangled in the sheets, his hot eyes never leaving you as you unhooked your bra.

Reason 2: When he's all serious about business and gets that intense look in his eyes, you'll imagine he's recounting that ill-advised night or brooding about how much he wants you. In reality, you killed that opportunity the minute you snuck out of his hotel room, and drove another nail into the coffin of your would-be affair when, in a desperate attempt to keep him at a distance, you accused him of only hiring you to get you in bed. *Real smooth.*

Reason 3 (as if there needs to be another): You're around him *a lot,* and though you're absolutely strong enough to resist the intense pull of sexual attraction, you're not sure how you're supposed to resist *him.* The way he values family above everything else. The way he rarely smiles, but when he does, it lights up his face first, then the whole damn room. The way he treats your little boy as if he's the most precious thing in the world. The way he makes you want things you believed you were okay with never having.

"Are you even listening to me?" Brayden asks, but I'm so hung up on Reason 1 and memories of his tanned skin against white sheets that I'm really *not* listening. At all.

I chew on the inside of my cheek and nod, digging through my mind to recall what made him approach my table at the back of Jackson Brews. "You don't like the shirts," I say, but I'm still so sucked in by the memory of his mouth on my neck that the words come out like a purr.

Brayden frowns. "You're not in *trouble,* Molly."

I shake my head, trying to snap out of it and more than a little grateful that he mistook my turned-on voice for insecurity. Reluctantly, I pull my gaze off Brayden and to the new Jackson Brews shirts on display at the far end of the bar—or what's left of them. They've been selling fast. "Levi approved them."

"Why did I think it was a good idea to let him do the marketing?" He glances around the bar, his eyes landing on each of the half-dozen staff members in their brand-new T-shirts. The Jackson Brews logo is on the front, and on the back, the new tagline my friends and I came up with while drinking on our last girls' night.

Jackson Brews
The bar. The beer. And . . . oh, Lord . . . the BROTHERS.

Levi thought it was hilarious. Jake just smirked and shrugged. Ethan rolled his eyes, and Carter grinned and gave me a little once-over that seemed to say, "You know it." I didn't think Brayden would *love* the design, but he tends to stay out of it when he disagrees with my executive decisions. *Not this time.*

"How do you think that shirt is going to make Nic and Ava feel?" he asks.

I snort. It's almost adorable that he thinks his brothers' significant others *wouldn't* like the shirts. As if they aren't proud as fuck of their hot Jackson men. "Who do you think helped me come up with the idea? They claimed the first shirts. Even Ellie got one." Ellie, who's currently *not* with Levi Jackson but is clearly in love with him. We all know they'll be back together for good any day now.

Brayden scowls. "You're kidding me."

I laugh. "It'll be okay." Then I make a rookie mistake—I reach out and squeeze his arm.

Christ. His biceps bunch beneath my hand. My life would be so much easier if this man weren't so dedicated to his morning workouts. It's just not fair. He runs a *brewery*, for heaven's sake.

When I worked for Brayden as his northeast territory sales manager, I put on ten pounds in the first two months. Everyone thinks it's the coolest job in the world—working for a growing craft brewery—but the reality is driving around to bars, drinking beer, and subsisting on greasy bar food while you try to get buyers to put Jackson Brews beer on their tap lists.

Somehow the Jackson brothers defy all odds. I think they have a genetic mutation that transforms beer into muscle mass. It's the only explanation.

Brayden should be soft and have a beer belly that hangs over the waistband of his pants. Instead, he's all hard lines and corded muscle. The only soft thing about Brayden is the look in his eyes when he talks about his family. And his face, the night we slept together.

A shiver races down my spine at the memory of dark eyes fixed on mine, hands stroking my curves with reverence, and his body, hot and attentive as he moved over me.

I bite back a moan. *This is why you don't sleep with your boss.*

"Is everything set for the Yuseki luncheon Thursday?"

I nod and pull my hand away. I should probably enforce a *don't touch the boss* rule. "Yep. Everything's good to go."

"Staffing's covered? The food's ordered? The hiccup with the linens is all resolved, and you've confirmed the headcount?"

I fold my arms. "I'm trying not to be insulted."

He rolls his shoulders back and exhales slowly. "Sorry. Old habits."

"You hired me so *I* could do this. Not so you could have another pile of tasks on your plate."

"I know. And I trust you."

"Then act like it," I say, my tone gentle. Giving up control doesn't come naturally to him, and despite what I said, I don't take it personally. His family's always giving him a hard time about how much trouble he has letting go, and he's nagged Levi as much about the taproom grand opening as he's nagged me about the banquet center. Hell, Levi probably has it way worse as the little brother.

From the moment I interviewed to work for Jackson Brews last spring, I've noticed how Brayden's siblings are always trying to get him to delegate more. His impulse to micromanage wasn't all that noticeable when I was working as a sales manager eight hundred miles away, but up close and personal, it's impossible to miss.

"You're as territorial with your business as Noah is with his Pokémon cards," I say.

Brayden's eyes warm at the mention of my son. "Where is the little rascal tonight?"

"Mom wanted to take him to the movies." Which means I have a kid-free night off work—a once-rare occasion that has become more commonplace now that I live in the same town as my mother. I put in another ten-hour day at the banquet center today, so I have every intention of using my free evening to drink a very tall beer and gorge myself on Jake Jackson's fried delicacies.

"How's everything working out with Veronica?"

I grin at the mention of my son's nanny, a woman with a newborn son of her own. "Noah loves her so much. And baby Jackson . . ." I shake my head. "Noah's newest mission is to convince me he needs a little brother of his own."

Brayden's brows shoot up into his hairline.

I roll my eyes. "Relax. This uterus is closed for business."

Of course, Brayden's brother Jake chooses that exact moment to appear at my table with my beer and food. His gaze shifts back and forth between me and his brother. "Is there a reason the two of you are discussing Molly's uterus?"

"Noah wants a baby brother." I snag the plate of fried goat cheese from his hands, unwilling to wait another minute for those sinful bits of honey-coated heaven. "It's not happening." I pop a piece into my mouth and moan. "How do you make these so damn good? Did you sell your soul to the devil, or what?"

Jake sighs. "Do you really want to know my secret to good food?"

"Here we go." Brayden groans, crossing his arms.

"No, seriously," Jake says.

I tilt my head to the side, considering the cost of this information. "Why do I feel like Eve being offered an apple?"

Jake wags a finger at me. "I don't try to make food low-fat or low-carb or low-sodium or low-anything. I just make food with fresh ingredients and let it be what it'll be."

"I'm proof of the consequences of that attitude." I frown down at my black skirt. Half of my other skirts don't fit, and this one has become my new favorite, since it's stretchy enough to make room for the added pounds. "At this point, I either have to give up bar food or buy a new wardrobe. And since I have a pathetic bank balance and expensive tastes"—I pop another piece into my mouth and close my eyes—"my diet starts tomorrow."

Jake gives me a hard look. "Listen, I know better than to tell a woman she doesn't need to lose weight—losing battle. But do me a favor and don't let Ava hear you talking about dieting, okay?"

I frown. Ava is Jake's wife and my stepsister. She's tiny and perfect and currently has the world's most adorable baby bump. The last thing she needs to worry about is her weight. "Why not?"

Jake shakes his head. "She's feeling frumpy. It doesn't help that one of the teenagers at the theater told her she was carrying the baby 'in her thighs.'"

I flinch. "Ouch."

Brayden scowls at his brother. "You don't actually let her believe that shit, do you?"

"*Let* her? As if I can control what she thinks?" Jake shakes his head. "Don't give me that look, Brayden. I tell my wife how beautiful she is every day, but apparently my opinion doesn't count." His huff expresses just how disgusted he is by *that*.

I bite back a laugh, and a super-awkward snort slips out. "Boys are so cute and clueless."

"Everything going okay with her otherwise, though? The baby's good?" Brayden asks.

Jake beams. "Regardless of what Ava seems to think about the way her body is changing, everything is going beautifully."

"Molly, there you are!"

Jake, Brayden, and I all turn to see the front door swing closed behind my landlord, Tom Eckles. He makes a beeline to my table, tracking snow in with every step.

"I was hoping I'd catch you here," Tom says. He drags a hand through his snow-speckled dark hair.

"I'd better get back to the bar," Jake says with a curt nod to Tom. I can tell by the change in his expression that he doesn't like my landlord. *Join the club.*

My gaze locks on Brayden in hopes that he might hear my silent plea not to leave me alone. It must work, because Brayden takes a seat in the booth across from me. "Hey, Tom," I say, wariness making my voice thin. "What's going on?"

11

Tom seemed like a nice enough guy when he coached the girls' volleyball team in high school. And he seemed like a nice enough guy when he agreed to rent me his late grandmother's tiny two-bedroom cottage on the west side of town. I *wish* I could say he seemed like a nice guy last week when he made a pass at me and I declined, but nice guys don't grab your ass and then call you an uppity bitch when you tell them to back off.

"Hey, Brayden," Tom says. "I just needed to talk to Molly for a minute."

Brayden lifts his chin, showing no sign of moving from his spot, thank God. "Hey, Tom. Talk away."

Tom pulls off his leather jacket and slings it over his arm as he shifts his attention back to me. "Hey, I'm sorry to do this to you, but I'm gonna need you and Noah out by the end of the week."

I blink at him, sure that I've heard him wrong. He didn't just say—

"You're evicting her with a week's notice?" Brayden says.

Tom makes a face. "Not an *eviction*, exactly. I just need her to move. I wouldn't if I didn't have to. But my niece is moving back to town next Monday, and she needs a place to stay."

"But you said . . ." He gave me a deal on renting his grandmother's house and said Noah and I could stay there as long as we wanted. He even acted like he was doing me a big favor by not "locking me into a contract," made me believe I wouldn't need one anyway because "any day now" his siblings were going to come around to selling the house to me.

"Sonofabitch," Brayden mutters. "Where are they supposed to go?"

12

Tom lifts his palms, but I see the way he instinctively backs away from Brayden. "My niece is pregnant, and my sister wants to see her settled before Christmas. The dad's not around, and we're just trying to help a young girl out." He shifts his gaze to me. "*You* understand, I'm sure."

I understand because I'm a single mom, or . . . ? "I need more than a week."

There's something cruel in his gaze as it tracks over me slowly before coming back up to meet mine. I see the residual anger in his eyes. *Uppity bitch.* "I wish things could have worked out differently."

He wishes I would have let him grope me when he tried to turn an awkward hug I didn't want into an investigation of my ass. He *wishes* I'd spread my legs for him. He felt so entitled to what I didn't give that now he's fucking me over to punish me for it.

"I hope I can count on you to leave the place as nice as it was when you moved in," he says.

I wrap my fingers around my glass and take a long swallow of beer to keep myself from chucking the contents in his face. He knows how much I've done to that house in the three short months I've been there. He knows I've used my free time to tear down old wallpaper and paint, to pull up the ratty old carpet and reveal the original hardwood floors waiting beneath. He'd dropped hints that it would all be in my favor in the end, and that it was only a matter of time before his siblings felt emotionally ready to let go of their grandmother's home. Any work I put into it would be well worth it when his brothers and sisters finally agreed to sell to me.

I'm such an idiot.

"You're a real sonofabitch, Tom," Brayden mutters.

Tom's gaze slides between Brayden and me, and his expression slowly transforms into a smirk. "Oh, I get it." He waggles a finger between us. "I see how you got your job, Molly. Typical."

The blow strikes as hard as he intended it to, but I hide my flinch. "Jealous?"

"Get the fuck out of my bar," Brayden growls, and I wonder if Tom notices the way Brayden's hands have curled into fists.

He sneers at Brayden and shrugs back into his coat. "Word of warning? I'd be sure to wrap it if I were you."

Tom turns toward the door, and Brayden lunges out of the booth, but I grab his arm and squeeze. "Don't."

His muscles bunch under my hand, but he doesn't take another step, *thank God.* I don't need Brayden fighting my battles. I knew what I was getting into when I moved back to Jackson Harbor—knew that a reputation like mine isn't one you get to escape just because it's been eight years.

Only when Tom is out the door does Brayden turn to me. He studies my face for a beat before sliding into the booth across from me. "What are you going to do?"

I shake my head. *Three weeks to Christmas, and he's kicking us out.* Noah was so excited to be in a *house* for Christmas—one with a fireplace and chimney so Santa could come in the "right way." And I foolishly fed that excitement by telling him all the cool things we were going to do. Now I'll have to break it to him that we'll be spending the holiday in a hotel.

"The only thing I can do." I push my food away, my appetite vanishing right alongside my plans for a relaxing evening. "I'm going to start packing . . . and find somewhere else to live."

"I can't believe he's doing this. What a jackass."

"It is what it is." I swallow back the emotion threatening to break free. *Don't freak out.* "But thank you for sticking around while he was here. It was nice to have . . ." *A friend.* I don't say it aloud. I don't know if Brayden considers me that at all. I'm his employee. I'm the woman he slept with once. I'm his sister-in-law's stepsister. But friend? Maybe it's strange that I could jump into bed with him so easily in New York, but the idea of calling him my "friend" makes me feel too vulnerable.

Typical Molly.

Maybe I haven't changed as much in the last eight years as I'd like to think. Tom obviously didn't think so, or he never would have tried to make a move on me.

"Anytime," Brayden says.

I don't like the way he's studying my face—like he can see my thoughts and all the broken pieces I keep hidden under this pretty-girl façade. I lift my beer to my lips, but my stomach churns, and I put it down before taking a drink. "I'll see you at the office tomorrow?" I ask, more to change the subject than anything because, truthfully, it's a stupid question. Brayden isn't the kind of guy not to show up. Ever.

He nods. "I'll be there."

Slinging my purse over my shoulder, I head to the bar, where I wave at Jake to indicate that I want to settle my tab.

"Molly?"

I turn to Brayden, who frowns at me.

"You don't have to do this alone."

I close my eyes at the offer couched inside those words.

He'll help. His whole family will step up and help. That's what the Jacksons do. He doesn't owe me that. He doesn't owe me anything. And yet . . .

"She doesn't have to do what alone?" Jake asks, handing me my bill.

Brayden turns to his brother. "Molly's landlord evicted her. He wants her out by the end of the week."

"What an asshole," Jake mutters.

Brayden nods in agreement, but I'm barely aware of them, too focused on imagining Noah's face when I have to tell him our Christmas plans have changed. If my mom hadn't just sold her house and moved into a small apartment, I could go stay with her.

The idea of sleeping in my stepfather's house has bile rising in my throat. Maybe it's a blessing that moving in with her isn't an option, because I know I'd do it. If it meant giving Noah the Christmas morning he's been dreaming of, I'd do it. Even if it meant facing demons I've spent the better part of a decade running from.

Two

BRAYDEN

"This is it." I lead Mom into the new Jackson Brews taproom. She didn't want to see it until it was finished, but after months of construction, we're finally getting there. Thursday is our grand opening, and I want her to see the space dedicated to our father before we open it to the public.

Her eyes widen as she scans the room—the long, polished walnut bar with the live wood edge, the high-top round tables lining the bank of windows that overlook the harbor, the dark tiled floor, and the muted turquoise walls. She takes in every detail, and the emotion in her eyes fills me with a pride I can hardly speak around.

"What do you think?" I manage to ask.

A big chalkboard for our offerings spans the space between the open shelving on either end of the bar, and beneath it is the dedication plaque.

In loving memory of Frank Jackson, who dared to chase his dreams.

Mom presses a hand to her chest. "Oh, your father would be so proud of you."

"This is all because of him." My voice sounds like sandpaper. Selfishly, I'm glad I decided to bring her here alone instead of making it a family affair. My siblings will get their chance to celebrate with her during the grand opening.

Mom shakes her head. "Oh, no, Brayden. This is because of you—all of my kids, but mostly you and Jake, of course. All the hard work you've put in turned your father's little dream into something bigger than he ever could have imagined." She swipes at her cheeks, at the tears that flow easily. "And now Levi is part of the legacy too. Your father would be proud indeed."

The door to the kitchen swings open, and a dark head flies past us in a flash, little limbs pumping. "You can't catch me!" Noah shrieks.

Molly emerges behind him, her face glowing with joy as she chases her son. "Wanna bet?"

He circles back and moves to dart behind the bar, but Molly wraps him into her arms before he can pass her. She lifts him off the floor and swings him around. He giggles madly in response. "Faster! Faster!"

I'm vaguely aware of my mother beside me—the way she watches me watching Molly—and I school my expression the best I can, giving away nothing of what this sight does to me.

Molly's love of Noah transforms her face from beautiful to radiant. And maybe it's because I was thinking about my father or because bringing Mom here has my emotions at the surface, but seeing Molly like this and witnessing the bond between her and her son does something to me. It reminds me that she isn't just the beautiful woman I took to my room one night. And she isn't just my employee. She's this beautifully layered and complex human who has become one of the brightest spots in my life, whether she knows it or not.

And she's completely off-limits.

My chest goes tight with the longing I've done my best to ignore since she returned to town. It's hard to ignore something that grows with every passing day.

Molly spots us and stops spinning. She was so lost in her time with Noah that she ran right past. Some of that raw joy fades from her eyes and is replaced by caution. "Oh, hi." She lowers her son to the ground. "Sorry, we didn't know anyone else was here. Noah just got done at preschool, and we were having lunch together in my office before I take him to Veronica." She holds his hand, as if trying to keep a leash on that wild energy now that they have an audience. "How are you, Kathleen?"

Noah waves at us with his free hand. "Why are you crying?" he asks Mom. "Are you sad?"

Mom shakes her head. "I'm just fine."

"'Cause it's okay to be sad," Noah says, nodding solemnly. "Mom said it's okay to cry too. Even for boys."

Mom beams at Molly, and if my mom hadn't already been half in love with my new banquet center manager, I know Noah's words have sealed the deal. "Your mom's right, but these are happy tears."

Noah frowns as if he's trying to make sense of that. "Why?"

"Because I have so much happiness in my heart, it bubbles up and leaks out my eyes," Mom says.

"Oh. Okay." Noah nods, seeming content with this answer and ready to move on to something more interesting.

"I was showing Mom the taproom," I tell Molly. "I wanted her to see it before the grand opening."

Molly hoists Noah into her arms, and the boy wraps himself around his mom, leaning his head against her chest like I've seen him do a hundred times in the few months they've lived here. "Have you seen the banquet rooms?"

Mom shakes her head. "This is the first time I've been to this location. I wanted to wait until everything was ready."

"I can give you the tour," Molly offers.

Mom grins. "I would love that, if you have time."

The banquet center has its own entrance on the opposite side of the building, but Molly leads the way through the kitchen, showing off the setup she painstakingly picked out as she prepared the space. "I brought the chef on early so she could help me design the kitchen," she says. "In addition to having a modest selection of small plates for the taproom, we want to be able to serve full meals for as many as two hundred and fifty guests at a time on the banquet side, so we needed a design that could accommodate both jobs in as little space as possible, since we're paying for prime real estate on the water."

Mom flashes a look to me, a single gray eyebrow arched. My siblings have made enough comments over the last few months that I can guess what she's thinking.

"This is Molly's project," I say, reading the question in her eyes. "She made the decisions. I wasn't exaggerating when I said this wasn't going to be another responsibility on my plate."

"Don't believe him." Molly laughs, shifting Noah in her arms as she leads the way to the hall that runs behind the kitchen and banquet center. "He keeps careful tabs on everything I do here, so the banquet center has *definitely* added work to his plate." She shrugs. "But it's true that he let me have the reins and gave me the final say on design. I know—wonders never cease."

Mom huffs. "To say the least. But maybe he just needed someone like you in his—"

"I'm working on it," I say, flashing a warning look to Mom. I'm really not in the mood to fight her matchmaker instincts today.

"Our offices are all off this hallway," Molly says, pointing out each. "Levi's, mine, and Brayden's."

"You've finally given yourself an office away from home," Mom says. She squeezes my wrist. "It's about time."

I never wanted an office at the bar, even when Jake offered to give up his apartment for me to set up shop above Jackson Brews. It seemed easier and quieter to work from home, but not having a work space for business meetings has been an obstacle over the years. When we were designing this space, Molly suggested I could put my office here and hold meetings in the small conference room. It made sense, and it seems like it's going to work out great.

"Down at the end of the hall is the stairwell," Molly says. "You can take them up to get to the employee entrance of the rooftop terrace, and down to get to the locker room and break

21

room in the basement."

Noah wiggles in her arms. "Down," he says, wiggling with more vigor until Molly sets him on the floor.

"On the other side of the stairwell," she says, pointing, "is the storage room, and beyond that, a kitchenette that leads into two smaller party rooms and the small conference room. Off the hall opposite that is the main banquet hall."

I lead the way, opening the door just as Noah races past me and into the big, empty room. The lights are off, but the wall of windows overlooking the lake provides enough light to illuminate the vast space.

"Oh, it's absolutely stunning!" Mom scans the room as if she can imagine what it'll look like when it's set for a reception—the floor filled with tables and fine linens, the far alcove made into a dance floor, the rustic wooden rafters overhead draped in tulle. I was never very good at imagining such things, but once the space was ready, Molly had it set up, and a photographer came in to take pictures for the website. Now potential clients don't have to use their imagination. They can see for themselves how every detail was planned for elegance.

Noah races to the alcove at the end of the room and shakes his booty. "This is where you dance!"

Molly grins, and a little sound escapes, like she's biting back a laugh. "That's right, Noah."

"Come dance with me, Kathleen!" he calls.

Mom watches him with the same delight I see on her face when she's around my niece, Lilly. "You've done a spectacular job, Molly," she says, and I'm not sure if she's talking about the banquet center or Noah. Probably both, and I would have to agree.

"Thank you," Molly says.

Mom heads to the sunny alcove to dance with Noah, and Molly shifts her gaze to me. "I hope you don't mind me bringing him in. I wanted to spend a little time with him before I have to go house hunting. I didn't think anyone else would be here."

"I don't mind at all." I shove my hands into my pockets. "House hunting?"

"Rental hunting, at least. There isn't much available in my budget. After looking at them online, I'm not very hopeful." With a sigh, she shrugs. "Can't hurt to look, right?"

"Right." I follow her gaze to where Mom is doing her best funky chicken. Noah laughs so hard that he drops to the floor in delight. "Let me know how I can help."

She shakes her head. "It'll be fine. We've been through worse."

I know it's true, but that doesn't mean I like it.

Some of the worry on her face fades as she studies her son. "Come on, Noah. We have to get going."

The boy folds his arms and pouts. "Aww! Why, Mom?"

"Because Veronica's waiting."

He lights up at the mention of his babysitter and races across the room to his mom.

"I'll lock it all up on my way out," I say.

Molly nods, then calls to my mom, "It was good to see you, Kathleen."

"And you too, Molly," Mom says. "Bye, Noah."

"Good luck," I say, watching Molly and her son leave through the back.

"Bye, Rayden!" Noah calls over his shoulder.

I don't even notice Mom's moved until she's standing at my

side. "She's a lovely woman," she says softly.

"I know."

"And a good mom."

I nod. "That she is."

"And she looks at you like you walk on water."

I frown. Mom sees what she wants to see. "Resist the urge to set me up, please."

Mom just laughs and shakes her head, walking back to the tasting room. "I'm hungry, Brayden. Could I talk you into taking an old lady to lunch?"

MOLLY

"I'm so sorry," Teagan says, frowning into her beer.

"Why are you apologizing?" I drain a quarter of my beer in one pull and sigh. It's been a long afternoon spent looking at the best rental homes and apartments Jackson Harbor has to offer. It turns out that Noah's Santa-friendly chimney requirement is the least of my concerns, because 1) hardly anything is available right now, and 2) my budget is laughable in this town. "You warned me it'd be slim pickings."

"That doesn't mean I wasn't hoping that one of them might have been a hidden gem. Sometimes they look worse in the pictures, but the potential is clear when you see them in person."

"Sadly, none of these. If anything, I should apologize to you. You wasted an afternoon off work."

"Oh, I had my own selfish reasons," she says. "I have a perfectly good alarm and don't need a four-year-old bunking with me and waking me up at ungodly hours."

I laugh. "I promise Noah and I won't be crashing at your place. That's what hotels are for."

Teagan frowns, and I know she's no happier about that potential solution than I am.

Today was hard. When I woke up this morning, I had to fight an old heaviness to get through my normal routine. Life should feel easier. We buried my asshole stepfather almost two months ago, and I finally don't have to worry about him finding out about my son. My stepbrother, Colton, is out of rehab, and I'm preparing for the very first event at the Jackson Brews banquet hall. Despite my looming homelessness, everything is amazing. And yet I woke up this morning feeling the old ache of loneliness gnawing at my bones, and it hasn't let go all day.

Jake emerges from the kitchen. He's in such a good mood that he's damn near swaggering. "Smile, ladies," he says, leaning on the edge of the bar opposite us. "It's snowing. We've got beer. Life is good."

I'm not in much of a smiling mood, but I can't help but obey when I realize he's wearing one of the new Jackson Brews T-shirts. As I suspected, Brayden's the only one who doesn't think it's funny.

"Easy for you to say," Teagan says. "You're not going to be homeless at Christmas like poor Molly here."

Jake grimaces as he turns his attention to me. "Shit. I'm an ass. I forgot."

I roll my eyes. "She makes it sound like Noah and I are

going to spend our Christmas sleeping beneath the overpass and huddled around a burning trash barrel. We'll be okay." That's what I keep reminding myself—it's not ideal, but it's okay. We're always okay, my boy and I. This is nothing but another bump in the road that's turned Noah into the most awesome tiny human I know.

"Hey!" Teagan nudges me with her elbow. "Don't ruin a perfectly good guilt trip."

"No luck finding a place?" Jake asks.

I shake my head. "Maybe I'm too picky, but . . ."

"I saw there's a small house on Crawford for rent," he says. "It's close to the park."

I stifle a shudder at the memory of the rat-infested two-bedroom on the east side of town. "Saw it. Hard pass."

Ava comes out from the kitchen, smoothing her skirt down around her baby bump. If Jake's long stare at his new wife didn't give away what they were doing back there before Jake emerged in a suspiciously cheerful mood, Ava's flushed cheeks would. The new husband and wife can't keep their hands off each other, and her pregnancy hasn't seemed to slow them down at all.

A tug of longing rips through my gut, sudden and unexpected. My pregnancy was long, lonely, and wrought with too many fears for the future. Noah was worth every bit of it, but to get the joy of a child without all those moments of terror and self-doubt . . .

I push my envy aside and paste on a smile. Wishing I'd had just a little of what she has doesn't change that I want it for her or how happy I am that she and Jake finally found their way to each other.

"What are you all talking about?" Ava asks.

"Molly was house hunting today." He waves to someone in one of the back booths. "There's nothing good available."

The next thing I know, Brayden's standing beside me at the bar. Brayden, who was so sweet with his mom at the banquet center this morning. Brayden, who wasn't annoyed at all to see I brought my wild child into the office, but instead lit up at the sight of Noah running through the place. I didn't realize he was here.

"How'd the house hunt go?" he asks.

"Bad," Jake says.

"The place on Crawford was actually pretty nice," Teagan says. "If you don't mind rats."

Jake mimes puking into his hand.

"I was hoping you'd get lucky." Brayden scans my face like I've been in some awful accident and he's looking me over for injuries. "Are you okay?"

"We'll be *fine*." Dear Lord, if I have to take one more pitiful, sympathetic stare aimed in my direction, I might lose it. Those looks make me feel like I'm six again and being told my father isn't coming home. I *hate* pity. I'd prefer a high school full of assholes calling me Blowjob Molly to even a handful of people feeling sorry for me.

"What kind of guy kicks his tenants out before *Christmas*?" Anger twists Ava's normally smiling face. "Did he really *just now* find out his niece needs a place to stay?"

"Who knows?" I shrug. I'm too ashamed to admit what I believe to be the real reason behind my sudden eviction. "Maybe I can make it up to Noah and find a hotel with an indoor pool."

"The hotel on the interstate has a pool. A slide, even," Jake says.

Brayden shakes his head. "Didn't they shut down for some sort of asbestos removal?"

I grimace and take a deep breath. "Somewhere else, then. There are plenty of vacation homes in this town. Surely one of them has the holiday available." I can already feel my credit card groaning at the possibility of paying holiday rates to stay in a Jackson Harbor vacation rental.

"Why don't you just stay at Brayden's?" Ava asks.

I stiffen at that, and Brayden stills beside me—just enough of a reaction that I understand exactly how he feels about that possibility. "Don't be ridiculous," I say, trying to wave away the words like she never spoke them—because I'd prefer that to the awkwardness that's settled between my boss and me.

"He's in that big house all alone," Jake says. He turns to his brother. "You probably wouldn't even notice Molly and Noah were there."

I'm surrounded by crazy people.

I'm pretty sure all the Jacksons know that Brayden and I hooked up in New York last spring. Secrets are a rare commodity in this family. Given that, you'd think it would occur to *someone* that it's not a great idea to put us under the same roof.

"The whole reason you didn't sign a lease with Tom was because you were looking for a house to buy, right?" Ava asks. "If you just move in with Brayden temporarily, you don't have to worry about finding a place to stay until a house comes on the market."

"It would be ideal," Teagan says softly, breaking her silence, but from the way she's looking at me, I feel like she understands why this "ideal" solution would also be complicated in ways I don't want to admit out loud.

I meet Ava's eyes, trying my best to silently communicate that this is a bad idea. Am I the only one who's noticed how still Brayden has gone? God, he's probably desperately trying to come up with a polite way to take Ava's naïve offer off the table.

I do it before he can. "I wouldn't intrude like that."

"We don't want you to spend your Christmas at a hotel," Jake says.

Ava chimes in, oh so helpfully, "The last thing you need is a vacation rental gobbling up your hard-earned down payment, should you finally find a house you want. Staying at Brayden's is a logical solution. And since you could put all your rent money into savings, you'll be that much closer to buying your own home."

"Noah and I will find our own place."

Ava leans forward on the bar, her expression serious. "The Jacksons are going to drag you and Noah to the cabin with them anyway, and every other family event they have. It's their—*our* way," she says, seeming to remember that she's a Jackson now too. "There's room for everyone, whether you want them to make room for you or not."

"And it's really sweet." I keep my eyes on Ava. I can feel Brayden watching me, but I don't want to see what's in his eyes. "It really is, but it's unnecessary."

Making an excuse about needing to get Noah, I pay my tab and hurry out of the bar before they can subject me to any further attempts to convince me, and before Brayden's silence can slice into me any further.

The truth is that the idea of sleeping under the same roof as my boss and seeing him when I wake up every morning . . . I don't want to put on my mom hat and go retrieve my son. I want to put on my sexiest underwear and start drinking.

No matter how tempted I am to sleep with Brayden, I shouldn't, and I especially shouldn't plop myself right in front of that temptation at the loneliest time of the year.

Three

BRAYDEN

The door has barely closed behind Molly, and I'm still thinking about the way her hips sway in that fitted black skirt, when my sister-in-law smacks me on the shoulder. "You jackass!"

I gape at Ava's uncharacteristic outburst and look to Jake for some backup, but my brother just glares at me. "What the hell did I do?"

Jake's brows shoot up into his hairline, and Ava mimes pulling out her hair.

Teagan hops off her barstool and shakes her head. "I'm staying out of this." She swings her purse over her shoulder. "Have a good night."

"Staying out of what?" I ask.

But she just whispers, "Good luck," and heads out the door.

"Ugh." Ava scowls at me, turns on her heel, and stomps back

into the kitchen, growling, "I'm too hormonal for this crap!" as the swinging door swishes in her wake.

Jake cuts his eyes in the direction of his wife's retreat before his sympathetic gaze turns to me. "I didn't mean to corner you like that. I just assumed you'd agree."

"Corner me?" I must be slow as shit today, because I finally realize why Ava's mad at me. I drag a hand through my hair. "I don't care if Molly and Noah stay with me." It's a moot point, isn't it? The look on Molly's face at the suggestion screamed that she'd rather eat glass. And hell, she's made it clear where we stand. Our night together was *a mistake*. I'm her boss and nothing more. She wants to forget we ever crossed those lines. I've been working damn hard to check all those boxes for her.

"If you don't care, then why didn't you say something?" Jake asks.

I scowl at my brother. "Did it ever occur to you that you were putting *her* in an uncomfortable position? That maybe she doesn't want to stay with me?"

Ava's shout from the kitchen is loud enough to be heard through the whole bar. "You still could have said something."

Jake bites back a smile at his wife's outburst.

I roll my shoulders. Ava's as sweet as they come, and I don't like her ire directed at me. "I didn't realize my silence was a problem when I knew she'd likely prefer a different solution." I lower my voice so Ava can't hear me in the back. "Come on, you can't tell me you don't see this as Ava's blatant attempt to play matchmaker." Never mind the ideas such an arrangement would put in Mom's head. Jesus—Molly and Noah living with me. Mom would *love* that.

Ava returns from the kitchen with a plate of fries, but her pout tells me I'm not forgiven.

Jake shrugs. "Maybe, but I'm not sure there's a better solution. She and Noah would have to camp in the nursery if they moved in with Ava and me. She could stay with Levi, I guess."

Ava smacks her husband on the arm. "Seriously? Ellie and Molly are only recently on friendly terms after the whole ordeal with Colton. There's no way Molly would move in with Levi when it would raise brows, and people would gossip about Molly and Levi being together."

Jake frowns. "Everyone knows Levi's in love with Ellie."

Ava shrugs. "People can be assholes who are much more interested in a juicy story than they are in the truth. Molly knows that better than anyone. And anyway, let's not put any obstacles between Ellie and Levi reuniting."

"Agreed," I mutter. Ellie and Levi are taking some time apart after a messy ordeal that involved Ellie losing her memory and Levi falling hard for his best friend's girl. We all know it's only a matter of time before she lets herself be with him, but he's giving her the space she asked for. Inserting Molly into that is a terrible idea.

"Shay would happily take her, but the three of them in that little apartment?" Jake shakes his head. "I guess Nic and Ethan could move Mom to the guest room upstairs and let Molly and Noah have her apartment behind Ethan's garage."

Ava squeaks in protest, and I glare at Jake. "Mom isn't moving anywhere. That's unnecessary." I don't have to say the rest out loud—that I don't like the idea of her climbing the steps at Ethan's all the time, that even though she's recovered from chemo and is officially in remission, she's still weaker than she was before and wears out easily. She broke her ankle in a fall last summer and gave us all a scare. No way I'd risk adding a broken hip to our worries.

Jake nods. "I guess Carter might be able to—"

"Shut the fuck up before I knock you out."

Jake presses a hand to his chest, feigning innocence. "I'm so sorry. Is there a reason you don't want your beautiful *employee* living with your flirt of a single brother?" He makes a face as he scratches the back of his neck. "Because I could have sworn you told me you weren't interested in her like that anymore."

I said I didn't intend to *pursue* anything with Molly. Never that I wasn't interested. But I'm not about to point out the difference to Jake when he's dead set on making me feel like an ass. "I'll make it clear she's welcome to stay with me, but I'm telling you now she'd probably rather risk the rats at that Crawford Street rental than have to sleep in the same house as me."

Jake's lips twitch. "If you say so."

MOLLY

"With the ice festival, it's considered peak season. You'd be surprised how many people want to spend their holiday in Jackson Harbor."

I pinch the bridge of my nose and count to five. I've had this conversation half a dozen times today in my attempts to negotiate better rates on vacation properties. "I understand. I just thought that if I were staying a month or two . . ."

"If you pay two months upfront, I can offer a ten percent discount," the woman says. "But that's the best I can do."

Two months at these rates would be like a wrecking ball to the meager savings I've scraped together since moving here. I have a good job, but too many months living in New York unemployed put me in a hole I haven't fully climbed out of. "Let me think on it. I'll call you back tomorrow."

"Okay. I'm sorry I don't have better news, but the owners don't mind it being vacant over the holiday. They enjoy hopping over from the city for a night or two when they can, so they're not very motivated to lower the price."

"I understand." I swallow. Spending Christmas in a hotel room is looking more and more inevitable. "I'll be in touch."

We end the call, and I close my eyes and take two deep breaths. Maybe Jackson Harbor has made me soft. I've dealt with much bigger blows than pre-holiday relocation. I can certainly handle this.

But I'm far too aware that I haven't broken the news to Noah yet, and maybe I should have. Instead, I've decided I'll wait until I know exactly where we're heading at the end of the week. I don't want to make any more promises I can't keep.

I shut down my computer, grab my purse, and head out. I have an appointment with a guy who's trying to sell his house on contract. It's the last possibility between me and Christmas in either a hotel or on Mom's couch.

As I step out into the back lot, I tug my peacoat closed against the sharp chill in the air. Winter never waits to hit Jackson

Harbor. It likes to visit in November to remind us what it can do, and then settles in for good by early December. This year is true to form, and Noah has been so excited about building a snowman in our own front yard that the white powder covering my car is just another reminder of what's on the line.

"Molly." Brayden's deep voice stops me right as I reach my car.

I turn slowly. "Hey, what's up?"

I keep my eyes on his face. Not on that strong chest that I remember feeling so warm beneath my cheek, and not on the hands that took me by surprise when they first touched me—rougher than I'd have guessed for a man who spends the majority of his workday behind a desk.

"I just wanted to extend the invitation myself—for you to stay with me. Ava's right. I have more than enough room, and it's a reasonable solution."

Reasonable solution. Hardly a glowing invitation.

I can see it in his eyes. He's as wary about this as I am. "Thanks, but I'm not sure it's a good idea."

"You've found a better option?"

"I have some promising leads."

He arches a brow, then whispers, "Liar."

The word throws me back to our night in New York together when I called him a liar for pretending the text from Ethan didn't mean anything.

"Okay, so the leads aren't *promising*, but I do have some leads." Maybe it's irrational, but I resent Tom for making me deal with this now instead of a month ago. Christmas as a single mom means wearing a cape and doing all the things, and this year, the holiday is happening right alongside the grand opening of the banquet center and my public debut in my new role with Jackson Brews. I'm determined not to screw any of it up, but I'm feeling more than a little overwhelmed. "It's too much to ask, Brayden."

"It's not. Not at all. I do have the room."

I swallow. I know he does. He lives in the big house where his parents raised him and his five siblings. When his mother moved out to live in the apartment behind Ethan's garage, no one was ready to see her sell the house. Apparently, Brayden moved in as a temporary solution, but the family continues to gather there every Sunday and for any major holiday that they can't celebrate at their family cabin.

"You're looking at me like I'm offering you a room in my dungeon."

I shake my head. "Sorry. No. I mean, this is incredibly kind of you." I want to be the woman who can hold his gaze through what I need to say next. But I'm not. So I study a crack in the pavement at my feet instead. "I was thinking that after our ill-advised night in New York—"

"Christ." Something like anger flashes over his features, and he looks toward the traffic inching down Lakeshore Drive. "Despite what you might think about our night and my ulterior motives for hiring you, this *isn't* about getting you in my bed."

I am the world's biggest bitch. "Brayden—"

"I regret how I handled everything. And that my decisions that night made you feel—"

"Stop!" I desperately want to go back to being the Molly and Brayden who don't talk about that night and who never, *ever* mention the shitty accusation I made. "Please. Can we just . . ."

When he turns back to me, his expression is guarded. "Just what, Molly?"

"Pretend I didn't say that?" I swallow, but the shame doesn't go away. "I never believed you would hire me just to sleep with me, and I promise there's no part of me that thinks you're offering space in your home just to get in my pants."

"Good." He nods, but this conversation pulled that old hurt to the surface—pain that *I* am responsible for—and the sight of it makes me feel so small and unworthy of everything he's given me. "So you'll consider it?"

"I'm worried that sleeping under the same roof might end up more complicated than either of us wants."

He stuffs his hands in his pockets and rocks back on his heels, and when I drag my gaze back to his face, the corner of his mouth twitches in amusement. "Am I that irresistible?"

I snort. "Oh, fuck off."

"No, I totally get it. If having me around would distract you from your work or prove to be a bigger temptation than you can handle—"

"I can handle it just fine." I handle it every freaking day, *thankyouverymuch*.

He holds my gaze. "Then move in. You and Noah can have the second floor all to yourselves for as long as you need. I never go up there, so you don't need to worry about any accidental seduction."

I roll my eyes. "I'm not worried about *accidental seduction*."

"Then what are you worried about?"

I search for a reasonable objection but come up empty. The only reason not to stay with Brayden is because I'm attracted to him and don't want to make the same mistake I did in New York. Then, it was a mistake because he was my boss. Now he's more than that. He's . . . my friend. The label might scare me, but it's true. As a single mom, I need his friendship far more than any bedroom chemistry that simmers between us. "I'm worried about taking too much from you."

"It's not too much. Not at all."

"Then I'll consider it. Thank you."

He grins—really grins that rare, full smile that transforms his whole face. Warmth spreads from my tummy all the way out to my fingers and toes. This guy doesn't smile enough. "You're welcome." He looks at my car. "Where are you headed?"

"I'm looking at another house. This one's a rent-to-own kind of thing just outside of town. The commute wouldn't be too bad, and we could move in right away."

"Want me to go with you?"

For a flash, I imagine it—what it would be like to have Brayden in my life as more than my boss and friend, what it would be like to have a partner who helped me make decisions when they overwhelmed me . . . What it would be like to have him look at me the way his brothers look at their women. "No, that's unnecessary." I force a smile. "I've been picking places to live on my own since I finished undergrad. I've got this."

"Do you need any help packing?"

I shake my head. "I don't have much, so it shouldn't be too bad. I'll rent a truck for the move, though, and I could use some help loading the furniture if you think you could talk your brothers into it."

He shakes his head. "Save your money on the truck. Between

Jake's and Levi's, we can get you taken care of."

"Thank you," I say. But it doesn't feel like enough. I know it's not enough.

"Whatever you need, Molly," he says softly. "I mean that."

Despite the chill nipping at my cheeks, I melt.

BRAYDEN
Seven months ago . . .

"This one is good." Molly nudges the tasting glass back toward the bartender. "But I think it would be better if they toned down the hops a little." She turns to me, her cheeks flushed from the beer samples, her eyes bright from a long but successful afternoon. She's stunning, and every time she looks at me, I feel myself being tugged toward her, a magnetic pull that might be stronger than my own willpower.

"Agreed," I say, nodding to my own sample. "There's a lot of nice citrus, but it gets lost."

"I like IPAs as much as the next girl, but sometimes it's like the breweries are trying to outdo each other for the hoppy-est beer available."

The bartender—my buddy Raine from college—grins at

41

Molly like he's a smitten schoolboy. She has that effect on guys. "These hipster assholes come in here trying to tell me the shit they brew in their basement is better because it has higher IBUs."

Molly shrugs. "I mean, it's possible. I've had some delicious homebrews, but homebrew IPAs are tough."

"Sure," Raine says, "me too. I've also had some that taste like the bottom of an unwashed gym sock."

I grimace at the description. "I've had those too, unfortunately."

Raine rocks back on his heels and surveys my newest employee, no doubt taking in Molly's wide smile and blue eyes, and the killer curves under her professional attire. I resist the urge to move closer—to stake a claim I don't have. Molly is my employee, and our day of training was a success. She has the perfect personality for sales. She's bright without being too bubbly, and informed without being obnoxious. She's got the face for it, too. She might punch me in the nuts if I admitted it out loud, but a pretty face is an important part of sales. I learned a long time ago that the purchasing managers for these pubs are far more receptive to a beautiful woman's sales pitch than mine.

"I wondered if you'd ever get over Sara," Raine says. "It's good to see the evidence with my own eyes."

Molly flashes me a questioning look, but I shake my head at my old friend. I'm not sure why he's bringing up Sara now. "It's been ten years." I grab my next sample—a dark, rich porter—and sniff it before bringing the glass to my lips.

"Looks like things worked out for the best." His gaze shifts to Molly then back to me. "So how long have you two been together?"

I choke on my beer.

Molly bites back a grin. "Do we look like a couple?"

Raine arches a brow. "Shit. Are you not?"

"No." I cough the beer from my windpipe. "Not at all." I could swear I see hurt flash across Molly's face. *Seriously?* Surely she knows a guy like me would trip over himself to be with her. "I'm still in Jackson Harbor. Molly lives in Brooklyn."

Raine folds his arms. "She loves beer and has the face of an angel, and you're going to let a few hundred miles come between you?"

"Try eight hundred miles," I mutter, not bothering to pretend I haven't thought about it.

"I work for him," Molly says quickly, but I don't miss the way she directs her gaze at her beer now. The way she's avoiding my eyes. This whole situation is embarrassing the shit out of her, and I feel like a dick for not making our relationship clear to Raine from the start.

"I see," he says, though the look he's giving me says he doesn't see at all and thinks I should make my move now.

I wish I could. Hell, I've been thinking about it all day. She's . . . tempting. With every laugh that passes her lips, and every flush of her cheeks at my praise, I think about it.

Molly points a thumb over her shoulder. "Does that old jukebox actually work?" she asks Raine.

Nodding, he reaches into a jar behind the counter then drops a fistful of quarters on the bar. "Knock yourself out."

She takes the coins with a subdued smile then slides off her stool and weaves through the tables to the jukebox on the opposite side of the room. I watch every step.

"I'm sorry," Raine says softly. "If I made things awkward, I mean . . ."

I shake my head. "Don't worry about it."

"She doesn't look at you like you're just her boss."

I arch a brow, waiting for him to explain what he means by that, but he shrugs and moves down the bar to help another patron.

Molly's staring at the musical offerings, her fingers digging into the back of her neck like she's trying to work out a knot.

I drain my sample before heading across the room. Since Raine turned the conversation toward awkward, we might as well address the elephant in the room.

I stand beside her as she flips to the *Purple Rain* album and studies the songs. "Prince?"

"My mom . . ." Swallowing, she shakes her head. "Before Mom and Nelson got together, Mom and I were obsessed with Prince. I'd get home from school, and she'd turn on *Purple Rain*, and we'd dance in the living room to every song on the album, laughing and playing air guitar." She blinks back tears. "We didn't have much back then. Music was my treat. My reward." She drops quarters into the machine and punches a few buttons. "I Would Die 4 U" starts to play.

"Nice choice."

She flashes me a smile before lowering her gaze back to the jukebox. "They're all good choices."

"We've never talked about it," I say softly.

Judging by the way she tenses, I don't have to define *it*. She knows what I'm referring to. That night, eight years ago, when she was just a kid and I found her at that party, blitzed out of her

44

mind, and dragged her out before she could get in more trouble. "I didn't think you wanted to."

"Shouldn't we clear the air?"

She shrugs. "I'm not sure. I'd probably rather box it up and put it in storage with all the other memories best left undisturbed."

"I can do that. If that's what you want."

She brings her gaze up to meet mine. Those blue eyes sear into me, and I wonder what she sees. "I think I want . . ." Her pink lips curve into a sultry smile. "Dinner."

"I can do that too."

MOLLY

I was eighteen when I climbed into bed with Brayden Jackson. He was twenty-seven. It wasn't the first time I'd offered my body to a man as a pathetic sort of gratitude, but it was the first time I was turned down. Now, eight years later, Brayden's my new boss, and every time I look at him, I think of that night and my *relief* when he grabbed me by the wrists and stopped my hands from moving down his bare chest. I should have been mortified, but instead I was just grateful that *one guy, one time,* saw me as more than an easy lay. That on some level he understood I didn't really want to give what I was offering.

"So, what do you think after today?" Brayden asks. He gives the waitress a polite nod as she clears our plates, then leans back in the booth. He looks like he should be in a magazine spread with those intense eyes, the stubble on his cheeks. His sleeves are rolled up to his elbows, revealing the corded muscles of his forearms, and the top two buttons of his shirt are undone.

"About the job?" It takes a force of will to take my mind off his sex appeal and onto a professional conversation. In truth, I'm dying to know what he made of that night eight years ago and if he still thinks I'm a foolish, reckless girl who needs to be rescued. "I think it's fun."

The day has been full and somehow simultaneously exhausting and exhilarating. We went to bars, liquor stores, even other breweries, and talked about Jackson Brews beer. After giving introductions, Brayden would let me lead the conversation, noting the gaps in the location's offerings and suggesting Jackson Brews products that could allow them to have a better selection.

"You impressed me." He settles his arms on the table and leans forward, his eyes bright. "I thought I'd have to step in with details about our less-popular selections or at least answer some questions, but I don't think you needed me here at all."

"Well, you gave me enough study materials that I should be able to write a dissertation on Jackson Brews at this point." I grin. It was fun to show off a little—to prove to him and myself that I deserve this opportunity. I wouldn't put it past the Jackson family to give a struggling single mom a job, even at a loss to the company. But if pity motivated them to put me on the payroll, I want to do such a good job that they never regret it.

His phone buzzes on the table beside him, and he puts his hand over it. "Do you mind if I check this?"

"Of course not."

He picks it up and unlocks the screen. I take advantage of

the opportunity to study the rugged lines of his face. "Jake's just checking in," he says, tapping out a reply.

I feel my smile falter at the mention of his brother. I used to have the biggest crush on Jake. I've never slept with a Jackson brother, but Brayden's not the only one I've crawled into bed with.

What a slut. Such typical Molly behavior.

Brayden's attention's still on his phone, and he doesn't seem to notice my mood slip. "And Ethan sent a video of my niece practicing her lines for *Charlotte's Web*." He chuckles, and little wrinkles crease at the corners of his eyes with his smile. "Come here. You have to see this."

Swallowing, I climb out of my seat to take the spot beside him.

He tilts his screen toward me and turns up the volume so I can hear the little girl recite Fern's lines with the dramatic flair of a Broadway hopeful. When I look back at Brayden, his expression has softened and his eyes are full of love.

"She's precious," I say. Then, because it's so foreign and wonderful, I say, "Family is everything to you, isn't it?"

He nods. "Everything."

I shift my gaze back to the screen as another text comes through from Ethan.

> Ethan: Hope it's going well tonight. Do yourself a favor and make your move. You deserve a little fun in

I don't get to read the rest before Brayden curses under his breath and pulls the phone away. "Sorry."

"Make your move?" I ask. "On me?"

Red creeps up his neck and into his cheeks, and if he weren't so fucking *sexy*, I might call it adorable. "Ethan's just . . . It doesn't mean anything."

I lick my lips. "Liar."

He swallows and studies my face, then his gaze drops to my mouth. "I wish you didn't work for me so I could be honest." He turns away and studies the photograph hanging by our table. "I've obviously had too much to drink, or I wouldn't have even said that much."

My heart pounds harder. Faster. I've had a couple of beers with dinner and a few samples throughout the afternoon before that. My skin is warm, my body relaxed. Maybe that's why I slide closer. Or maybe it's just because I love the way he was looking at me before he turned away.

I lift my hand to his face, relishing the brush of stubble beneath my fingertips. With a gentle nudge of my hand, I turn his face back to mine. "Be honest. Pretend I don't work for you for a minute. I want to know what you're thinking."

His gaze drops to my mouth and his tongue darts out to touch his bottom lip. The sight sends pleasure bolting through me. "You want to know how much I want you?"

I cup the back of his neck and lean forward, brushing my lips across his. Just once. "I offered myself to you before, Brayden."

His Adam's apple bobs as he swallows. "You were a kid."

"I was eighteen. Totally legal."

"You were drunk."

I thread my fingers through his hair and keep my eyes on his. "That never stopped anyone else."

When he rescued me from the party that night, I'd seen him

48

as the cold and hard eldest Jackson brother. All the Jackson boys were and still are gorgeous, but where his brothers were full of laughter, smiles, and jokes, Brayden was always too serious. Too hard. But that night, after he pulled me out of that party and away from those boys who were plying me with shots of cheap vodka and circling me like turkey vultures, there was tenderness in his eyes. I begged him not to take me home. I hadn't expected compassion from a man like him. I've lived a life where I've learned not to expect that tenderness or compassion from anyone, and especially not from men.

I swallow hard, thinking of the text Brayden's brother sent him. "Do you want me?"

He huffs out a dry laugh and searches my face. "More than you can imagine."

I lean closer. "Then do something about it."

His hand is hot, his fingertips searing as they find my thigh beneath the table and inch upward under the hem of my dress. "Are you drunk now, Molly?"

My mouth brushes his ear as I whisper, "I've had enough to be brave, but not so much that I don't know what I'm doing."

One hand grips my thigh and the other plunges into my hair. He turns my mouth to his and kisses me. His lips are soft, coaxing, and I think I moan when his tongue touches mine. He's heat and hunger, and his kiss lights a fire in me I haven't felt in years.

I ignore the voice in my head that chants, *Slut, easy, whore,* the one that whispers all the cruel words they flung at me in Jackson Harbor. I lock that voice away and press into Brayden, loving the feel of his calloused hand inching up my thigh and aching for more, for everything he'll give me.

Tonight, I'm going to pretend I'm worthy of a man like him, because tomorrow he'll fly home, and it won't matter that he deserves better than me. It won't matter that I can never be more than a one-night stand.

BRAYDEN

"Let's get out of here," Molly whispers against my mouth. She's so damn sweet. I can hardly think straight.

I trace the line of her jaw with my thumb, and she shudders. "Where do you want to go?"

"To your room," she says. I stroke my thumb higher, and her breath hitches. "Is it close?"

"A few blocks." God, I've never done anything like this. I'm not the kind of guy who puts his hand up a woman's skirt in public, but her skin is so soft and I love the sounds she makes with each brush of my thumb. I'm dying to feel the heat between her legs and taste her moans against my mouth. I've never been so undone. I don't give a shit where we are. "Are you sure?"

She laughs. "So sure."

"You're not drunk?" I asked before, but it matters.

She sucks my earlobe between her teeth, and blood rushes to my cock. "I know what I'm doing."

I throw money on the table, and we scramble out of the booth and out of the restaurant. The streets are wet, and rain pounds down on the sidewalk, so we stop short under the awning.

"I'll get us a cab," I say, holding her by my side.

"I won't melt."

"Fair warning?" My voice is husky with desire. "If you come back to my room, I plan to make you melt completely." Part of my brain warns that this is too fast, that I'll scare her off if I don't slow down, but for the first time in my life, I ignore that voice of reason and focus on the woman in front of me.

"That sounds like a promise."

I drag my gaze over her, lingering on her legs and the hem of her dress, remembering the heat of that skin, thinking about how close my fingers were to the apex of her thighs. "Oh, it's absolutely a promise, Molly."

She takes my hand and threads her fingers through mine, all smiles and giggles as we race down the street to my hotel.

The whole way to my room, I can't stop touching her. A hand on her elbow as we cross the street, an arm around her waist as we push into the hotel, a quick kiss on the back of her hand as we wait for the elevator, and then a slower, open-mouthed kiss on her neck as we ride to my suite.

After using my key card to get us into my room, I open the door for her and follow her in. The door has barely clicked closed behind me when she peels off her soaked sweater and unzips her dress, letting it fall from her shoulders and to the floor at her feet.

When she steps forward, she's in nothing but a black satin bra, matching lace panties, and pink heels I imagine hooked over my shoulders. "Christ, you're beautiful." My heart's racing so fast and my blood roars in my ears. "Every time you've come back to Jackson Harbor the last few years, I've wanted to tell you that."

"Why didn't you?"

I grin and step forward, closing the distance between us and settling a hand on her hip. "You barely gave me a chance. You're rarely in town, and when you are, you only stick around a day or two."

Something flashes in her eyes that I don't understand—a secret—but she blinks and it's gone. "And to think I've spent the last eight years believing you just didn't like me."

"Why on earth would you think such a thing?"

"I crawled into your bed that night. You wouldn't even let me touch you."

I took her back to my place because she'd begged me not to take her home. I assumed she was afraid she'd be in trouble for drinking, so I agreed to let her stay with me and set her up with a blanket and a pillow on my couch. She was still drunk when she woke me up an hour later, her hands on my chest, her mouth on my neck. "My reaction had nothing to do with what I wanted."

"Hmm." Her fingers go to the buttons on my shirt, undoing them one by one. "Has anyone ever told you that you're too noble for your own good?"

I wrap a hand around each wrist and still her hands. "I don't regret it. You were beautiful, and I was . . . tempted." I don't even want to admit how tempted I was. She was so sexy but too damn young. Legal, sure, but it wasn't about the law. It was about being able to look at myself in the mirror the next morning. But I never forgot that night, or the way she melted into me when I wrapped my arms around her and whispered, *Just sleep, Molly.*

Her gaze flicks up to meet mine then drops down to my throat. Can she see the thrum of my pulse there? "Tempted enough that you've thought about it?" I'm still holding her wrists as she rises onto her toes and flicks her tongue at the pulse point in my neck. "Because I have. I went home that day and touched myself in the bath while I imagined your hands on me."

Lust surges through my blood at that image, and I release her hands. "I thought about it then and after, but . . . it was different in my fantasies."

"You wanted me sober."

"For starters." I dip my head and run my nose down the side of her neck. She hisses at the contact and arches into me as she unbuttons my jeans. "This is so much better."

She swallows, then steps out of my grasp. "On the bed." Her blue eyes rake over me, dark with lust. "I need a chance to redeem myself."

Chuckling, I pull off my shirt and climb onto the bed. I prop myself up on the headboard and put my hands behind my head, watching as she steps out of her shoes and reaches for the clasp on her bra.

The satin straps slip down her shoulders and to the floor. She saunters toward the bed, all feminine grace and sexual confidence. She straddles my hips. "Is this okay?"

"You think there's a chance in hell I'm going to stop you this time?"

She arches her back and shifts her hips, rubbing herself against the aching length of my shaft. "I hope not."

I thread a hand through her hair and bring her mouth down to mine, kissing her hard and telling her with my lips and tongue that I'm not going anywhere. This is exactly where I want to be.

She rocks into me, and pleasure bolts down my spine,

building too fast. I need more. I need her closer. Need to feel her heat.

I reach between us to rid myself of my jeans, and she's there too. We become a mess of hands and limbs as we work in tandem to pull them off. By the time we throw them to the floor, she's on her knees beside me, and we're both laughing. She straddles me again. "Next time, remind me to make you get naked *before* you get on the bed."

"Next time, I'm going to strip *you* naked." I dip my head and flick my tongue over her nipple.

"I'm not naked yet," she says, breathless.

"But I like you like this." I grip her waist and run my thumbs along the scrap of lace at each hip. "I could make you come like this."

She gasps, hands in my hair, and I suck the tight peak of her breast into my mouth. This time when she moves against my cock, I can feel her heat, feel how slick she is even through my boxers and her panties.

I pull her closer, and she picks up the pace, and when her nails dig into my shoulders, I know I could come like this too—from nothing but the friction of our bodies' instinctive dance.

I flip her over on the mattress and kiss my way down her body.

"Brayden." She reaches for me, but I just look up at her from between her legs and smile.

"This was worth the wait," I murmur. I lower my face and suck her clit through the lace. She moans and grips fistfuls of the duvet as she arches into my mouth.

She's so fucking beautiful sprawled out before me like this, but I want to taste her, to feel her and only her under my tongue, so I peel away that last piece of her clothing and toss it to the floor.

"What happened to making me come through those?" she murmurs.

"Next time." I hook an arm under each leg and draw up her knees, opening her. I lower my mouth to her inner thighs and sweep across that tender skin with my lips, then my tongue, then my teeth. When I finally bring my mouth between her legs, I hover above her and just . . . look. "You're beautiful everywhere."

She trembles, and I lower my lips to her clit. Her hips jerk, and she cries my name. Hands on her thighs, I pin her open and taste every inch, dragging my tongue along her before circling her opening. I'm drunk on her. On this night. On the whimpers and moans and pleas as she falls apart under my tongue.

"Please," she murmurs. "God, Brayden . . ."

I slide two fingers into her then and feel her body clench violently and the release of her orgasm rocking through her.

I stay between her legs and stroke her gently as she floats back down.

"Come here." She grabs my wrist and guides me up her body.

I settle over her, between her thighs, and frame her face with my hands. She's flushed, and her hair is a wild mess against the pillow. "You're perfect."

"I'm not. I—"

I press my mouth to hers and kiss away her protest. She opens under me, and my blood heats further when she licks her own taste from my lips. When her hips lift to meet mine again and she's moaning into my mouth, I pull away to shed my boxers and grab the condom from my jeans.

She watches me roll it on, and a surge of masculine pride jolts through me at the combination of satisfaction and anticipation on her face. She keeps her eyes on me as I climb over her, and doesn't break my gaze as I slowly slide inside.

"You feel . . ." I swallow hard and squeeze my eyes shut. I don't want to come yet, but I feel my release threatening to surge down my spine. "So good," I murmur. I move deeper and deeper with each pass, until her body adjusts to me and I thrust in fully.

"Brayden," she whispers in my ear. "Brayden, how can . . .? How can this feel . . .?"

I nuzzle her neck. "So good. Me too."

We find our rhythm easily, and I get lost in her. She smells like strawberries and something intoxicating. Her nails dig into my shoulders, and she squeezes around me, orgasm building again.

"Come for me." I thrust deeper, clinging to the scraps of self-control even as my own release threatens. "I want to feel you come like this."

The words push her over the edge, and she does, arching her neck and crying out. When her release locks her body tight around me, I follow right behind.

As we come down from our pleasure, I run kisses along her neck, her jaw, her lips.

I take care of the condom, and when I come back to bed, she's half-asleep. I pull her into my arms, loving the way our bodies fit together.

Next time, I want her in my bed, not in a sterile hotel made for strangers and secret lovers. Next time, I'll take it slow and show her just how much I've thought about this. Next time, and the time after that. "When can I see you again?" I whisper against her ear.

She hums, nestles into me, and falls asleep.

MOLLY

Present Day . . .

The tables are set. The water glasses are iced and ready. The kitchen is prepared to plate meals in twenty minutes. The staff members are dressed and know their stations, and I'm eighty percent confident that they're capable of doing their assigned tasks today—only eighty, because this is our first event and half my staff has never served before.

I scan the room one last time and cringe when the light catches on a handprint on the far bank of windows. I'm pretty sure that one was compliments of my son. *Shit.*

"Austin, run to the janitorial closet and grab the window cleaner." I point to the handprint. "I think our cleaning staff missed a spot."

"Sure thing, Miss Molly."

I cringe at the nickname but don't correct him. I *think* he's just trying to be polite. Austin's a cute kid, eighteen, and a senior at Jackson Harbor High School—the same school where I graduated with his older brother, Gabe. I did a lot more than *graduate* with his older brother, most of which I'd turn back time to erase if I had the choice. But it turns out Austin's much less lazy and more respectful than Gabe, and since he has serving experience, I'm thrilled to have him on my staff.

He heads toward the exit, but then stops and snaps a picture of the empty room with his phone.

I frown. "What's that for?"

He grins, his thumbs flying over his screen. "It looks awesome with the tables set and the linens and stuff. *Schmancy.* What's the social media hashtag campaign for Jackson Brews? I'm posting this sucker on Insta."

Oh, hell, that's kind of sweet. "The hashtag is *happeningatJacksonBrews*," I say. I should have thought of posting myself, but with everything else going on, it slipped my mind. "Thanks, Austin."

He winks at me. "No problem, Miss Molly. Done." He tucks his phone into the pocket of his black dress pants and disappears toward the janitorial closet.

I left my to-do list on my desk, and I'm feeling a little twitchy without it, so I head to my office even though I'm almost positive every item's been crossed off.

When I confirm there's nothing left to do, I plop down into my chair and realize immediately that it was a mistake. *What a day.* God, I'd give about anything to turn off the lights and close my eyes for twenty minutes.

"Are you okay?"

I lift my head and spot Brayden leaning in the doorway. "Everything's fine. Great, really. I think we're ahead of schedule."

He cocks his head to the side. "You look tired."

I wrinkle my nose. "Thanks."

He shakes his head. "I didn't mean to offend you. I'm just worried. You have a lot on your plate right now."

It's been a long day. After staying up packing until midnight, I woke up at four thirty and arrived onsite at six to make sure our new janitorial staff had the banquet center polished to my standards, but somehow I missed the windows. I'll have to chat with them about that.

I stayed through my scheduled midmorning break to monitor the kitchen staff, though they probably would have done fine without me. I am tired, but I've handled long work days on minimal sleep a hundred times before. What Brayden sees on my face is probably less about physical exhaustion and more about how anxious I am that I might screw this up.

Giving myself a little shake, I scan my list for the third time, confirming again that we're not forgetting anything. "I'm fine." I force a smile I'm too exhausted to make believable. "I promise to slap on some fresh lipstick so our clients don't think you're overworking me."

His gaze drops to my mouth and my bare lips. "I don't think you need it."

Snorting, I grab my purse. "You're just blinded by my inner beauty."

He doesn't reply to that—though, really, what can he say? Instead, he narrows his eyes and asks, "How was the house you saw yesterday?"

"A total bust. I don't need fancy finishes, and I know better than to expect them with my budget, but a working furnace in the middle of a Jackson Harbor winter is a must."

Brayden barks out a dry laugh. "Snob."

I laugh. "I guess so."

"Have you thought any more about my offer?"

A lot. Nonstop. Too much. My brain's been spinning with the implications and potential complications of moving in with Brayden. That's half the reason I stayed up so late last night. I knew I wouldn't sleep, so I figured I might as well get some packing done.

I bite my bottom lip. I know what I need to do. I know what the best decision is, for me, for my son. "It would just be temporary."

"I know."

"And you have to promise you'll tell me if we're in your way at all. Ever."

"I promise."

"I'd like Santa to visit Noah there on Christmas morning—presents under the tree and his stocking hung on the mantel and the whole bit. If that's not too much to ask. Because he's four, and Christmas is everything to him, and—"

"That's not a problem, Molly."

I nod sharply. "And I think we should agree that we won't sleep together." His eyes go wide, but I stumble on. "Because we've done that, and we know it's a bad idea and it'll only complicate things, and I know it's Christmastime and sometimes that can be kind of lonely so we might be tempted only to regret it later, and because I'm your employee and you're my boss, and I like this job so I'd rather not compromise it for physical gratification."

"That's a lot of reasons."

I swallow. "I have more." But no matter how many items I add to the list, I'm still afraid it'll fall short. Because he's *him* and I'm . . . I've never thought myself weak before, but our night in New York proves I have very little self-control when it comes to this man.

"Do you *need* more?"

Maybe. Probably. But he probably didn't need any reason at all, so it doesn't matter. "So we're agreed?"

"No sleeping together," he says, but I swear his gaze drops to my mouth for a beat, and my mind flashes to our night together, his eyes on my mouth, his hand on my thigh beneath the table. Is he thinking about it too?

Lust zaps through me at the memory. I close my eyes, only to be bombarded by a thousand more. *His head between my legs. His mischievous grin. The smell of him when he came back to bed and pulled me into his arms.*

When I look at him again, his expression has shifted to one of concern. Is he worried that I have feelings for him? Or that maybe I've been thinking too much about sleeping with him, and he hasn't thought about sleeping with me at all?

"You really do look tired. Is there anything you need me to do before the party gets here?"

Oh. *That.* Work stuff. Not hot, under-the-table, super-naughty, spank-bank stuff. "I'm fine." I clear my throat and can practically hear screeching tires. I mentally shift gears. *Work.* "If you want to greet Mr. Yuseki when he arrives, that would be great. I think he trusts me, but he's a little old school with the woman-in-charge situation."

"We'll greet him together," he says, and some of the tension I've been carrying all day melts. Because yes, Brayden takes his business very seriously, and yes, he wants this to go as well as I do, but he trusts me, and he wants Mr. Yuseki—a potentially huge client for repeat business—to understand that. "Be right back."

He disappears, and I dig in my purse for my lipstick. One look in my handheld mirror, and I see that he's right. I look like hell. Like a woman who has too much on her plate and is too stubborn to admit it. My boss isn't the only one who has trouble delegating.

When Brayden returns, he has a steaming cup of coffee in one hand and a glass of water in the other. "Caffeinate and hydrate," he says, setting them on my desk. "Rock this luncheon, and then tonight, after the taproom grand opening, *sleep*. If you need help finishing packing, I'll come over."

"I think you have enough to do without packing my stuff."

He shrugs. "Trust me, I've helped my siblings move enough times that I'm practically a pro."

I groan. "Why do you have to be so *nice*?"

His lips twitch like he's fighting a losing battle with a smile. "Would you rather have an asshole as a boss?"

"At least I know how to deal with assholes. I literally have *years* of experience."

He shakes his head slowly. "Drink your coffee, Molly. I'll come get you when Mr. Yuseki arrives."

"**H**ere's to Jackson Brews," Nic says, hoisting her glass in the air. "And another booming success."

"Hear, hear!" Teagan says, clinking her beer against Nic's.

The tasting room is so packed with the grand opening that the girls and I took our beers and snuck over to one of the small party rooms in the banquet center. Originally, I was going to manage the tasting room as well as the banquet center, but when interest poured in from people who wanted to use our facility for their events, it quickly became clear that we'd need someone for each position. Since Levi recently retired his motocross helmet to join the family business, it worked out perfectly. Tonight, that means I get to enjoy my friends and let him make sure everything up front is running smoothly.

Friends. Warmth sweeps over me at the realization. I spent years avoiding Jackson Harbor at all costs—avoiding my past and my family. Some days it feels like this incredible group of friends was my reward for finding the courage to return.

"And to Molly," Nic says. "I heard today's luncheon went off without a hitch."

I smile. "Mr. Yuseki already booked three more luncheons, so I would call it a success."

"That's awesome," Shay says. "Great work."

"Okay," Teagan says, glancing around the table. She points to Ava, who hasn't stopped yawning since we settled into our table in this quiet room. "You're knocked up and don't want to stay

64

out past eight most of the time." She turns to her right to point to Nic. "And your wedding is in two weeks, and you'll probably be knocked up shortly thereafter."

Nic shrugs. "I wouldn't mind, but I'd rather get through school first."

"So pretty much," Teagan continues, "it's going to be me and all you bitches with your fabulous sex lives and adorable babies."

"Um, hello?" Shay says. "Am I invisible or something?"

"Of course not, but your dissertation gets more of your attention than any hot guy in your bed would."

Shay shrugs as if to say "fair enough." She's Brayden's only sister, and though I haven't spent a lot of time with her since moving back home, I've always liked her. Even when half our high school was talking shit about me, Shayleigh Jackson was always kind.

I clear my throat and raise my hand. "No fabulous sex life here. I'm single, remember?"

"But you have an adorable little boy, so shut up."

"You want a baby?" I ask, arching a brow.

Teagan makes a face, her dark hair swinging around her face. "No. I'm just lamenting the fact that my fun, single friends are no longer . . ."

"Fun?" Ava supplies with a frown. "I don't feel like much fun, to be honest. I'm so tired and bloated. I slept through half my honeymoon. I mean, when we weren't . . ."

Shay holds up a hand. "We get the idea." She shudders. "I really need to find friends who aren't sleeping with my brothers."

"I think it's exciting," Nic says. "So much awesome stuff happening."

Teagan nods. "I'm happy for everyone. I just don't want you bitches to forget me when you're doing your playdates or whatever."

Nic wraps her arm around Teagan and squeezes her. "We're not gonna forget you."

"How are the wedding plans coming?" Teagan asks her.

I clear my throat. "Shouldn't you ask her official *wedding planner* that question?"

Nic beams. "I'm so excited. I can't believe I get to get married in front of the lighthouse. Lilly keeps calling it the *Frozen* wedding and is trying to convince me to bleach my hair so I'll look like Elsa." She shakes her head, love for the little girl all over her face. "Don't worry. We'll keep the ceremony short so you don't literally freeze."

I smile at Nic—my friend and the first bride to trust me with her reception. "Then we'll come back here and party. It's going to be perfect."

Jake appears in the doorway to the kitchenette, a tray of "The Jackson 5" flights in each hand. "I thought you ladies might be hiding back here." He steps up to our table and slides the flights into the middle.

"God, I miss beer," Ava whispers.

Jake winks at her. "Worth it."

"True." She blushes as his greedy eyes take her in, as if he hasn't touched her in a month and they *weren't* just caught making out in the kitchen thirty minutes ago.

Jake reluctantly tears his attention off his bride and turns to me. "Any luck on the house hunt?"

I shake my head. "None."

"What are you going to do?" Ava asks softly.

I'm honestly surprised the news hasn't already spread. Wildfire moves slowly compared to the Jackson family grapevine. "Brayden thought your idea made sense and offered to let Noah and I stay with him temporarily. I'm taking him up on it. Just until I can find something else. I told Noah this afternoon, and he's thrilled about it."

"Good." Jake smiles at me. "I'm glad to hear it."

"Speak of the devil," Ava says.

Brayden's standing in the doorway, his hand on Noah's shoulder. "Look who's here."

"Mama!" Noah shouts, rushing toward me.

Grinning, I turn in my seat, open my arms, and scoop him into my lap the moment he collides with my chest. "How was your day, Mr. Man?" I ask, burying my nose in his hair. He smells like his tear-free shampoo and Play-Doh.

"Ronica took me to the park, and I got to slide through the snow!"

I drop my jaw in an exaggerated show of surprise, even though Veronica ran the snowy park idea by me before she took him. "But it's so *cold* out! And it snowed all day! Are you an ice cube?"

He shakes his head. "No, Ronica made me wear a hat." He folds his arms and scowls. "I hate my hat."

"I'm glad she did, or you'd be Frosty the Snowman."

He giggles. "Would not."

I feel Brayden's eyes on us and look up. He's smiling. Really *smiling*. Warmth rushes through me at the sight of it, and when his eyes lock with mine, everything around me goes quiet and all

I can hear is the beating of my own heart.

"I hear you're *moving*," Ava says to Noah, and I could kiss her for the way she makes the word *moving* sound like the most exciting activity in the world.

Noah bounces on my lap and smiles at his aunt Ava. "We're going to stay with Rayden for a while! He said I can even stay in his old bedroom on the very top floor!" He turns those beautiful brown eyes to me and wraps a little hand in my hair. "How long are we staying, Mama?"

"I don't know exactly. Until after Christmas for sure."

His face lights up, and he turns to Brayden. "We get to spend Christmas with you? You'll be there when Santa comes?"

The room seems to go still, as if everyone around us is holding their breath.

Brayden's gaze flicks to mine for a beat before he nods at Noah. "I will."

"Will you help me open my presents?"

I tickle Noah's side. "Hey, who said you're getting presents this year?"

My boy doubles over, his sharp giggles filling the room. "I always get presents, silly."

The conversation turns to holiday plans. Everyone is smiling and relaxed, but I notice that Shay isn't smiling. No, Brayden's sister is watching me like she's a mama bear and I just stepped too close to her cubs.

BRAYDEN

"You're so much more badass than me," Shay says. "I hate running in the snow."

I tear my eyes off the glowing lights of my Christmas tree to survey my sister, who's in the kitchen doctoring her coffee. It's not even eight in the morning, but Shay was waiting in the kitchen when I got back from my run. I let her make coffee while I showered and got dressed. "I like running in the cold." I shrug. "Clears my head."

"You lost me at *I like running*. It's a necessary evil as far as I'm concerned."

I arch a brow. "You could work out with Carter and me at CrossFit if you hate running so much. You'd probably love it once you got going."

She shudders, then pulls her mug against her chest as if it can protect her. "And get callouses on my baby-soft hands? I'll pass."

I laugh. I haven't bothered to ask her why she's here. I know she's doing her typical sister thing and showing up to talk when no one else knows anything's bothering me. Usually, I'm grateful for her eerie perception. Today, I'm not sure I'm up for it.

Taking a seat on the couch beside me, she holds her mug in both hands as she folds her legs under herself, and we sip our coffee for a while, enjoying the comfortable silence of the crackling fire and an otherwise empty house.

"Are you ready to give up this quiet?" she finally asks. When I arch a brow in question, she says, "The house won't be this peaceful with a four-year-old living here."

I shake my head. "I don't mind. Noah's a pretty awesome kid."

My sister tips her head to the side as she studies me. "Hmm."

"Stop that," I growl.

"Stop what?"

"Stop trying to *read* me. You came over here for a reason. If you have a question, ask it."

"Really? You're *inviting* me to ask personal questions?"

"Aren't you going to ask them either way? Aren't you here for a recreational dig into my psyche, followed by a thinly veiled lecture on what you think I should do?" I wave toward myself. "Bring it."

"Okay, fine. Are you sure about this? I know having Molly stay here makes sense on paper, but if you have feelings for her—"

"I never said I have feelings for her."

"You didn't have to. I see the way you look at her."

I grunt. "You see what you want to see."

She rocks to the side and bumps her shoulder against mine.

"Come on, Brayden, you practically created a whole new business just so you'd have an excuse to bring her back to Jackson Harbor."

I open my mouth to object but close it again. I always planned to open the tasting room, but the banquet facility idea was born of a New York City conversation with Molly. One of our stops that day was to an event center, and she admitted how much she enjoyed the event-planning side of her not-for-profit work. She told me then that if I ever opened an event center, she wanted first dibs on managing it. She was joking—last spring, her stepfather was still alive and well, and that meant she had no intention of ever returning to Jackson Harbor—but I never forgot about it.

The tasting room morphed into something more because it was a good business decision, but maybe it was convenient that a good business decision also meant getting Molly closer. I won't deny I wanted that, even if she drew the line in the sand and made it clear that we'd never be more than boss and employee. I knew how much she struggled as a single mom with no family around, and I liked the idea of keeping an eye on her and being able to help when she needed it.

Shay's grinning at me. "You even get this dopey look on your face when you think about her."

"You're the only person in the world who thinks I'm easy to read," I mutter. And thank God. If everyone else could read my emotions as easily as Shay does, I'd feel like I was walking around cut open all the time.

"If only I could get a read on *her*," she says, wrinkling her nose. "I can't decide if she's just stuck between a rock and a hard place, or if she likes the idea of being closer to you on some level."

"Trust me. Her decision to move in has nothing to do with what happened between us."

"And what *did* happen? You never talk about it."

"I told you, we had a few drinks and . . . we connected, I guess. It was just one night." *A mistake.* Hell, nothing about it felt like a mistake. "No big deal."

Shay pulls her phone out of her pocket and plays around on the screen.

"What are you doing?"

"I'm adding up all the times you slept with a woman you didn't care about."

I blow out an exasperated breath. "Shut it."

"This is a tough one." She purses her lips and wrinkles her brow, the picture of thoughtfulness. "What's none plus never?"

"Are you really so well versed in my sex life, little sister?"

"I'm well versed in *you*." She gives me a pointed look that seems to say, *Tell me I'm wrong.* But I can't. I'm not a one-night stand kind of guy. I've just never seen the appeal. When I took Molly back to my room, I thought it was the beginning of something.

I was an idiot.

I swallow. "It makes sense to let her stay here. I have plenty of room." The truth is that I don't know how Molly really feels about this mess, but of the two options Shay presented for Molly's move, I'd guess *rock and a hard place.*

"It's not going to be weird?"

"It's a big house."

Shay takes a long pull from her coffee before shaking her head. "You're a stubborn ass."

"Thanks."

"And I'm afraid you're a stubborn ass who's going to end up hurt."

I have to laugh at that. Molly's never given me a reason to think we could have a relationship—quite the opposite, actually—so I'm not sure why Shay thinks my heart's at risk now. "I'll be fine."

"That's what I'm afraid of. You'll just be fine and never go after what you really want."

I cock my head. "I've lost track—are you trying to protect me from Molly or set me up with her?"

She frowns and mutters, "I haven't decided yet."

Rising from the couch, I pinch my sister's nose and shake my head. "I'm a grown boy, sis. Trust me to handle my life by myself."

MOLLY

"I'm already so tired," Bella says, whimpering dramatically as she collapses onto a breakroom couch.

Today is our first Saturday, and we arrived at five a.m. to prepare for a breakfast for the local Kiwanis club. My staff and I ate an early lunch and are wrapping up our break before heading up to start on the second party of the day—an eighty-person luncheon for Jackson Harbor Hospital. We'll finish cleanup from that just in time to go to tonight's Jackson Brews employee Christmas party.

"You'll be fine," I tell Bella, but I smile, because she did bust her ass this morning. She's earned a little whine. "Just a few more hours, and then we get the night off."

"Par-tay!" Austin says, grinning at me.

"My dad won't let me go to the Christmas party," Bella says. "He said someone my age has no business spending a Saturday night in a bar."

I frown. I'll have to talk to Brayden about that. Every year, they shut down the Jackson Brews bar for the employee Christmas party, but this is the first year we've had underage employees. Maybe next year we should do the party in one of the banquet rooms instead.

"That blows," Austin says from his spot at the table. He's been playing on his phone but puts it down to look at Bella. "You should come anyway. You're eighteen, aren't you?"

"Yeah, but I still live at home."

"So? What can your dad really do about it?"

I take a breath and move toward the locker room and away from the conversation. While I certainly want Bella to be able to come to the party, I'd rather not be part of a conversation that encourages her to go against her father's wishes.

The locker room door swings shut behind me, drowning out the words of their argument. I can't help but smile as I take in the space.

Knowing how long Saturdays can be in the catering and food service business, Brayden and I decided to dedicate some of our limited space to our employees' comfort. We wanted there to be a place to relax during breaks, and even shower if they needed to. So in addition to the casual relaxation space on the other side of the door, we invested in this locker room.

I dig through my purse for my lipstick but hesitate when I see my reflection. I look as tired as Bella feels. There are dark bags under my eyes, and my cheeks lack their normal color. It's been a long week, but I'm almost through it. Considering how well everything's going with the first banquet center parties, it's worth a little exhaustion.

I sweep pink over my lips, and the locker room door swings open.

Austin pushes in. "Everyone else went upstairs to clock in."

I nod, happy to hear my staff didn't have to be reminded what time their break was over. "I'll be up in a minute."

He clears his throat and holds my gaze a beat too long in the mirror.

Frowning, I turn to him. "Are you okay?"

He hesitates, then shakes his head. "I'm fine. I just . . ." He smiles. "You're a good boss. I thought you should know you're doing a great job."

"Oh." My shoulders sag. For a second there, I thought he'd come in here for something else. I was actually worried about this *kid* catching me alone when he just wanted to give me a compliment. Man, I'm screwed up. "Thank you, Austin."

"You're welcome." His eyes sweep over me slowly, lingering a little too long at my breasts and hips. "See you upstairs."

I stare at the door for a solid minute after he goes, trying to shake the slimy feeling that interaction left me with. He's just a teenage kid trying to butter up his boss. Any awkwardness I felt comes from me and my own baggage.

I shake it off, but make a mental note not to schedule him

to work alone with me. At least not until this uneasy feeling has passed.

I have a few minutes before I need to greet the next party, so I head to Brayden's office. I don't need to report to him, but since he's here—*cough*, workaholic, *cough*—I might as well let him know how well breakfast went. I stop a few steps outside the door when I hear another voice.

"If Nic's happy, I'm happy."

I smile at the sound of Ethan Jackson's voice. He must have come in to talk about wedding plans. I know I might never get a couple as easy to work with as him and Nic, so I've been making sure to enjoy how laidback and easygoing they are.

"Well, if you need anything else, just say the word, and Molly will make it happen."

I take another step, prepared to reveal myself, when Ethan says, "Speaking of Molly, you feel good about that? I know you didn't want to hire her, but it seems like she's doing great."

I take a step back. *Didn't want to hire me?*

"I think it's okay." Brayden is silent a beat, and I frown. *Okay?*

"You don't have to hide with me," Ethan says softly. "I get it. I see it when you look at her."

Brayden groans and mutters a curse. "She's just so . . ."

I'm frozen in place, waiting, knowing I don't want to hear him finish that sentence but unable to move my feet.

"On my bad days, I wish I'd never brought her on," Brayden says. "But I try not to be such a selfish ass most of the time. She's broken and she doesn't even know it. If I'd had any idea what kind of baggage she was dealing with, I would have never—"

I take one step back, then another. I don't want to hear any more. Humiliation roars in my ears. I stumble my way down the hall and toward the banquet room, where my staff is filling water glasses.

I bring a trembling hand to my lips. I hate the idea of anyone thinking of me as broken, but the idea that *Brayden* sees me that way, that he thinks my messy past makes me somehow less fit for this job? The words are so heavy that I can hardly fill my lungs.

Think about it later.

I lock away the hurt and focus on the job my boss wishes he'd never hired me to do.

BRAYDEN

"**You** wish you'd never slept with her?" Ethan asks gently.

"I wish I wouldn't have rushed things that night. I was just another asshole hooking up with her, and it was too easy for her to walk away."

"And now she's moving in with you."

I meet my brother's eyes, looking for what he's not saying. My younger brothers were always buddies, their own unit, and then Ethan and I were close, but life got in the way. Hell, maybe my workaholic tendencies got in the way. Or maybe things changed between us after he lost his wife, and I hated that I couldn't fix it. We've only started to reconnect in those old ways since Nic's been around.

Ethan knows about my night with Molly—knows more than

anyone else—and knows I wish more had come of it.

I drag a hand through my hair and stare up at the ceiling. I'm not big on sharing my feelings, but hell, if anyone will understand, it's Ethan. "At first, the attraction was mostly physical. But seeing her with Noah and working next to her all the time . . . Jesus, she's the best employee I've ever had, and I know we need her here. I *know* it. But I keep wondering what would have happened if I'd never hired her."

"If you hadn't hired her, she'd still be in New York."

I sigh. "*Details.* It's just that she puts the job above anything else, and I wish she wouldn't. I know I don't want to."

Ethan's eyes go wide, and he shakes his head. "Wow."

"What?"

"I can't believe Brayden 'Workaholic' Jackson wishes he could put his personal interests ahead of his business."

I shrug. "It's my own damn fault." If I'd taken things slower and we'd not spent the night together, maybe she'd look at me differently now.

"I'm not judging. Hell, it's refreshing, brother. You deserve a life of more than endless paperwork."

"It doesn't change anything. She works for me, and she doesn't want a relationship with her boss." She's made that more than clear.

Ethan folds his arms and smirks at me. "You know, Nic was my employee before she was my girlfriend. Maybe it's not ideal, but if you really want her and she wants you, I'm sure you can work it out. When it's real, it's worth the risk."

My gaze goes to the hall behind my brother, as if I could magically will her to appear. I see her almost every day, but when she's close, it feels like I'm waking up. When she's not, I catch myself finding excuses to go to her. "I'm not sure she wants me in return."

Ethan shrugs. "She's moving in with you. I can't imagine a better time to find out."

Seven

MOLLY

Usually, I'm a beer girl. Not that mass-produced tasteless stuff. God no. I work for Jackson Brews, and drinking any beer with the word "Lite" in its name would probably get me fired or shunned at the very least. No. I love beer like I love art—complex, effortful, rich, and layered. Porters, barrel-aged stouts, saisons with a fruity back end.

But tonight, I skipped the beer and went straight for the tequila. One shot upon arriving at the Jackson Brews employee Christmas party, and another shot every time I thought about Brayden Jackson wishing he never hired me. Calling me *broken*.

I'm on shot number five . . . a shot for every hour that's passed since I heard him say those words.

I nudge my empty shot glass toward the bartender. She's a server from Howell's, but the Jacksons brought her on for tonight so none of their staff would have to work the Christmas party—an event that's a work gathering for half of us and family reunion for the other half.

"I can't." The peppy bartender bites her lip as she looks to someone standing behind me. She brings her gaze back to meet mine. "You've been cut off."

I turn around to see who she was looking at and spot Brayden. He's cut me off, and he's watching me with the same worried look he's been subjecting me to since I walked in the door and started tossing them back.

He saunters toward me, giving Kitty a nod that sends her scurrying to help someone on the opposite end of the bar. "You okay?"

The worry in his eyes, and his words—God help me. The tequila surges in my stomach. *Poor Molly.* I'd rather face the sneers of a hundred mean girls than be pitied. I thought I earned this position, even if it was initially given as a favor, but Brayden still sees it as a pity job for a broken girl. "I'm fine, so you can stop looking at me like that."

"You've been avoiding me all night."

"I haven't been avoiding you. I've been celebrating." I force a smile. "That's what we're here for, isn't it? To celebrate another great year for Jackson Brews?"

He looks into my eyes for so long that I want to turn away from him or, at the very least squirm, but I'm too stubborn, and I only lift my chin.

"If seeing me cut loose makes you *uncomfortable*, I'll go home. Just say the word."

"Did everything go okay at the banquet center today?"

I grunt and catch myself reaching for my empty shot glass. "Surprisingly well, considering." *Considering you never wanted to hire me. Considering you regret the decision.*

He frowns. "Considering what?"

"Don't you have employees you need to schmooze with or something? Or maybe new hires to sweet-talk into your bed?" It's a low blow, and I regret it the minute the words pass my lips.

Something flashes in his eyes. "You're a mean drunk, Molly."

When he walks away, I keep my ass glued to my barstool instead of running after him like I want to. Hell, he saved my ass when he hired me, so I should be grateful, pity or no.

A man lowers himself onto the barstool beside me. He's built and tall—maybe not as much as Brayden on either count, but impressive nonetheless. His light brown hair slides over one eye, and when he brushes it back, I can't help but notice the size of his hands. Big hands. Nice hands. Brayden has nice hands too—big and a little rough.

Don't think about Brayden. He doesn't want you. Not even as an employee. You're broken.

So I throw all my energy into focusing on this new, very attractive man beside me as he studies the tap list on the chalkboard.

"What's good?" he asks, not looking at me.

"That depends." I like to think that my words can pass for husky and not drunken and slurred. "What do you like?"

"Blondes," he says before tearing his gaze off the menu and turning to me. I arch a brow, and he laughs, grimacing only slightly when I flip my hair. "I mean, blonde beers, but, well, also . . ." *Damn.* Is that a blush creeping up his neck? "Yeah." He extends a hand. "My name's Jason, and I swear I'm not typically so awkward."

I take his hand. Big. Warm. Softer than Brayden's, but—

I cut off that train of thought before it can go any further. It's been seven months since my ill-advised night with my boss, and I still can't stop comparing guys to him. One night with his hands and mouth, and my body decided he was the gold standard by which all other men should be measured. *So irritating.*

"I'm Molly," I say softly.

"You're the one managing the banquet center," Jason says, a smile curling his lips.

"That's me. And what about you? A sales manager?" I ask. It's a reasonable guess, since this is an employee party. There are sales managers all over the country though.

"I'm . . . not exactly on the payroll." He grins and waves to the taps behind the bar. "Can I buy you a drink?"

"It's an open bar," I say, not willing to admit that he couldn't even if I wanted him to. *Because my boss thinks he needs to babysit me.*

He grimaces and shakes his head. "Right. Sorry." Then that grin again.

Before I know what I'm doing, I'm tracking Brayden across the room. I hurt his feelings with my jab about seducing new employees. I should apologize. Or thank him for putting up with me despite my brokenness. Or maybe I should just go home before I do something stupid. Or, worse, *someone.*

"You're from Jackson Harbor, aren't you?" Jason asks. "Where have you been?"

I do my best to lock up the tangle of emotions that flood me every time I think of Brayden telling his brother he regrets hiring me, pull my attention back to the man in front of me, and smile widely. "I've lived in New York for the last eight years. What about you?"

BRAYDEN

Molly is dancing with Jason Ralston. They're *dancing* together in the middle of my bar like this is some dance club and not a fucking brewpub. She has her arms wrapped behind his neck and is laughing as if he's the funniest guy she's ever met. *Fucking fantastic.*

I'm trying not to glare, but it's hard not to be irritated. She's avoided me since she walked in the door, but Jason fucking Ralston makes her light up like that?

Carter smacks me between the shoulder blades. "You're staring, brother."

I tear my gaze off Molly. Off her long legs, exposed in that short red dress. Off her hips, swaying to the music. Off the grin she's been giving Jason. I thought she was just busy when she avoided me at work earlier, but she barely spared me a hello when she got here tonight, and then upped the stakes when she went for the tequila.

I've been keeping one eye on her all night, but maybe a little more since Jason arrived. I *thought* I was being inconspicuous. Apparently not.

"They seem to be hitting it off, huh?" Carter asks, frowning toward Molly and Jason.

"Seems like it." I shake my head and give my attention to the rest of our guests. We do a Jackson Brews Christmas party every year. We shut down the bar and eat a big meal, give everyone gifts for another year of service, drink, and party. It's never been my thing, but I was excited about it this year. Now I'm not sure why. Did I think Molly and I would hang out tonight? That she'd change her tune and suddenly start looking at *me* like that?

Jason whispers something to Molly before heading toward the restroom.

"I'll be right back," I mutter to Carter. My brother sets his mouth in a thin line and tilts his head. His expression says, "Don't do anything stupid," but he's wise enough not to say it out loud.

I'm not about to be the creep who follows a guy to the urinal, so I wait in the hall for Jason's return. He lights up like a Christmas tree when he sees me, and meanwhile, it's all I can do not to scowl. "Brayden!"

I take his outstretched hand and shake it hard. "Thanks for coming tonight."

"Happy to, man. Happy to."

I take a breath. This is awkward, but I'm not about to keep my mouth shut when I see the way he looks at Molly and I know how much she's been drinking. "You met Molly?"

"Yeah. Christ, she's fantastic, isn't she? She's going to be great over at the other facility. I just know it."

Sure. Act like you've been feeling her out for business reasons. "I agree," I say stiffly.

Jason tilts his head. "But you didn't corner me back here

because you wanted to talk to me about her work ethic," he says. "You two are . . . involved?"

I cough. *Shit.* "No. Not at all. We're . . . friends." I might hate that word.

His shoulders sag. "Well, that's good, because she can't take her eyes off me."

My hands flex into fists. "About that . . . She's had a bad day." I don't have any idea what would have made her reach for the tequila tonight, but this isn't normal behavior for her. Something's wrong.

His eyes narrow. "Shit. What happened?"

I don't know. She won't talk to me. "It doesn't matter. My point is that she's not herself tonight. Don't . . ." *Don't fucking touch her?* Yeah, I'm pretty sure Molly would cut off my balls if I overstepped to that extreme. "If you two are going to start something, tonight might not be the time."

Jason tucks his hands into his pockets. "I've never been a patient man."

"She's drunk." My unspoken *asshole* hangs in the air between us. Jason's not stupid. I'm sure he can see it in my eyes.

He smacks me on the shoulder. "I'm sure she appreciates you looking out for her. Like a big brother, right? No worries, Bray."

Bray. I fucking hate that. Only douchebags who think their money entitles them to the world call me *Bray*. But there's nothing else I can say. I warned him. I made my concern clear. Now all I can do is hope that he'll listen or that Molly's sobered up enough that she won't make any decisions she'll regret tomorrow.

When I return to the party, Molly and Jason are back at the bar, and she's drinking—no, *chugging*—Jason's beer. That's the last thing she needs, but if I interfere, Jason will think I'm trying to come between them.

Carter's watching them too, and he frowns at me. "I know we need that fuckboy to invest in the new bottling facility, but I hope that doesn't mean I have to like him."

"Is this the singles corner?" Shay pushes to stand between me and Carter.

Carter sighs. "It appears so."

"Am I a bad sister for hating them a little?" she asks.

I follow her gaze to Jake and Ava. It appears they took the lead from Molly and Jason, because they've abandoned their game of pool to dance. Jake's hands are all over his wife, from her hips to her softly rounded belly.

"That's not hatred," Carter says, smiling at the two of them. "That's jealousy."

"They're just perfect together," Shay says. "I'll never, ever find that. But after growing up and seeing Mom and Dad love each other so unconditionally, I can't bring myself to settle for less."

"Nor should you," Carter says softly.

I catch a flash of blond hair and turn my head just in time to see Molly tugging Jason into the kitchen behind her. "Where the hell are they going?" I mutter.

Shay squeezes my shoulder in silent sympathy. If I wanted to hide my feelings for Molly from my family, I've done a piss-poor job of it. "I didn't realize they knew each other."

"Who says they do?" Carter asks.

"Has Ralston decided if he's going to buy in?" Shay asks.

I shrug, unable to say more when my thoughts are on what Molly is doing with him in the kitchen.

"You can leave," Carter says. "You've done your duty as Mr. Bossman, and Shay and I can take it from here."

I flash my brother a grateful look. If I stay, I risk barging into that kitchen and pulling Jason off Molly. I want to keep her from doing something she'll regret tomorrow, but I know it'll come off like I'm some overprotective father—the last thing I want to be to her. "I think I will."

Sliding my hand into my pocket, I palm my keys and eye the door to the kitchen. I'm parked in the back, but I'm self-aware enough to know passing Molly and Jason on my way out is a terrible idea.

Shay seems to read my thoughts. "Maybe go around front."

"Good call."

She bumps her shoulder against mine and smiles. "See you in the morning for the big move."

I meet Carter's eyes. "Make sure she doesn't try to drive home."

He nods. "Of course."

Eight

MOLLY

"Christ, you're gorgeous," the guy whispers into my neck. I blink, my head spinning as I try to remember where I am and who I'm with.

My mouth tastes like lime and tequila. Sleep tugs at me, but I shake my head to chase it away and try to focus on the guy I'm straddling. We're in a car . . . his car?

He trails kisses across my collarbone and snakes a hand down the front of my dress to cup me through my bra. I focus on pinning down my thoughts, but it's like catching snowflakes. They melt away each time I reach for them.

His car. Yes, this is his car, and he's . . . I blink at him, and he grins at me. I met him at the party. I smile back, drunkenly proud of myself for piecing this much together.

We're in the back of his car in the Jackson Brews back lot,

and his name is . . . *Jason. Jason who likes blondes.*

"I spotted you the second I walked in tonight." He tugs my dress down and scrapes his teeth over the top of my breast. "Wanted to do this from the moment I saw you."

My eyes float closed, and my head lolls to the side. It's freezing out here, but my skin is hot. Too much. I drank too much. And there are too many hands on me all at once. At my waist then palming my breast, my ass, in my hair. Another slides up my thigh.

"Stop. I . . ."

He pulls back and meets my eyes. "Are you okay?"

I swallow hard and nod, my day coming back to me in a rush. Remembering Brayden's conversation with Ethan makes an old, ugly feeling rise in my chest. Like a blooming weed that steals the sun from everything else. I just wanted to forget everything. And then this guy . . .

I press my mouth to his, trying to chase the thoughts away with his touch. His hands resume their exploration, and he tugs down one side of my wide-necked dress to reveal my lace bra.

"So hot," he murmurs, lowering his head.

I rock into him as he sucks my nipple through the lace, loving the way the sensation obliterates everything else. He tugs the other side of my dress down and off my arms until I'm in nothing but my bra from the waist up.

I'm broken, and no amount of proving myself will ever be good enough, but here—in the arms of this stranger—I can forget all that. I can be sexy. Wanted. Not a charity case like Brayden sees me.

The thought has a sob ripping from my throat, and I press

my palms against Jason's chest to push him away.

He blinks at me. "What's wrong?"

I scramble off his lap, sitting sideways on the seat beside him. Shit. What am I doing?

"Hey, it's okay," he whispers, reaching for me.

Blowjob Molly. God, I promised myself I wouldn't be that girl again, but here I am, hooking up with a stranger in a dark parking lot.

Another sob tears out of me. *Slut. Easy. Whore.*

"Are you okay?" he asks. His eyes are wide. Panicked.

I reach for the door handle and lunge out of the car, spilling onto the gravel lot and rushing away from the car on my hands and knees. *Not that girl anymore. I don't want to be her.*

The cold air hits me like a million tiny pinpricks. My dress is down around my waist, my bra exposed.

"Molly?"

I lift my head to see Brayden. His nostrils flare as his gaze shifts from me to Jason, who's climbing out of his car. I don't have time to say a word before Brayden takes three long strides forward and swings his fist, connecting with Jason's jaw and sending him to the ground.

"Stop!" I scream.

"What did you do to her?" I've never heard so much menace in Brayden's voice, and I jump off the ground and grab his arms before he can swing again. He's stronger than me by miles and could shake me off if he wanted, but he doesn't.

"What the fuck?" Jason cries, holding the side of his face.

"He didn't do anything." I tug Brayden away from the car. He lets me, but his hard glare stays on Jason.

"You're half undressed, crying, and running away from him. Doesn't sound like nothing."

"Fuck you," Jason says. "I'm not a fucking rapist. She just flipped out for no reason."

"Then why was she crying?"

Jason throws up his hands. "Fuck if I know." He meets my eyes, and guilt washes over me, nearly drowning out the shame of becoming that girl again. "Did I do something that scared you?"

"I'm sorry." I'm not sure who I'm talking to. Maybe everyone. This is such a disaster. I tug up my dress. God, it's freezing out here, and I have snow all over my bare legs from crawling on my hands and knees through the parking lot. "I just had a bad day and I thought I wanted . . . I'm sorry."

"She's obviously trashed, and you took advantage," Brayden growls.

"I'm fine." I tug on Brayden's sleeve. "I'm just drunk and I want to go home."

"You're a piece of work, Jackson," Jason mutters. "I'm going to have to rethink our partnership."

"That makes two of us," Brayden says.

Partnership? The cold air zips along my skin, clearing my mind and marginally sobering me.

"I'm sorry." I don't know how many times I've said it, but it's not enough. I just want this to be over. I want tonight to have never happened. I want to rewind the day and start over so I never listen in on Brayden's conversation with Ethan.

"Get in the car," Brayden says without looking at me. "I'll take you home."

"Please," I whisper. "I'm sorry."

When some of the coiled tension leaves his shoulders, I release him and climb into the car. Brayden climbs in the driver's side and starts the engine without looking at me.

"Who was that?" I ask.

Brayden's jaw twitches, but he still doesn't look at me. "You were half-naked in the back of his car, and you have to ask me who he is?"

"You know what I mean. Who is he to you? To . . ." I close my eyes, realizing what I should have thought of much sooner. Anyone at that party should have been off-limits, because everyone at that party is affiliated with Jackson Brews. "What's his connection to Jackson Brews?"

"He's an investor. He was considering helping us expand our bottling facility."

I bite my bottom lip. *Was.* Past tense. Because I screwed it up. Blowjob Molly screwed it up. I can't blame Brayden for wishing he'd never hired me, can I? "I'll fix it," I promise, but I have no idea how.

Brayden drags a hand through his hair. "Did he hurt you or try to—"

"I said he didn't."

He flashes me a look that says he still doesn't believe me. "You were crying."

I turn away, looking out my window at the pretty lights lining Main Street. "It was a bad day."

He doesn't say another word until we pull into the driveway of my rental, and he cuts the engine. "Do you need me to stay and take care of Noah?"

My blood cools, and the shame in my chest flips to

indignation. "You think I'm going home to my son like this? That I'd go home drunk to my four-year-old?"

"I didn't think you'd get trashed at a work event and grind against a potential investor like you're . . ."

I glare hard. "Like I'm *what*?"

His jaw twitches. "Never mind."

"Like I'm easy? Like I'm a slut?"

"You're putting words in my mouth," he says tightly.

"You're an asshole." I climb out of the car and race to the house, all too aware of Brayden following me. I unlock the front door and push inside as fast as my limited coordination will allow.

Before I can close the door behind me, Brayden stops it with one big hand. "Molly."

I lift my eyes to his, studying his face in the porch light. "Noah is at my mom's."

He nods slowly, studying my face but not saying a thing. He's so damn stingy with his words, and it drives me insane.

"I wouldn't have had more than a drink if he weren't somewhere safe for the night. I'm a lot of things, Brayden, but I'm not a bad mom."

"I didn't say you were."

"You implied it." I close my eyes, nausea rolling over me. My living room is littered with boxes ready for tomorrow's move, and I don't even know if Brayden wants me to move in with him anymore. I take a breath. "I'm sorry if I screwed something up with Jason. I'll talk to him. I'll fix it somehow."

Brayden bristles. "I don't know if I want you talking to him alone." He stares at me, looking me over again and again, as if he expects to see injuries. "Tonight . . . it looked bad."

"I know, but he didn't do anything wrong. I was fine, and then suddenly I wasn't and I just needed to get away." I fold my arms, imagining how it looked from Brayden's point of view: me scrambling out of the car with my dress around my waist, sobbing. "It was a bad day."

"Are you okay now?"

No. I'm not okay. Because Brayden's right. I'm broken, and there's no fixing me. I'm a shattered bone that was allowed to heal without ever being set. "I'm fine."

I see the word in his eyes: *liar.* But he doesn't say it. Instead, I get a single nod. A final once-over, as if he still doesn't believe I wasn't assaulted. "Good night."

"Good night." And I'm proud of myself, because I manage to lock the door and make it to my bedroom before my tears return.

I wake up to someone pounding on the door, and bury my face in the pillow.

Moments from last night flash in my mind. The shots. The pity on Brayden's face. The guy . . .

I roll over in bed and press my hand to my forehead, and I remember Brayden driving me home, the twitch in his jaw, the anger blazing in his eyes. His rage was so much better than the pity I saw in his eyes when he said good night.

The pounding continues, and I force my eyes open to look at the clock. Eight a.m. Who the hell is at my door at eight a.m. on a Sunday— *Shit*! I'm supposed to move in with Brayden today.

I climb out of bed, race to the door, and yank it open.

Carter Jackson's standing on my front porch, and he blinks at me before turning around and putting a hand over his eyes. "We'll wait here while you get dressed," he says, discomfort evident in every word.

I look down and wince. A T-shirt I don't remember changing into and a pair of boy-cut panties. Could have definitely been worse, but if I'd given half a thought to my appearance before rushing to the door, I'd have at least pulled on some pants.

On the sidewalk beyond Carter, Brayden scowls and runs his eyes over me in a way that is one hundred percent disapproving and zero percent sexual. *Figures.*

"Come on in." I pull the door wider. "I'll be right back." I want to rush to my room and hide, but pride makes me keep my head high and sway my hips as I walk away.

Once I reach the privacy of my room, I shut the door behind me and change quickly, trying to ignore the relentless pounding in my head that begs me to send them away and crawl back in bed. I was the idiot who got drunk last night. Now I get to pay for it by feeling like death on moving day. Frankly, it's not punishment enough if I truly screwed up Brayden's relationship with a potential investor.

I drag a hand over my face. I need to talk to Jason tomorrow. I'll have to get his information somehow, since I doubt Brayden's going to hand it over. I need to apologize for what happened. Explain that I didn't dart out of his car because of him but because I panicked.

Once I'm dressed in a pair of leggings and a loose-fitting

long-sleeve T-shirt, I brush my teeth and hair then wander out to the kitchen. Apparently, more Jacksons arrived while I was dressing. Now, in addition to Brayden and Carter, Levi, Shay, Jake, and Ethan stand in my kitchen. At least they didn't *all* see my panties.

"I brought coffee." Shay shoves a mug into my hands. "Thought you'd need it."

I flash her a grateful smile and take a long sip. "Marry me," I whisper, and she grins.

"So what's the plan?" Carter asks.

"I say we load up the furniture and the stuff for the storage unit first," Levi says. "Then we'll get the stuff for Brayden's moved."

I tuck away my discomfort at the whole situation and turn to the group. "I'm not moving much to Brayden's. Mostly clothes and some of Noah's favorite toys. Those things are labeled. Everything else will go into storage."

The brothers nod and disperse, setting to work on the piles of boxes in my living room.

I meet Brayden's eyes. After last night, does he want to rescind his offer to let me and Noah stay with him? If his siblings knew I might have hurt the family business, would they still want to help me today?

Brayden just gives me a barely perceptible nod, as if he can read the questions on my face.

"You're sure about this?" I ask softly.

"Absolutely." That's quintessential Jackson behavior. Unconditional acceptance. I was raised by a stepfather who put conditions on everything, and I never know what to make of this group and their kindness. But after the mess I made last night, I need to know he hasn't changed his mind.

"Can we speak privately for a minute?"

He nods, and I lead the way down the hall. I was going to take him to my room, but I turn into Noah's at the last minute, because bringing him into mine feels too . . . intimate.

I shut the door behind him. "Do you want me to find another place to stay?"

"No. I already told you I'm sure."

"But after last night . . ." My cheeks heat. I spent years rewriting my identity, only to have one bad day send me spiraling back to my teenage habits. In the sober, hungover light of morning, I'm ashamed. "I made a mistake."

He wanders to Noah's desk across the room, toying with the Power Rangers sitting in a box. "So did I. I should never have assumed . . . anything."

"Noah and I can find somewhere else. There are hotels and even some apartments that would be . . . acceptable." I swallow hard as he turns. He knows how I feel about my options, and I hate the pity I see in his eyes. "We'd be fine."

"I've already promised Noah the attic bedroom and to be there on Christmas morning to see what Santa brought." He shrugs. "I'm a man of my word."

I straighten, trying to hide the way his promise to my son makes me melt. Letting Brayden know he makes me feel all melty inside—letting him know how easily I could want more—is dangerous territory. "Thank you."

"Go eat some breakfast," he says. "It'll help with the hangover."

"Hey, asshole!" Levi calls from the hall. "Wanna come out here and help us with this couch, or what?"

Amusement flashes over Brayden's face, and he gives me one final searching glance before leaving to join his brothers.

Nine

MOLLY

With all the Jacksons helping, the move goes much faster than I anticipated, and we're dropping the last of my bags in one of Brayden's upstairs bedrooms by lunchtime. I chose the room with the soft blue walls and the dark mahogany queen-size bed.

"I found one more box in the back of your car," Brayden says behind me. He plops it onto the end of the bed. "Are you okay?"

"She's broken and she doesn't even know it."

If he didn't want to hire me, surely he didn't want me to move in. But the promises he made to Noah are as important to me as they are to him, and being able to give Noah a good Christmas is more important than my pride. I'll endure the humiliation of Brayden's pity until after the holidays. Then I'll find a new job and somewhere to live.

"I'm fine." I focus on organizing the clothes I tossed on the middle of the bed, all too aware that Brayden is still in the room.

"Are you still feeling sick? Or is it something else?"

"I just wish you didn't have to let us stay." I force myself to turn, to meet his eyes even when shame makes my cheeks hot. "I have some leads for houses that are supposed to be available for rent at the beginning of the year."

He frowns. "I told you there's no rush. Stay as long as you want."

"Brayden, would you come down here and cut the ham?" Kathleen calls up the stairs.

"Be right down," he says, not taking his eyes off me. "Just give me a shout if you need anything, okay?"

"Sure."

"Oh, and this box wasn't labeled. Where do you want it?" He pulls open the flaps of the box he set on the bed when he entered. "Looks like there are some washcloths in here. And . . ." He lifts a stack of washcloths and peers at the contents beneath. His eyes go wide. "Oh."

The moment my brain registers what box he's looking at, I lunge for him and smack a hand over his eyes. I intentionally put that box in my car, separate from the others. And I *forgot*.

Brayden's chest rumbles with laughter, and I want the floor to open up and swallow me whole.

Brayden Jackson just saw my entire vibrator collection.

He gently pulls my hand away, revealing eyes full of mischief.

I squeak. "Don't look in that box again."

His lips twitch. "But I really, *really* want to."

I point a finger at him. "Don't you dare."

He presses his lips into a thin line, amusement dancing in his eyes. Then, as if he can't help himself, he asks, "Are they *all* pink?"

"Shut *up!*" My cheeks are on *fire.*

His voice is the softest caress of a whisper when he says, "Molly, your cheeks are almost as pink as your vibrators."

I smack both hands against his chest. "You did not just say that word!"

"Vibrators?" He grins. Not one of his smirks or half smiles, but a *grin*, and damn me and my stupid chemical attraction to this man, because it makes me want to slam the bedroom door closed and climb him like a tree. "If you don't like the word, why do you have—"

I throw my hand over his mouth. "Don't say it. We agreed we'd keep our relationship professional—that's what we both wanted. So don't say it. Don't even *think* about it." Then, because I realize his lips are pressed to my palm and it reminds me too much of our night in New York when his lips were *everywhere,* I back away.

The warm amusement in his eyes turns to heat. "First of all," he says, his voice like silky steel, "those were your rules, not mine. I agreed for you, not because that's what *I* want." He drags his gaze over me, and my heart pounds so fast it feels like a hummingbird's trying to escape my chest. "Second, even if I tried not to think about you using your little collection of pink toys, I'd fail miserably." He dips his head, and I can feel his breath against my ear as he says, "I'm already thinking about it, and I will be for a long time yet."

I swallow and try to ignore the heat pooling low in my belly, dipping lower. "I'd rather you didn't."

With a shrug that seems to say *too bad*, he winks at me and leaves my room.

As soon as he goes, I press my hands to my hot cheeks.

I take the box and hide it in the back corner of the closet, but I can't stop thinking about the way Brayden looked at me, about his words. *"I agreed for you, not because that's what I want."*

What does that mean? Just yesterday, he was telling his brother he thought I was broken, but now he wants more from me? I don't understand what he feels about me, but something tells me that trying to figure it out will put me in dangerous territory.

Mom's on her way over with Noah, so I push my embarrassment and confusion to the side, head up to the attic loft, and put Noah's Batman bedding on the bottom bunk. I make the bed and line his favorite stuffed animals up along the wall. The second I hear his happy screech of delight, I grin and rush to the stairs.

Noah's already on his way up. "I want to see my room!" he shouts as he flies past me.

I let him go and smile at my mom, who's making her way up behind him. "He certainly has a lot of energy," she says, pride in every word.

"How was he last night?"

"Perfect, of course."

I snort. Noah could be a holy terror, and Mom would still think he was perfect. I'm so grateful for that. For her unwavering adoration of her grandson. "Did he sleep through the night?"

"He got up around three for a drink and then went right back to bed. This morning, he helped me make muffins and ate three while they were still piping hot." She glances down the hall toward my bedroom. "It's nice of your boss to let you stay here."

"It is." *Please don't ask if this means something more. Please don't make me talk about my feelings for Brayden.*

"I'll find a bigger house," she says, surprising me. "As soon as everything's settled with Nelson's estate." Her calm expression falters when my stepfather's name passes her lips, and my breath catches and my eyes burn.

Originally, I planned to keep what her husband did to me a secret forever. I never wanted her to know about those years of feeling dirty and scared and ashamed—as if the abuse was somehow my fault. As if it was my fault when he raped me again, years after I thought I'd escaped him for good.

"I'll find somewhere to live where you and Noah can come any time," she says, her voice trembling. "I should have gotten a place of my own years ago." Her eyes fill with tears, and I wish again that I could have saved her from the heartache of the truth. "I never want to fail you again," she whispers, and the words tug on a loose thread inside me, unraveling emotions I keep locked up tight.

This has been such a hard year. My stepfather disappeared and was murdered—his dirty business dealings finally came back to get him. My stepbrother, Colton, was the prime suspect in the investigation, and as a result, I found myself coming forward and admitting that my stepfather sexually abused me for years.

As a teenager, I kept busy so I wouldn't have to be close to him. If I wasn't at a sporting event or volunteering with one of my groups, I was at a party like the one Brayden rescued me from that night—drinking and trying to prove my worth by giving myself to any guy who slid a compliment my way. When I left for college,

I did everything I could to never return to Nelson's house. I took internships and school trips and shitty summer jobs—anything to keep myself out of my stepfather's reach. But the summer I graduated from college, I came home before starting graduate school, and one night he got drunk and held me down.

For almost five years, I hid the results of that night from everyone in Jackson Harbor but my mother. But even though my mother knew I was pregnant, she didn't know the child was Nelson's until last month. Before then, I'd let her believe Noah was the result of a drunken night between me and Colton, and she believed I was keeping Noah a secret in order to shield my child from Colton's addictions. I spent years lying to her and hiding from everyone else, just to protect her.

My eyes burn and my throat thickens. I squeeze her arm. "It wasn't your fault, Mom."

She opens her mouth to reply and is cut off by the sound of tiny feet racing down the attic stairs.

Noah darts around the corner and grabs his nana's arm. "Come see my room!"

"Your *temporary* room," I remind him. "We're only visiting. Not staying forever."

He ignores me and drags his nana up the stairs. Mom shoots me a smile over her shoulder as she goes.

With Noah occupied, I decide to use the time to unpack my room, but I don't even get through the door before Shay is at the foot of the stairs, shouting at me to come down and join them for lunch.

"Be right there," I call.

I head up the stairs to the attic. Mom is sitting in the middle of the floor with Noah, her legs crossed under her as she watches her grandson play. "Noah? Let's go have some lunch."

"I'm not hungry!" he says, his eyes on the Power Ranger he's flying through the air.

I smile, knowing I hold the trump card. "I saw cinnamon rolls down there."

Noah drops the Power Ranger and races out the door and down the stairs. Mom and I laugh and follow.

"Would you like to stay?" I ask her as we reach the bottom of the stairs.

She shakes her head. "I wouldn't want to intrude."

"The Jacksons always say there's room for everyone."

She pulls me into a hug. "That's sweet, honey, but I need to run some errands. I'll see you soon."

I hug her back and kiss her cheek before pulling away.

Ava joins us in the foyer. "Are you leaving already, Jill?"

My mom nods at her stepdaughter before embracing her. "I'll stay another time," she promises. When she pulls back, her eyes are on Ava's growing belly. "You look great. Are you feeling okay?"

"I feel great."

"Mom!" Noah shouts from the kitchen. "Can I have *two* cinnamon rolls?"

I point at my mom before she can tell him yes. "Don't you dare," I whisper, then call to my sugar-holic son, "Only one!"

Mom laughs. "Love you both," she says to Ava and me before heading out the door.

Ava leads the way to the kitchen, where Jake is helping Noah fill his plate with food from the massive spread. I knew the Jacksons would do their typical family Sunday brunch after the move, but I thought they might do something simple, since they were busy all morning. Instead, they've prepared a feast. The kitchen peninsula is crowded with dishes: cinnamon rolls, fruit salad, hash brown casserole, ham, eggs, sausage, and enough bacon to feed an army.

I think I must be gaping, because Shay laughs. "We're gluttons on Sundays," she says. "You get used to it."

"More bacon," Noah tells Jake, who's already put two pieces on my child's plate.

Jake musses his hair before adding another two pieces. "That's my kind of kid."

Noah heads to the dining room with his plate and takes a seat beside Ethan's daughter, Lilly.

Jake hands me a plate. "Since this is your first Jackson family brunch, you're required to stuff yourself until you feel mildly nauseated."

I arch a brow and open my mouth to protest, but across the room, Nic shouts, "It's tradition."

"Well, who am I to buck tradition?" I fill my plate and follow the Jacksons to the massive dining room table. Within seconds, everyone is eating and talking. Noah's smile grows and grows.

He's never had this—a meal with a big, happy family like this. Until six months ago, the only family he knew aside from me was my mother, and she didn't get to see him very often because I lived so far away. Now I've told everyone about my son and why I had to keep him a secret.

Even as my heart aches that I couldn't give him this big family experience myself, I know I'll never stop feeling grateful for the Jacksons for showing him what family should be.

"Come on," Jake says, waving a plate of cookies in my face. "You have to try these."

"They're his best cookies," Ava says.

They smell so good my mouth waters, but I just finished a big brunch-style lunch, and I don't need to heap on the calories from one of Jake's decadent cookies. I pat my stomach. "Did you know that in the few months I worked as a sales manager, I gained ten pounds? I still haven't gotten that weight off."

Carter looks me over. "You look fine to me."

My cheeks heat, not because of Carter's innocent approval, but because of the way his words make Brayden's jaw twitch, something like a warning flaring in his eyes as he turns to his brother. It's not the first time Carter has given me a compliment, only to have Brayden tense. Is it jealousy, or does he not want his brother involved with someone as *broken* as me?

"He means you're curvy in a hot way," Shay says. "Lucky bitch."

I laugh. "Nevertheless, I have a perfectly lovely wardrobe, and half of it currently doesn't fit me. I'd rather lose the weight than buy new clothes."

"Why don't you come work out with us?" Carter says.

"Don't do it!" Shay's eyes are wide, and she shakes her head vehemently. "It's a trap!"

Carter chuckles. "It's no trap. My brothers and I like to work out together. It's all in the name of good health."

Shay snorts. "They treat their workouts like competitions.

They think they're professional CrossFit athletes or something."

"It makes what would otherwise be a tedious hour in the gym a good time," Jake says. "Come on. Join us."

I turn to Shay. "It can't be that bad."

She folds her arms. "It's your funeral. The last and only time I worked out with them, I couldn't walk down stairs for a week. I had to grip the handrail like a ninety-year-old woman. And sitting on the toilet to pee? Lord help me."

Carter bites back a smile, but Brayden looks at me with a cocked brow. "What do you say? Join us?"

I hesitate. I didn't realize Brayden works out with his brothers. I always imagined him working out alone for some reason—maybe because he's so private about everything else in his life—but backing out now will make it look like I'm avoiding him. "You wouldn't mind?" I ask Brayden. He sees me at work, got stuck giving me a place to stay, and now he can't even work out without facing poor, broken Molly.

But Brayden shrugs as if it's nothing. As if he didn't tell Ethan how much he regrets hiring me. "I think it's a good idea. Just ease in slowly so you don't hurt yourself."

"When do we start?"

Carter grins. "Can you meet us at the gym at eight tomorrow morning?"

I nod. "Sure. I'll come after dropping Noah off at preschool." I turn to Shay. "Will you come with me? *Please*?"

"No. Just . . ." Shay wrinkles her nose and shakes her head. "No. And when you can't walk in two days, don't come crying to me."

MOLLY

*S*hay was right. Working out with her brothers was a terrible idea, and my Monday morning started with fifteen minutes of utter hell. *Only fifteen minutes,* I thought when they described the workout. *How bad can it be?*

I drop the barbell and collapse to the floor. My lungs are on fire, and every muscle in my body is screaming at me about my bad decisions.

Note to self: You can *die* in less than fifteen minutes. And I'm pretty sure I almost did.

"Are you okay?"

I open my eyes and find Carter grinning at me. I would scowl, but even my face hurts. "Do I *look* okay?"

He hands me my water bottle and chuckles softly. "You did great."

"Don't condescend to me," I mutter, pushing up. "You guys did way heavier weights and twice as many reps."

"We've been working out like this for a while," Jake says from his spot across the room. I feel a little better when I see he's on the floor too. He's lounging against the wall, chest heaving as he catches his breath. Brayden and Levi are already wiping down our barbells, like they just went for a light jog or something. "I promise, when we first started, we weren't going this heavy or moving this fast."

Shay was right. The brothers are competitive. And they all pushed to beat each other in the workout, trying to get the most repetitions, but Levi ultimately won today. If the quivering in my legs is any indication, I'm guessing she was right about the other part too, and I won't be able to walk tomorrow.

Groaning, I push myself off the floor. "You're all evil. I hope you know that." I sense Brayden watching me but avoid his gaze. I've been avoiding him since I moved in yesterday. It was easy enough to do, since I had to unpack last night, but tonight I might not have an excuse. "I need to go shower," I say to no one in particular.

"Will you be here tomorrow morning?" Carter asks.

I'm not even sure I'll be able to get out of bed tomorrow morning, but I say, "Wouldn't miss it." I turn into the back hallway and am pushing into the locker room when Brayden calls my name.

He hands me a towel.

If my heart weren't still racing from that torture they call a workout, it would speed up at the sight of him—shirtless and sweaty, his athletic shorts hanging low enough to reveal the indent of muscle by his hipbones.

I mutter a thanks for the towel and pull my gaze away. *He thinks you're broken. Everything he does for you is out of pity.*

The reminder makes me nauseated. Or maybe I have the workout to thank for that.

"Are you okay?" he asks.

"I'm not dead, so that's something."

He runs his gaze over me—quick, assessing—and I'm glad he can't see just how much my quads are burning right now. My pride couldn't handle it. "I told you to take it slow."

I shrug. "I'm fine. You don't need to protect me."

He narrows his eyes, but I push through the locker room door before he can say anything else.

BRAYDEN

Ralston & Taylor Investments is two blocks down from Jackson Brews. Far too convenient for me to pass up the opportunity to apologize to Jason Ralston on Monday morning. Unfortunately.

I don't want to apologize for shit. When Jason arrived at the party on Saturday night, Molly was already drunk, and whether she willingly climbed into the backseat of his BMW seems like a moot point. Drunk women can't consent. My father taught me that before I ever had a sip of alcohol. Sure, those lines get a little blurry when you're dating or when you've been drinking too—hello, night in New York—but it's a rule of thumb I've stuck by, and I'll be damned if I'm not going to judge this asshole for not giving it a second thought, for plying her with more beer when I already warned him she was drunk, then for taking her to the back of his car in a cold parking lot, of all places.

Molly might not know she deserves better, but *I* do, and I'm going to make sure Ralston knows too.

Molly's been distant, and my reaction with Jason is no doubt part of the problem. I'll apologize for her sake. If that means we still have our new investor, that's just an added bonus.

The receptionist beams at me as I walk through the front entrance. "Good morning. How can I help you today?"

"Good morning. I'm here to see Jason Ralston."

"May I tell him who's here?"

I'd rather you didn't. But I smile like I'm not asking to see the guy I assaulted two nights ago. "Brayden Jackson."

"I'll let him know." She waves to the leather couches in the waiting area. "Please, have a seat. Make yourself comfortable."

I nod and wander in that direction, but I don't sit. I'm too restless to be still. I stand by the window and watch the street outside. Snow-covered cars roll by and bundled-up pedestrians rush to their Monday-morning destinations.

"You can follow me," the receptionist says from behind me.

It's a power move, I realize. Making me go to him on his turf instead of coming out here to greet me. I was hoping to have this conversation on neutral ground, like the coffee shop across the street, but my temper got me in this mess, so my pride is going to have to step aside while I clean it up.

She leads me into Jason's office, where he's waiting, seated behind his desk. The large space has rich wooden paneling, a dual-screen computer, and a couple of leather chairs on the opposite side of his desk. "Would you like anything to drink?" she asks.

I shake my head. "I'm fine. Thanks."

With a nod, she backs out of the office, shutting the door behind her as she goes.

Jason doesn't stand. He rocks back in his chair and studies me. I wince when I see the purple bruise under his left eye.

I shove my hands into my pockets. "I came to apologize."

He arches a brow but doesn't reply.

"I saw Molly scrambling out of your car, and it looked bad."

"You made assumptions."

"I did."

"You realize how insulting that is? That you think I'd force Molly . . . or *any* woman?"

"You would have done the same thing in my position."

He opens his mouth to protest, then snaps it shut and sighs. He drags a hand through his hair. "Hell. I probably would have."

"I'm sorry about the black eye." I shove my hands into my pockets. "And I'm sorry about the assumptions I made in that moment."

Jason studies me and then nods slowly. "Okay. Forgiven."

"But I don't want you dating Molly." That was unplanned, but the second the words are out, I'm glad for the change of direction.

He pushes his chair back and stands. "Excuse me?"

"She's had a tough year and—"

"That's Molly's choice to make. Not yours."

He's right. I fucking *know* he's right. But that doesn't stop me from saying, "She deserves better than what you have to offer."

"You don't know shit about what I have to offer."

"You have a *reputation*."

He grunts. "So does she."

Every cell in my body lurches forward at those words, but I force my feet to stay rooted in place. Punching this sonofabitch again isn't going to put me in Molly's good graces or do a damn thing to change what assholes assume about her. "You *didn't* just say that." My voice is deadly calm.

He slowly walks around his desk to stand in front of me. When he stops, he tucks his hands into his pockets and mirrors my posture. "You know the difference between you and me, Jackson?"

I hold his gaze but don't answer.

"You want to pretend she doesn't have a reputation—that the pretty blonde you're chasing after isn't the same girl who got on her knees for half the guys in her high school."

Adrenaline spikes in my blood, and my hands curl into fists. "*Don't.*"

"Whereas I," he says, his voice low, "don't give a shit about her past."

"You don't give a shit about anything but your dick." This isn't going well. I came here to apologize, but now I don't feel sorry for that bruise beneath his eye. In fact, I'd really enjoy giving him a matching set.

His lips twist into a smirk. "We can't all be perfect like you, Brayden. And if you try to make Molly into someone she's not, I think you'll find she can take herself out of your life as completely as my cousin did."

I flinch at the mention of Sara, just as he intended me to.

"Is that really what you want?" Jason asks. "To make another woman feel like she has to disappear to escape you and your unreasonable standards?"

He's trying to piss me off. Trying to pick a fight here, where Molly isn't watching and he can swing back. But his words—and the mention of Sara—make the fight drain out of me.

I turn around and leave his office without another word.

Eleven

BRAYDEN

"**D**o you want to watch a movie with me?"

Molly has been sitting at the kitchen table with her laptop and a cup of tea since she put Noah to bed an hour and a half ago. I've found half a dozen excuses to come in here since then, and she's managed to avoid looking at me every time. When I try to start a conversation, I get one-word answers. She's been distant since the day of the Christmas party, but her silence tonight has been remarkable.

"No thanks," she says without looking at me.

I roll my beer between both hands, searching for patience. "Are you going to tell me why you're giving me the silent treatment, or am I supposed to guess?"

Molly's mug drops to the table with a clatter. She closes her laptop and blinks up at me. "I'm not giving you the silent treatment."

"Aren't you? You've avoided saying more to me than absolutely necessary since moving in." God, I'm being an immature ass. I should keep my mouth shut and let her ignore me, but I hate it. "Is this about Saturday? About me punching Jason?" Either that, or my comments regarding a certain pink toy collection pissed her off.

Her teeth sink into her bottom lip as she studies me—but at least she's actually looking at me, unlike the masterful avoidance she's managed the last two nights. "A little bit." She swallows. "I wasn't going to say anything until after Christmas, but I guess it's only fair that you know I'm looking for another job."

Dread twists my stomach. *She's leaving.* I force myself to keep my face neutral. "Why?"

She's silent for several pounding beats of my heart, and I can see the war on her face as she tries to decide how much she wants to tell me. "I heard you talking to Ethan in your office on Saturday."

I still, beer halfway to my mouth. Slowly, I lower it to the table. *Shit.* If she heard me talking to Ethan, she knows how I feel about her. She knows I want to try to pursue something personal, despite our professional relationship. But what the hell—I revealed as much when I opened her private little collection, didn't I? "You did?"

"Yes, and I never would have taken the job if I'd known you didn't want me."

That's . . . *What?* "What exactly do you think you heard me say, Molly?"

She scans my face and swallows. "I heard him say you never wanted to hire me. And you said you wish you hadn't."

"Jesus." I rub my forehead. "Did you hear the rest of it?"

"Why would I want to?" Her blue eyes fill with tears. "I'm really proud of the work I've done for you—both as your sales manager and banquet center manager—but I'm not going to cling to a position where I'm not wanted. After Christmas, I'll help to find and train my replacement, and I'll get out of your hair."

"You need this job." I laugh, because this is so ridiculous. "More than that, the banquet center and your staff need you. *I* need you."

She blinks at me, as if those words surprise her. I must be the shittiest boss ever if she doesn't understand what an asset she is.

"I can't stop you if you want to leave, but certainly don't do it because you think it's what I want or what's best for the business."

She shakes her head. "I don't need your pity, Brayden. This is just like Saturday night when you assumed you needed to protect me and—"

"You were drunk, and I told him not to start anything with you. I told him you'd been drinking, but the sonofabitch took you to his car anyway."

She slowly pushes back from the table and stands. "You did *what*?"

"Come on, Molly. You were downing tequila like it was your job. You wouldn't have let him touch you if you weren't trashed, and he knew it."

She stalks toward me. "Are you so sure of that, Brayden?"

"Yeah. I am. You were in a mood, and—"

She slams her palms against my chest. "You don't know shit about me, and you had no right to tell him he should or shouldn't touch me. Jesus. I'm a grown woman. *I* chose to drink too much. I chose to get in that car with him, and when I changed my mind, I chose to get back out."

You were crying. I swallow back the words and meet the anger in her eyes with my own stubborn stare. "Jason has a reputation for sweet-talking women into his bed and then dropping them. Do you want me to be sorry that I was looking out for you?"

"I want you to apologize for interfering in my life. You had no right. I don't want you punching guys for me, and I don't want you giving me jobs you don't want to give me. Quit treating me like I'm some breakable doll who needs protecting."

Her hands smack my chest again, and I ball my hands into fists at my sides to resist the urge to pull her into my arms. "I never said you were breakable."

"You're right. You didn't say I was breakable. You said I was *broken.*"

I close my eyes, trying to remember exactly what I said and imagining how those words sounded to her. Less than two months ago, I found out the real reason she avoided Jackson Harbor for the last eight years. She wasn't just trying to keep Noah a secret from everyone here. She was protecting her son from the man who abused her most of her childhood. The man who raped her when she came home from college. "You have had a brutal year, and half of that was on *me* for bringing you back here." It's true, if not the full truth. I've had a lot of time to regret my role in returning her to the hellish reminder of her past. "If you'd stayed in New York, the mess with your dad wouldn't have happened."

"Don't you think I know that?" she whispers. "Don't you

think I realize that my returning here set Colton off? But it was my decision, Brayden. Not yours. I hate that I brought such a mess to your family when I moved home, and I'm sorry that learning about my past made Colton turn to his addictions again, but it was *my* choice. That wasn't your fault."

"You had a horrendous childhood. If I had known about what you'd been through when we met in New York, I never would have—"

"I'm *glad* you didn't know." She throws her hand over her mouth, as if she's trying to stop herself from saying more, but she whispers, "I wish you'd never known."

I try not to care, but it stings. I want her to let me in, let me closer, and she wishes I didn't know about her past. *A reminder of those lines she drew, Jackson. Employee. Friend. Nothing more.* "Please don't find a new job—at least, not because of what I said to Ethan. You're truly irreplaceable."

"Can you look me in the eye and tell me you aren't employing me out of pity?"

I don't hesitate before meeting her eyes. "I'm not employing you out of pity. I gave you your first interview out of pity, sure, but I hired you because I believed you'd be an asset to the company. I asked you to take this position because I believed you'd be an even bigger asset here. And you are. You're damn good at your job, and if I have my way, you'll work for my company for a very, very long time."

"So wishing you'd never hired me was about *me*, not about the company?"

About you. About me. About us. "I shouldn't have said it like that when what I really meant was that I wished things had turned out differently—easier for you."

She smacks my arm. "Damn it, Brayden. I've been sick with stress thinking you don't want me."

The problem has always been that I want you too much. How can she not know that? But I shrug. "I guess if you're going to eavesdrop, you need to stick around and hear the whole conversation." But if she had, she'd know how I feel. That would scare her away, and if having her anger directed at me the last two days has taught me anything, it's that I don't want to scare her away. I'll take whatever Molly has to offer.

MOLLY

Brayden is *always* working.

I knew he put in a lot of hours, but I never would have guessed how much trouble he has turning off once he's home for the night.

I poke my head into his home office and find him exactly where I expected: in front of his computer, a notepad to his side. "Do you want to join us for dinner?" I ask. He's been tiptoeing around me since our talk last night, and I want to smooth things over. Make things easy between us again. "Nothing fancy. Just oven fries, chicken, and maybe a simple salad."

"Oh, hey. Sorry, I guess I forgot I have company."

I smile. "I don't expect you to entertain us, but I thought you might want to take a break to eat something."

"That sounds great. Let me shut this down, and I'll come out and help you."

"No need. You're giving us a place to stay. The least I can do is make you dinner."

He clicks his mouse a few times then stands, frowning as he takes in my Jackson Brews shirt—the new design he hates. "Oh, Lord, the brothers," he mutters. "What does that even mean?"

I laugh. "Fishing for compliments tonight, are you?"

His lips twitch. I catch myself holding my breath as I wait for one of those rare smiles, but it doesn't come, so I have to settle for the twinkle of amusement in his eyes. "Only if you want to give them."

"Go ahead and pretend that the women in this town aren't all crazy about the Jackson brothers. Y'all are smoking. Everyone thinks so."

"Everyone? And what do you think?"

I shrug. "Objectively speaking, I'm surprised women don't combust when you're all in the same room. Especially at the gym." Because at the gym, they get sweaty and shirtless and . . . *Holy shit*, I could lose hours of my day just appreciating the view of a sweaty, shirtless Brayden. The promise of that view was the only thing that made me turn toward that special hell on earth this morning instead of coming back home for another cup of coffee.

"All of us? Not one of us in particular?"

I snort. "You're really shameless, aren't you?"

He studies me. "Maybe I noticed you checking out Carter at the gym this morning."

I roll my eyes. "I was *not* checking him out. I was *glowering*.

Jesus. That man tried to kill me. Again." Today was my third day and the worst yet. We started with heavy back squats—which were killer on my sore quads and glutes—and then did a workout with kettlebell swings, jump rope, and walking lunges. I thought it was going to be easy, since the weights were light. I was so wrong. "These workouts had better make me hot fast, or I'm going back to being a sloth."

"Now who's fishing for compliments?"

"Oh, shut it. The scale isn't lying about those sales rep pounds."

He drags his gaze over me slowly, over my breasts and down to the fitted yoga pants I pulled on when I got home from work, all the way to my toes and just as slowly back up. My skin tingles beneath my clothes, as if every cell is raising its hand and asking to be inspected next. When he finally meets my eyes, he opens his mouth, but before he can say anything, Noah barges into his office.

"Rayden, look what I drawed!" He shoves a piece of paper into Brayden's hand.

Brayden stoops to his haunches and studies the drawing. "Oh, wow. Tell me about it, buddy. Who are these people?"

"It's you and me." He points to the paper. "And that's Santa."

"This is so good. You're a very talented artist."

"You can keep it," Noah says, his little chest puffing with pride.

"Are you sure?"

Noah nods eagerly, and Brayden takes the drawing to the bulletin board between his big office windows. The board is filled with work schedules, marketing plans, and other official-looking documents, but Brayden tacks my son's picture in the center.

I place my hand over the funny feeling in my chest. Like something in there is surging and growing and freezing all at once. Hope and gratitude and terror.

"I'll put it here so I remember Christmas is coming every time I get stressed with work." He bends down and scoops my son up into his arms. "What do you say you and I cook the chicken on the grill and let your mom relax until dinner?"

"Can I help you?" Noah asks eagerly.

"Yeah, bud. You have to be careful around the grill, but you can make sure I don't burn anything."

Noah wraps his arms around Brayden, and they head out of the office toward the kitchen. My heart swells even as my protective instincts wash over me. Brayden would never intentionally hurt Noah—I know it in my bones—but eventually Noah and I will move out, and Brayden will move on with a life that doesn't include my son. I want to protect my boy from heartache, but I can't keep him from connecting with Brayden while we're here. He's been drawn to the man since we moved to Jackson Harbor and Noah met him for the first time. I know Noah is better off with more people in his life. He needs more than his mom and nana.

I follow the boys to the kitchen. Brayden has already positioned Noah on a stool in front of the sink and is helping him wash potatoes.

I open the fridge to pull out the salad fixings.

"What are you doing?" Brayden asks when I put the tomatoes on the counter.

"Helping?"

He shakes his head. "Pour yourself a glass of wine and sit. Noah and I've got this, don't we, bud?"

"We got this!" Noah says.

BRAYDEN

Molly is always gorgeous, but I think the lounging, pre-bedtime Molly might be the hardest to resist.

She's sitting on my couch with a book. She's still wearing that ridiculous Jackson Brews brothers T-shirt and those black yoga pants that hug the curve of her ass, and her blond hair is piled in a messy knot on top of her head. After four days here, she's finally getting comfortable. The first three nights, she asked for permission before turning on the TV or sitting in the living room with a book—always so worried she was going to disturb me. But tonight, after she put Noah down, she grabbed her book and sprawled out on the leather sofa in the family room, her legs stretched out before her, her feet bare.

Dinner was a success, but more importantly, Molly actually sat down and let Noah and me prepare it for her. She insisted on helping with cleanup afterward, but at least I got her to let me make the meal. With the exception of the thirty minutes she relaxes with a book or a TV show at the end of the day, she's always going, and I considered it a personal victory to get her to sit down before dinner.

She lifts her gaze from her book and narrows her eyes at me. "Why are you looking at me like that?"

Because you're stunning. "Like what?"

She frowns and puts her book down. "Like you're trying to figure me out."

I don't try to pretend I wasn't staring. Why bother? When she's close, I can't help but look. "I'm just wondering how you do it all. Supermom, employee of the year, life of the party—you're everything to everyone."

She snorts. "Trust me, I fail often. But I'm holding you to the employee-of-the-year thing."

"Oh, absolutely. I've already ordered the trophy."

"Ha! I'm sure you have. Too bad I won't be around to see it."

I frown. "I thought we got past that. Still planning on leaving me?" My voice cracks a little on the *me*, and I feel exposed. *Don't go. Jesus, please don't go.*

"No, not that." She rolls her head to the side and rubs her shoulder. "I won't be around because you and your brothers are trying to kill me with those stupid workouts."

"Sore?"

Closing her eyes, she nods. "So sore."

"I was going to soak in the hot tub tonight." I hold her gaze. "You could join me."

"My swimsuits are in storage."

I arch a brow. "Who said you needed a suit?"

It's too fun—watching the pink flush of her cheeks, her mouth opening and closing for a beat before she remembers her tough act and lifts her chin. "We're not climbing into that hot tub together naked."

I might have been offended by the chill in her voice if I didn't see the heat flicker in her eyes. The same flicker I saw when I told her I had every intention of thinking about her and her collection of pink vibrators. "Shay has a bikini in the laundry room. I'm sure she'd be happy to let you borrow it."

I leave it at that and head to my bedroom to dig up my swim trunks. We have a privacy fence in the backyard, and the hot tub is right off the back door, so I only bother with the trunks when I have company. Maybe she'll join me or maybe she won't, but I won't press the issue. I think we both know I want her out here for reasons beyond her sore muscles.

I throw on a robe and head out toward the back patio. I'm tempted to grab a bottle of wine and a couple of glasses on my way, but that would be more likely to scare her off than relax her, so I resist the urge. I adjust the lights at the back of the house, flipping off the bright patio lights and turning on the string of lanterns strung from one lamppost to another along the patio's edge.

The night air is cold, but not bitter or too windy. My favorite weather for a soak.

I pull off the cover and turn on the jets before climbing in and taking a seat in the back corner. I close my eyes to stop myself from watching the back door—to stop myself from willing her to appear—and lean my head back as the water eddies around me, the jets at my back working into my own sore muscles.

Ethan's right about the catch-22 of my situation. I wish Molly didn't work for me so she'd be willing to give me a chance, but if she didn't work for me, I might never see her, and not having Molly in my life at all is far worse than having to settle for *boss* and *friend*.

"It's freezing out here." Molly dances around on the cold concrete, a towel wrapped around her breasts.

I bite back a smile. "Then get in already."

She starts to remove the towel, then freezes. "Close your eyes first."

"You didn't find a suit?" I swallow hard and remind myself I'm perfectly capable of sitting here with a beautiful, naked woman without trying to touch her.

"I did, but Shay is . . . *smaller* than me, and it doesn't fit right."

My lips quirk. "Sounds promising."

"Shut up and close your eyes until I get into the water."

"As you wish." I let my lids float closed, but all of my other senses kick into overdrive. The water swishes around me, rising slightly as she sinks into the tub.

"You can open them now."

I obey and study her in the soft lantern light. She's right. The suit doesn't fit her. She and Shay might be a similar size on the bottom, but Molly has more curves than my sister, and while the scrap of bikini top covers the most private bits of her breasts, it doesn't do much to contain them. I grin. "I think it fits just fine."

"Men," she mutters, spine straight.

I laugh, grateful things are easy between us again. I'm lucky she didn't stay angry with me after overhearing my conversation with Ethan. After I said she was *broken*. I realize how it must have sounded to her. How the word must have made her feel. *Broken*.

But, hell, aren't we all?

She squeezes the back of her neck with a soft moan that whips heat through my blood. "I'm skipping the gym tomorrow, but tell Carter it's because his workouts are too easy for me."

I chuckle. She's impressed the shit out of me with the way she's taken on the workouts my brothers put together. She's tough and more competitive than she'll admit. "I'll happily lie about your absence if it makes you feel better. Of course, he'll see right through me."

"Of course." Sighing, she sinks into the water and tilts her face toward the winter night sky. She arches her back and stretches those long legs out. Her feet brush mine, and she squeaks and pulls back. "Sorry."

"Afraid I might be poisonous?"

"No. I . . ."

I lean forward in the water and reach out until my hands come into contact with her foot. She doesn't say anything but watches me cautiously as I pull it into my lap and dig my thumbs into the arch.

She gasps, then moans—a long, low sound that reminds me I should be careful of exactly where I position her foot if I don't want to come across as a creep.

MOLLY

I close my eyes and let Brayden rub my feet. A tiny part of me screams that this is too intimate, that letting Brayden touch me in any way is a slippery slope that could easily lead me back to his bed. The rest of me tells that little part to shut up and enjoy his strong hands.

He finishes one foot then takes the other into his lap and gives it the same treatment. Maybe I should be embarrassed about the moan that slips out, but every muscle in my body is sore, and I don't care how I sound.

"If you want to come here, I can rub your shoulders," Brayden says, releasing my foot.

A shudder moves through my body at the silky promise in those words. Does he want me to sit on his lap, or . . . ?

He must see the hesitation in my eyes, because he smiles. "Just sit beside me." He drags a hand through his hair, and when he pulls away, it sticks up in two different directions. I like him like this. A little mussed. A little off his game. He's always so put together, and I'm realizing how much I like at-home Brayden. The only problem is trying to remember he's still my boss. Still off-limits.

"Do you give all your employees back rubs?" I ask as I scoot around to his side of the hot tub to sit beside him. I angle my body so my back is to him, but I hate that I can't see his face.

"Only my favorites," he murmurs.

I close my eyes the second he touches my shoulders. The heat of his calloused hands lights my nerve endings on fire and reminds me of our night together. His hands skimming over my breasts, my hips, gripping my waist as I straddled him.

I can't regret that night, and I suddenly wish he knew that. Wish he knew that it's one of my favorite memories.

His touch is soft at first, and I wonder if his thoughts have gone in the same direction as mine. He lightly kneads the tight muscles under my skin before moving to my neck to do the same. I roll my head to the side as he rubs the muscles along the ridge between my neck and shoulder and digs a little deeper there. His touch takes away my tension while wrapping my mind in the memory of his mouth, his whispers against my skin. Thoughts of that night send a buzz through me every time I let them surface, but now, with him touching me like this—kneading my muscles and reminding me of the strength of his hands, the skill of his mouth—I know I'd let him take me to bed if he asked.

I hear the moan before I realize it's mine, and Brayden chuckles, as if he understands what my memories are doing to me—what his touch is doing to me.

"I need to schedule a massage," I say softly. If he doesn't believe the sounds coming from deep in my throat can be blamed on my tight muscles alone, he doesn't call me on it.

"How often do you do that?" he asks. "Go for massages?"

It's a luxury I've only allowed myself when it's been gifted from a friend. "Maybe once a year if I'm lucky?"

His thumbs dance along my spine before pressing into the muscles on either side. "You need one."

I groan. "Maybe I'll treat myself with my Christmas bonus." The words come out as a husky whisper, because sweet baby Jesus, his *hands*.

"Why do I feel like you've already conspired with Santa Claus to spend said bonus on Noah?"

My laughter is hollow, and I shoot him a look over my shoulder. "Can you blame me?"

"Not at all. I'd do the same." He squeezes my shoulder. "If you want, we can go inside and I can work on you a little more." My eyes narrow, and his lips twitch. "Just a massage between friends, Molly. No expectations."

But I want more than that. Even though I shouldn't. Even though I've promised myself I won't.

Swallowing, I nod, sliding away from his touch and climbing out of the hot tub, all too aware of the skimpy fit of Shay's bikini on my breasts and his eyes on me as I reach for my towel. Do I go to his room or mine? Maybe just the couch?

The questions swirling in my head make me hot enough that I almost don't notice the winter air nipping at my wet skin.

He seems to see the question on my face. "Go to my room," he says gruffly. "The bed's higher and will make it easier to work on you."

I turn so I can see his face. "Are you sure about this?"

"I used to date a woman who was a massage therapist. She taught me a few things." His expression is unreadable. "It's up to you. No pressure."

I swallow. Hard. My body is practically begging me to climb in his bed. For the massage he's offering. And for more.

I drew the line between us. He's my boss. We're friends. And now . . . roommates. Are we crossing that line if I let him rub my back?

"Tell me what you're thinking," he says.

I wish things were different. I wish I were different. "I'm thinking you're right about my Christmas bonus, so I hope your girlfriend was a good teacher." I grin, totally casual, not at all turned on by what's about to happen. "I'll meet you inside."

I tuck my towel around myself and race into the house and up to my room. I'm sure he doesn't want me on his bed in a wet bikini, so I dry off and put on a thin tank and a pair of shorts—modest enough but not too much to get in the way.

When I get back down to his room, he's shirtless and in a pair of flannel sleep pants. His bedside lamp is on, and he waves me toward the massive four-poster bed. "It's not as ideal as a massage table, but I think I can make it work."

Dear Girly Bits: I'm going to lie down in Brayden Jackson's bed and let him put his hands on me. Do not get any ideas. This isn't for you.

I lick my lips then stare at him, the bed, then him again.

He cocks his head. "Does this make you uncomfortable?"

It makes me hot. It makes me want things. "I feel a little selfish, I guess." I shrug, as if it's nothing. "Maybe you can teach me, and I can massage you next. *Quid pro quo*, or whatever."

He grimaces at my word choice. "It's just a massage, Molly. If you want it."

Just a massage. Just his hands on my body for the first time in seven months. Just the very thing I fantasize about on a nightly basis.

I climb onto his bed and lie on my stomach, closing my eyes. I've been sore all week—not just from working out with the Jackson boys but from putting in too many hours at the banquet center. I know this will help. What I don't know is whether I'm letting him do it because I want relief from my sore muscles or because I'm so desperate for his touch.

He runs his hands lightly down my back, over my tank, moving up and back down and adding pressure with each pass.

"Tell me about your masseuse ex," I say. Maybe if we talk about a woman from his past, my brain will remember that this touching—this delicious, perfect touching—is platonic.

He scoffs. "Don't let her hear you call her that."

"Call her what? Your ex?"

"No, *masseuse*. She hated that word. Said it's too associated with people who give *happy endings*. She had an athletic training degree and preferred the term *massage therapist*."

"Oh, wait." I turn my head to look at him and put on my best innocent mask. "Does that mean I shouldn't count on a happy ending to go with *this* massage?"

His grin is damn near lecherous, and his gaze sweeps down my body, leaving little chills of pleasure in its wake. He crouches beside the bed until our faces are level and his mouth is inches from mine. "Struggling with some tension in other places, Molly?"

So much tension. My breasts are full and aching, my nipples too tight and sensitive against the mattress. I should look away from those dark, seductive eyes, but I don't.

He holds my gaze as he rubs the tight band of muscles at the small of my back, right above my waistband. "Do you need me to use some of your pink tools to help me reach those deeper muscles?"

"I don't know what you mean." My voice is husky.

He takes my hand and strokes my fingers one at a time without taking his eyes from mine. His fingers toy with the web

135

of skin between my thumb and index finger. Lightly. So lightly that the touch reminds me of what those skilled fingers can do between my legs. I don't care about the secret box at the back of my closet. All I need are those hands. "You set some pretty clear boundaries between us, and I'm not about to violate those. But if you change your mind and want to adjust the rules because you need something *more* from me . . ." His fingertips slide over my palm, and I swear I feel it between my legs. "Just say the word, and I'd be happy to help you out. With or without your collection of toys."

He stands and returns to the muscles on my back, as if nothing has happened. As if he hasn't just offered to get me off. I close my eyes and try to ignore the pulsing ache between my legs, try to ignore the devil on my shoulder who's telling me to roll over and drag him down on top of me.

Could I take him up on his offer without ruining everything? Does he mean it? Or is he just teasing me? No matter how much I want him, I need to think this through.

We're quiet for a long time, him working my muscles into putty and me willing my body to calm. "You didn't tell me about the massage therapist girlfriend," I say, if only to make myself think about something else.

He swallows loud enough that I can hear it, and I wonder if he's struggling to get hold of his thoughts too. "We met at Jackson Brews back when the bar was still a hole in the wall and Dad was running everything. She was here for law school, and we dated for a couple of years." His tone says it's no big deal, but there's something beneath the words that makes me think she was more than just a casual girlfriend.

"What happened?"

His hands move to my calves, and I nearly fly off the bed when he presses into a particularly tender spot. "Sorry," he murmurs, smoothing over it with a whisper-soft touch. "She left."

"You were in love with her." I squeeze my eyes shut at the tug of jealousy those words bring. To be loved by Brayden Jackson. I wonder if she had any idea how lucky she was.

"I wouldn't have been with her so long if I didn't love her."

"She's an idiot if she walked away from you."

He stills, then starts working on my other calf, his thumbs melting away the knots and tension. "Thank you." I hear it in those words—vulnerability, old hurt I never suspected.

I can tell he doesn't want to talk about her anymore, so I let it go. I relax into his skilled touch and eventually find myself drifting off to sleep.

I don't wake up until my phone alarm beeps at me from the bedside table. I'm still in Brayden's bed, the covers pulled over me. I turn off my alarm. Brayden must have brought my phone in after I fell asleep, but why not wake me up? Why give me his bed?

I pull myself out of bed and go to the kitchen to find a pot of freshly brewed coffee and a note from Brayden.

Hope you slept well and are a little less sore this morning. I'll let Carter know you're a total badass and went in search of a better workout this morning. I'll see you at the office.

-B

137

He undoubtedly spent his night in one of the upstairs bedrooms, but surely he would have slept better in his own bed.

As my fingers skim over the blocky letters on his note, I realize part of that steely will I've cultivated to resist my boss has already melted away.

thirteen

MOLLY

Jason Ralston is leaning in my office doorway later that morning, arms crossed, worry written all over his face. "Hey, beautiful."

"Oh, hey." I save my spreadsheet, close the program, and stand, wiping my hands on my jeans. "You got my message, I take it."

He studies me. "I decided I'd rather talk in person. I hope you don't mind."

I nod. He's right. Better to do this face to face. "I feel awful about Saturday."

He drags a hand over his face. "You and me both," he murmurs, stepping into my office. That's when I see it. The bruise around his left eye. From Brayden's right hook.

"Oh, no. Look at you. I'm so sorry."

139

He shakes his head. "Nah. I owe *you* the apology. I typically read situations better than that, and I read you all wrong." He searches my face. "I promise I'm not some brute who forces himself on women."

"No. Of course you're not." I walk toward him, my shoulders tense. "When I dove out of the car like that, it wasn't because of you or anything you'd done."

Swallowing, he tucks a lock of hair behind my ear. I nearly pull away from the intimacy of the gesture, but the vulnerability in his eyes keeps me still. A bolt of regret slices through me. "Then what was it?"

"Things were just moving too fast, and I . . ." I glance over his shoulder and realize we have an audience.

Austin is lounging against the wall between Brayden's office and mine, toying with his phone. I take Jason's hand and gently urge him farther inside so I can close the door. When it clicks closed behind him, I say, "I panicked."

"I'm sorry. About moving too fast. I shouldn't have . . . I mean . . ." He grimaces. "I swear I'm usually better at this." His lips tilt into a lopsided smile. "You're just so beautiful, and I'm scared I screwed up my chance by moving too fast. Frankly, I was relieved when I got your message that you wanted to talk."

His chance? I step back, just out of his reach. "I like you, Jason. You seem like a really nice guy, and I'm sorry if Saturday night gave you the wrong idea. I'm not looking for a relationship."

"Oh?"

"I have a four-year-old son." I wait for him to withdraw. Mention of a kid does the trick most of the time.

He turns up his palms. "So you're not allowed to date?"

"Dating is negotiable, but I'm not interested in a relationship that would lead to a meet-the-kid moment. Not yet, at least." I shrug. "That doesn't mean that I don't like you or that I wouldn't enjoy spending time with you, but my son is my priority."

"You're sure this isn't about Brayden?"

I blink. "No. Not at all." Why would he think that? "He's my boss and my friend."

He arches a brow. "I heard you moved in with him."

I fold my arms across my chest. "He offered Noah and me a place to stay temporarily. But it's a completely platonic arrangement." He just gives me massages, offers to get me off any time I want, and lets me sleep in his bed. Maybe we're not dating, but I'd definitely categorize our relationship as *complicated*. "We aren't involved romantically."

He grunts. "Does *Brayden* know that?"

"Saturday wasn't about him." The words slip out before I recognize them for what they are: a lie. Saturday was too much about Brayden. My mood. The tequila. Trying to lose myself in Jason. It was about my past and my identity, and how I'll never be the kind of woman I'd need to be to belong with Brayden Jackson. It was about hearing from his own mouth that he thinks I'm broken. Even knowing he didn't quite mean what I first thought doesn't change how much that word hurt. *Broken.* I shake my head. I don't want a relationship anyway—not with anyone, and especially not with my boss. So why does it hurt so damn much to know I can't have it? "Brayden is just a friend. He can be protective, but there's nothing more between us."

"Does that mean you'll go out with me this weekend? Casual. No expectations." He smiles slowly and gives me a once-over that should make my toes curl. Instead, it makes me think of Brayden and the way he watches me at home when he thinks I don't notice. The way he sets my body on fire. The way it shouldn't.

Maybe that's why I say, "My son's staying with his nana tomorrow night."

He grins. "It's a date."

BRAYDEN

The giggly blonde picks up the darkest beer of The Jackson 5 flight and swishes it in the glass. "So this one's the IPA?"

I try not to wince, but it's the third time I've been through the list—which is also written on the board in front of the glasses. "That's the porter." I've been stuck at this table with three giggling college girls for ten minutes, and while I don't mind answering questions about our beers, I get the distinct impression they're all playing the ditz to keep my attention. Does that actually work? Are there guys out there who prefer women who hide their brains?

She tosses her hair and dips her chin so she can look at me through her long lashes. "How do you know so much about beer?"

I clear my throat and try not to sound like a dick when I say, "It's my job."

Behind the bar, I catch Levi biting back a laugh, but the asshole doesn't do a damn thing to save me from these handsy girls who pulled me over the second I walked out of the back.

Her two friends lean closer, and one says, "You're, like, so smart."

"Older guys are so *sexy*," the brunette says.

Ouch. I try not to wince. I don't think of myself as the *older guy*, but compared to a bunch of college girls, I guess I am. Hell, compared to Molly, I kind of am.

She fell asleep in my bed last night, drifted off as I rubbed the knots out of her tight muscles. I couldn't bring myself to wake her up. I know she doesn't sleep enough, so I pulled the blankets over her and went to the guest bathroom to take a hot shower. I closed my eyes under the spray and let myself think about her as I took my cock in my hand. I thought about the heat in her eyes when I told her I'd be happy to get her off. Thought about the way her breath hitched as I toyed with the sensitive spots on her hand. But as my orgasm came closer and I gripped myself harder, my mind slid to the night in my hotel room when her body was mine to explore and my ears filled with the soft moans slipping from those perfect pink lips.

The release in the shower didn't feel like much of a release, not with the knowledge that she was still in my bed. Between thoughts of her and sleeping in an unfamiliar bed, it took me longer than usual to fall asleep.

"What are you doing tonight?" the brunette says, pulling my thoughts away from Molly—not that they've strayed far from her all day. "Maybe you should come to our place."

"We're roommates," the other two say in giggling unison. All three girls lean in.

Behind the bar, Levi bites his knuckle. I can practically feel

143

Shay's eyes burning holes through my back from down the bar. And I know Carter and Jake are around here somewhere too. We just wrapped up a board meeting to discuss potential investors for the new bottling plant. I'm not counting on Ralston coming back around—I'm not sure if I even want him to.

I'd rather my siblings not witness my pathetic attempts to let these girls down gently. I'm going to take so much shit for this later. "I'm sorry, ladies. I'm busy."

"Brayden?"

I turn from the trio and have to blink when I see the blonde standing three feet behind me. The worried pucker between her whiskey eyes, the dimple in her right cheek. It's like looking at a picture from my past.

"Hi," she whispers.

I blink again, then shake my head and half expect her to disappear entirely. But she's still standing there, as real as anything after ten years.

I consider my ability to prepare for the unexpected one of my biggest strengths. I always have a plan B and keep my cool when things don't go as expected—because nine times out of ten, they don't.

But I wasn't prepared for this. Sara was nowhere on my radar for tonight or any night, and the whole world slides out from beneath my feet as I take in the woman in front of me.

"Are you going to say anything?" she asks.

I open my mouth then close it again, unsure there are any words for what I'm feeling right now.

Good to see you?

Where the hell have you been?

Do you know how badly you fucked me up?

"You always said you were going to open this place." She tugs on a lock of hair—an old nervous habit I remember well—and looks around. "It looks like your dreams are coming true."

I'm vaguely aware of someone coming to stand at my side. When I force myself to pull my gaze off Sara, I see Shay standing next to me. She looks down her nose at Sara with a curl of her lip that tells me she's biting back the instinct to pick her up and toss her into the snow.

"Hey, Shay."

Shay's eyes are cold. "What are you doing here?" Maybe I should be glad she's asking the questions I can't seem to get out, but I'm not. I wish we weren't here at all. I wish I could deal with this—with *Sara*—alone, somewhere there aren't dozens of people shamelessly eavesdropping.

Sara has the good sense to lower her eyes. "This is a bad time. I should have . . ." Her gaze flicks to the door before coming back to me. "Can we talk?"

"He's busy," Shay says, my little sister acting like my fucking bodyguard. *Fantastic.*

I shoot her a look that tells her to back off. Shay rolls her eyes but walks away to give us space.

"Not right now, of course," Sara says. "I know you probably need . . . to think about it. But can we? Maybe have dinner next week or something?" She fishes a business card from her purse and hands it to me. "I have a new number."

I grunt. *No shit.*

"You don't have to decide now, and I wouldn't blame you if you never wanted to see my face again, but I would really like the chance to talk." She swallows. "To explain."

145

MOLLY

Shay rushes into my office, wide-eyed and flushed. "We have a situation up front."

"What kind of situation?" Jake asks, already standing to jump in. I was wrapping up for the day when Jake and Ava stopped by my office to say hi.

Shay shakes her head. "Not with the bar. Sara Jeffers is here. For Brayden."

That name means nothing to me, but judging by the way Jake's jaw drops, I'm guessing she's someone from their past. From Brayden's past.

Ava frowns. "*The* Sara?"

Sometimes I forget that Ava's been an honorary Jackson since she was a kid. She grew up next door to them and knows the ins and outs of their family history like her own. "Does someone want to fill me in?" I ask.

"Sara is Brayden's ex," Jake says softly.

I frown, and a memory clicks into place. The night Brayden came to New York, his bartender friend said something about him getting over Sara. "So his ex-girlfriend is here. Why are you all acting like someone died?" I don't mean to be insensitive. I'm sure it might be awkward for him to see her again, but Brayden's an adult. Surely a gorgeous, successful guy like him has plenty of ex-girlfriends.

Shay, Jake, and Ava all exchange a long look that tells me there's so much more to the story than the Jackson siblings are telling.

Shay folds her arms, then turns to me. "Molly, wanna do me a favor and head to the taproom?"

Ava's grin is a little evil. "Oh, I like where you're going with this, Shay."

Fourteen

BRAYDEN

Sara's changed her number, but mine is the same as it's always been. I wish she'd have thought to *use* it and warn me. My brand-new tasting room is the last place I want to deal with the shock of seeing her again. Especially tonight with all my family around. I would have prepared for this. I would have told her not to come here, where there are too many people who think they need to protect me.

One second, I'm staring at Sara, trying to decide how to respond to her frank invitation that we reconnect, and the next, Molly is wrapping an arm around my waist and grinning up at me like we're lovers. "Hey, you. Everything okay?"

Instinct alone has my arm snaking around her waist in return, but what the hell? "Everything's fine." With the exception of last night's massage in my bed, Molly doesn't stand this close

148

to me or touch me beyond the occasional brush of a hand—not since that one night. But right now, she's pressing against me like . . .

I catch sight of Shay standing at the edge of the crowd, a satisfied smirk on her face, and I realize exactly what Molly is doing.

God save me from meddling sisters.

Sara's gaze shifts between me and Molly and back, her face growing paler with each pass. "Oh. Are you two . . . ?"

I let the question hang there for a beat too long. Did she think I'd wait for her? Ten years and not a fucking *word*, and she's shocked to see another woman at my side?

The fact that I nearly did wait ten years only pisses me off more, but Molly either doesn't notice the tension in my body or she ignores it. She leans into me, so close I can smell her strawberry shampoo and feel her every curve. "I'm Molly," she says, extending a hand to Sara. "I'm sorry. I don't think we've met?"

Sara's gaze flicks between us again. "I'm . . . Sara?" The sight of Molly has her off balance. I flash a glare to Shay before stepping away from Molly. Shay might have led her to believe this would help, but I'm not interested in playing games.

Molly tugs her bottom lip between her teeth and looks up at me suggestively as she nestles closer into my side. It's sexy, and the look combined with the feel of her pressed against me might turn me on if it weren't so damn *calculated*. And if my ex wasn't standing in front of me looking for all the world like she wants another chance. "Is this the ex-girlfriend you told me about?" Molly asks. "The masseuse?"

There's not a doubt in my mind that Molly used that word deliberately.

The jab works, and Sara winces but tries to smile at me when she says, "Just let me know if we can talk." She turns and rushes out the door.

I watch her climb into a sedan in the parking lot and have no fucking idea how I'm supposed to feel. Relieved? Disappointed? The only emotion I'm sure of right now is confusion and frustration.

I set my jaw as I turn to Molly. "What was *that*?"

"Shay said she was your evil ex and we needed to save you."

"I didn't ask for your help." My head's a mess. I need to get out of here.

Molly bows her head, chastened. "Sorry. I . . ." She shakes her head. "Sorry."

"Don't blame her," Jake calls from behind the taproom bar, where he's stepped in to fill orders. It's getting busier in here by the minute. Thirsty Thursday, indeed. "We told her to intervene."

I don't need any of them *intervening*. "Call me if you need me, Levi," I say. I ignore the rest of my siblings and their curious stares, and head out the door to my car.

The cold bite of the winter air is more than welcome, and I don't even care that my coat is in my office. Maybe the cold will help me think straight, help me process this. *Sara is back. Sara wants to talk to me.*

Shay should have known better than to send Molly in like some fake girlfriend. If she had given it any thought, she'd have known I'd hate the idea, but she wasn't thinking about what I want, only how she could protect me.

"Brayden, stop," Molly calls.

"Why?" I ask, spinning around, but my anger melts when I see Molly's face. She feels like shit about this.

"I'm sorry," she says. "Seriously, Brayden. I should have stayed out of it."

"You should have." I exhale heavily and roll my shoulders back. "But it probably doesn't matter anyway."

"It does, though," she says. She takes me by the hand and drags me to the side of the building, out of sight of the road and the tasting room windows. "We're roomies, and I really, *really* don't want you pissed at me."

"I'll get over it." I release a breath. "I don't blame you for Shay's games. You didn't know."

"It's not all on Shay. I realized Sara was the one you told me about last night, and I didn't like it. I'm so sorry. Tell me what I can do to fix it."

"Why didn't you like it?" Sixty seconds ago, all I wanted was an excuse to leave so I could go home and be alone, but now that Molly's standing so close, all I want is an excuse to keep her here.

"What?" Her expression changes to an unreadable mask, and she backs up a step and then another until she's against the building.

I follow and rest my hands above her head, leaning into her as she tilts her face up to meet my eyes. "Why didn't you like my ex talking to me?"

She swallows, and her cheeks flush pink. With cold, or embarrassment? "I don't like that she hurt you."

"I never said she did."

"You didn't have to." She wraps her fingers around my

forearm, not pushing me away but locking us in place. "I know you, Brayden. Better than you realize."

My gaze drops to her mouth and her lips part. The pulse in her neck flutters faster. "I'm not sure you do." I swallow hard and make myself back away. "I'll see you at home."

When I get home, my sister's car is parked in the driveway, and I realize I'm not done talking about Sara tonight. Even if I want to be.

I park in the garage and come in the side door. Shay meets me in the hallway and hands me a tumbler of amber liquid. I sniff it, and my eyes go wide. "Dad's?"

She nods. "Seemed appropriate."

Sara is back and wants to *talk* to me, and Molly is living with me and falling asleep in my bed. I'd have to agree that tonight's the perfect night to break out the good stuff.

Dad loved fine bourbon. When he died, we divvied up his collection between the siblings. By some unspoken agreement, we only dig into it on really bad days.

I take a small taste and let the warmth coat my throat and chest. "Thanks."

"So, Sara's back. What an awful surprise," she murmurs, leading the way to the family room.

My mind's been a mess since I left the tasting room: Sara, Molly, where I've been, and what I want, respectively. Every time I think about Sara showing up like that, I'm more embarrassed than anything. I loved her. Planned to marry her. Until she erased herself from my life without any warning.

Shay plops into a recliner. A glass of wine is already sitting on the end table by her chair. While I was taking the long way home to clear my head, my sister must have been here planning her ambush. "Are you going to call her?"

"I don't know. She said she wants to explain."

"Explain why she's a heinous bitch?" Shay asks, and I shoot her a look. "I'm not sorry for how I feel about her. You deserved better than what she did."

"Maybe what she did wasn't about me. Maybe there are reasons we don't know."

Shay glowers. "She'd have to have one hell of a story for me to bite on that."

"I'd finally accepted that I'd ever see her again," I admit.

Shay sighs. "I think what worries me the most is that you might be able to forgive her, and the rest of us won't. I don't want to see you in that position—feeling like you have to choose between her and your family."

I drag a hand through my hair. "Not that it matters, but I think everyone would deal with it if we did get back together—and trust me, I'm not saying that's what's happening here." Honestly, in the months after Sara left, when I just wanted her back, whatever her explanation for leaving was, I worried about the same thing. What if I had an opportunity to make it work again, but my siblings and my mother could never forgive her? But the longer she was gone, the less of a concern that became.

"We might fake it for your sake, but things would never go back to the way they were." Shay looks into her wine and swallows. "It would be hard to trust that she wouldn't hurt you again."

"I keep asking myself if I want to hear her explanation, but I'm not sure it even matters. I needed to know her *whys* ten years ago, and hearing what she has to say to me now isn't going to change what not knowing did to me then." Or how it changed me. "But maybe the explanation isn't for me. Maybe it's for her. Maybe this is something she needs to do."

"You don't owe her anything."

I shrug. "I'm not sure that's true." I know Shay won't ask about it anymore—at least not today. She knows me too well to push too hard.

The sound of the garage door opening interrupts the silence.

"That's Molly," I tell Shay.

She snorts. "God, perpetually single Brayden is suddenly going to have to choose between the two women he could never resist. Maybe they'll fight over you."

I scowl at her. "You're hilarious. Despite that stunt you pulled earlier, that isn't what's happening here. And I don't want you putting poison in Molly's ear regarding Sara."

"Why not? Are you worried I might say something that could ruin their potential *friendship*?"

"I know you're angry with Sara, but let me figure this out by myself."

Sighing, Shay drains her glass and stands. "Okay. Let me know if I can help."

I huff a hollow laugh. "I'm not sure how you can."

Her smile is gentle. "I'm a good listener." She tears her gaze off me as the door to the garage clangs open down the hall. The house fills with the sound of little feet racing down the hardwood. "I think your fan club is here."

"Rayden!" Noah calls, rushing into the family room. "Rayden, I'm home! Come see the snow fort I maked in the backyard!"

"The snow fort you *made*," Molly corrects gently as she steps into the family room. She hands her son a blue-striped scarf and matching hat. "If you're going out back, you need to wear these."

"I'll be right back, buddy," I tell Noah. "I'm going to walk Shay out and grab my coat."

"Okey-dokey," Noah singsongs.

I follow Shay to the front, grabbing my spare jacket from the coat tree and shrugging it on as we step onto the porch.

"Why do I feel like you're escorting me to my car to make sure I don't stay and talk to Molly about Sara?"

I shrug. "So what if I am?"

She frowns at me. "I know you don't want my opinion—"

"Then don't give it."

"But I'm one hundred percent Team Molly."

"Is that so?" I walk around Shay's car and open the door for her. "What happened to being worried that Molly is on her way to breaking my heart?"

She shrugs and climbs into her car. "That was before Sara came back to town."

"Bye, Shay." I close the door.

She points her finger at me and shouts loudly enough that I can hear her through the glass, "Team Molly!"

Fifteen

MOLLY

"Can I get you two another round?" the waitress asks Friday night.

I raise my pint glass—which is still two-thirds full—and shake my head. "This will be all for me tonight." Last time I was at Jackson Brews with Jason, I was trashed and made bad decisions. Is that why he suggested we meet here? Was he hoping for a repeat of the night of the Christmas party? Or did he suggest the bar, hoping Brayden might see us together?

Jason frowns at his empty glass and then looks to me. "Do you mind if I have another?"

"Go for it."

"I'll have the Sunny Day IPA this time," he tells the waitress.

"Good choice," she says.

She heads to the bar to fill his order, and I pull out my phone to snap a shot of the chalkboard behind the bar and Jake at the taps filling a beer. Jackson Brews has a nice crowd lingering at the bar and filling half the tables tonight. I'll post the pic later with the happeningatJacksonBrews hashtag. The hashtag campaign was Levi's idea, and it's worked beautifully to raise awareness about all our offerings.

Jason folds his arms on the table and leans forward. "You know, I wouldn't judge you if you had a second beer."

I shake my head. "I have a long day tomorrow. Anyway, I don't like to have more than a drink or two at a time."

"Except for at the Christmas party?"

I sip my beer. I can't believe that was only six days ago. This week has been so damn long. "That was a bad day, and the tequila didn't make it better."

He smiles, and his hazel eyes scan my face. "Up until you started crying and I got a personal introduction to Brayden's right hook, I thought we were having a nice time."

"It was fine. I mean, you're great, and we were having fun, but . . ." I'm rambling. I take a breath and try to explain. "Drunken hookups were my typical bad-day fix when I was in high school. Saturday was a regression of sorts."

"Ouch," he says, but his smile softens it.

"*You* aren't the regression, just the way I acted."

He shrugs. "I'm pretty sure it takes two."

I smile. I appreciate that. Jason is . . . nice. He's been polite all evening, asks all the right questions, says all the right things, and I think he's sincerely interested in more than getting between my legs. But sober Molly isn't sure what drunk Molly was thinking. Hell, I'm not even sure what Thursday-morning Molly was thinking by accepting this date. I don't get any spark when I look at him, and my belly has been completely normal all night. There's no sign of the butterflies Brayden inspires with little more than a smirk across the room.

"Since I got to learn about the girl you were, tell me a little about the woman you've become." Jason reaches across the table and puts his hand over mine, rubbing gentle circles across my skin.

I fight the instinct to jerk away from his touch. "Well, for starters, now I prefer sober conversation with friends."

He arches a brow. The silence stretches between us for a few awkward beats before he nods. "I'll take friends if that's all you have to offer, Molly."

"It's just where I am right now."

"Because of your son?"

I nod. Because of Noah and, if I'm honest, because I have feelings for Brayden that would make intimacy with anyone else feel dirty. I was fooling myself when I accepted this date. I thought I could talk myself out of my feelings for Brayden or maybe just distract myself enough to forget them. *As if.*

"I'm not sure what Brayden's told you about me, but there's more to me than my reputation."

"You and me both," I say softly. Except sometimes, I don't believe it. The last time I was here with Jason, I believed I was no better than my old reputation and acted accordingly.

"You have an admirer." Jason nods toward the bar, and I twist in my seat to see Brayden standing there, watching us. His gaze flicks down to the table, where Jason's hand rests on mine. Once again, I have to resist the instinct to snatch my hand back.

Brayden turns on his heel and disappears into the kitchen.

"Do you want to tell me what's really going on between you two?" Jason asks.

I swallow and shake my head, gently pulling away my hand. "Nothing."

"I don't see 'nothing' when he looks at you." He sighs. "And I don't see 'nothing' when you look at him."

I turn my attention back to my date and frown. "Is that why you wanted to meet me here? You wanted to make him jealous?" It's not like it took any convincing to get me to meet him here. If anything, the idea put me at ease. Jackson Brews is home turf to me. I feel safe here and figured he knew that.

"I didn't want to be the guy you were sneaking around with." He shrugs. "I guess I thought if you'd meet me here then maybe you were truly interested. In retrospect, that was a bad call on my part. I'm pretty sure the only guy you're interested in is Brayden Jackson."

"We slept together once," I admit, surprising myself. "I immediately knew it was a mistake, and there's nothing between us now." It feels like a lie. Maybe there's been something between Brayden and me since that rainy night in the city when we raced through the downpour to his hotel.

"Is that why he told me to stay away from you?"

I blink at Jason, pulling my thoughts from my memories. "What?"

"You didn't know? The day he came to my office to 'apologize'"—he makes air quotes—"he insisted I stay away from you." He lifts one shoulder in a shrug that might look casual if it weren't for the irritation all over his face. "So whether or not you're involved, he certainly seems to feel some claim to you."

I push my beer away, anger flaring in my blood. "Will you excuse me?"

BRAYDEN

I cannot believe she's actually on a date with that sonofabitch. And I can't believe he brought her *here*. Like he wants to rub it in my face.

"You okay, brother?" Jake asks. He's working at the grill, making burgers and plating up meals.

I only came to Jackson Brews tonight because the house was empty. In truth, I was looking forward to a night at home with Noah and Molly, but they weren't there. Instead, Molly had left a note saying not to wait up. *And now I know why.*

"I'm fine," I growl, not sounding even a little fine.

Jake, wisely, doesn't call me on that, just nods and plates up his specialty bacon-barbecue donut burgers. If I had to guess, he already saw Molly here with Jason and knows exactly what's wrong.

Molly bursts through the swinging kitchen door, her eyes blazing, her cheeks bright. She stops in front of me and puts her hands on her hips. "What the hell is your problem?"

"My problem? I don't have a problem. If you want to date a guy who's going to try to take advantage of you when you're trashed, that's on you."

Jake clears his throat, and Molly spins on him. "Do you have something you want to say?"

He picks up the plates and shakes his head. "Not a thing," he mutters before pushing out of the kitchen and leaving Molly and me alone.

"You're such a freaking *hypocrite.*"

I fold my arms. "How do you figure?"

"You were all pissed at me for acting like I was your girlfriend to get your ex away from you, but you told Jason to stay away from me."

Busted. I should be fucking ashamed for acting like that, but I'm not. If she doesn't want me, fine. But Jason isn't good for her. "I'm just trying to protect you."

"You had no right. None. It's *my choice* who I date."

"I know that."

"I told you he didn't force himself on me. I *told you.*" She paces the length of the kitchen, only turning back to me when she reaches the walk-in coolers. She leans against the stainless steel and threads her hands into her blond hair.

"Why are you really so pissed, Molly? Is this about him?" I ask, stalking toward her. She's in a long-sleeve sweater-material thing that dips low in the front and shows off the swell of her breasts. The hem barely reaches the middle of her thighs. The sight of her in knee-high boots—the idea that she wore that sexy getup *for him*—fuels my anger as I stop in front of her. "Do you want him so damn much that you can't stand the idea that I might get in the way? Is he that perfect?"

She drops her hands to her sides. "No, you idiot. It's about *you.*" She swallows. "It's about you thinking you need to protect me."

I dip my head, bringing my mouth closer to hers. She gasps, but I stop when our lips are inches apart. "You know what you *didn't* hear that day I was talking to Ethan? When I told him that I sometimes wish I never hired you? Do you know why I said that?"

"Because you want to protect me from my past," she says, and I'm so close that her breath brushes across my lips. "You feel guilty that you brought me back here."

"That's only part of it."

"Oh?" Her voice shakes, like she's afraid of the worst, and I wonder, truly wonder, how she could not know the truth.

I tilt my head and graze my nose along the side of her neck. She arches, pressing her breasts into me. "I wish I hadn't hired you because I've wanted you from the moment you crawled into my bed eight years ago. I wish I hadn't hired you because if I weren't your boss, you wouldn't have run from me in the middle of the night. And if you had, I could have tried to win you back when you pushed me away." I run my mouth along her neck, a breath away from touching.

Her hand goes to my chest, and when I think she might push me away, her fingers curl into my shirt. "Then . . . why?"

"You made the rules. As long as I'm your boss, I'm not allowed to touch you. I'm not allowed to seduce you."

"Brayden . . ."

I pull back, finally meeting her wide blue eyes, praying it's enough, praying she understands. "*That's* why I wish I never hired you. Because I'm a selfish asshole when it comes to you, and I want to do all the things you told me I can't." I've crossed too many lines already, but I rub my thumb over her bottom lip, unable to resist one last touch before stepping out of her grasp. "Enjoy your date. I'll see you at home."

MOLLY

Brayden's house is quiet when I get home, and I miss my kid. I want the comfort of our evening routine, the joy of his easy smiles. I talked to him earlier, and my mom's bringing him home in the morning to spend a few hours with me before I have to head to work, but some primal part of me feels fractured when he's away. And maybe I also wish he were home to give me something to focus on other than Brayden's words tonight . . . something other than the ugly words I said to him.

Jason was gone when I returned to our booth, but when I checked my phone, I saw he'd sent me a text.

> *Jason: I don't want to get between you and Jackson. If you ever figure out what you want, you know where to find me.*

I hang my coat in the closet then look down the dark hall to Brayden's room. His door is closed, but I see the sliver of light coming from under it.

"*I want to do all the things you told me I can't.*"

A shiver of pleasure races up my spine at the memory of his words and the feel of his mouth so close to my neck, my lips. I want him, and he wants me.

Maybe it wouldn't matter if we gave in. Maybe our work responsibilities are disconnected enough that it wouldn't make a difference.

But I know Brayden's a family man, and I don't believe for a second that he doesn't eventually want a wife and kids. He'll be an amazing husband and father to someone. Thinking about it makes me wish I were in a position to gamble on that someone being me, but I know better, and that's a risk I promised myself I'd never take with anyone—at least not until Noah is grown and out of the house. Which leaves me here, climbing up the stairs in the dark to sleep alone.

BRAYDEN

I slept like shit last night, and since tonight is Ethan's bachelor party, I'm going to pay for it later. There was no avoiding it, though. I heard her come in, heard her climb the stairs, heard the water running in her bathroom as she got ready for bed. I waited, but she never came. I put myself out there, made it clear how I feel, and she never came.

If she doesn't want me, I'm just going to have to deal with that. Even if I feel the way she looks at me. Even if I can't believe this chemistry between us is one-sided.

At five, I give up on fighting for more sleep, make a pot of coffee, and return to bed with a mug of caffeine and a book. It takes a while, but eventually the thriller sucks me in enough to take my mind off the woman upstairs.

That's why I barely even realize Molly's in my bedroom until she's crawling into my bed. She takes the book from my hand. "We need to talk." She sits back on her heels and stares at me, waiting.

I push myself up and lean against the headboard. It's almost eight. "How'd you sleep?"

She shakes her head. "Not great, but I wanted to talk to you before Noah gets home." She scans my bare chest, my arms, lingering at the waistband of my flannel sleep pants. Her shorts are so tiny they could be panties, and her long-sleeve cotton shirt is so thin I can make out the outline of her nipples beneath it. Her hair's twisted into a sloppy knot on top of her head, and a few stray locks have fallen around her face. She looks like she walked right out of my fantasies and into my bed.

"Are you okay?" I lift my hand to tuck one of those stray locks behind her ear but drop it before I touch her. She needs to decide where the new boundaries are . . . assuming she wants to change them at all.

She takes a deep breath. "I like you, Brayden. I liked you before that night we spent together, and I like you now. But I don't . . ." She shakes her head and meets my eyes. "I don't *do* relationships."

I raise my brows. "I'm sorry?" It sounds like something an asshole guy would say—a throwaway line he'd use to get the girl to sleep with him. But this isn't some asshole guy. It's Molly, and she doesn't need a line if she wants to get me in bed. After all I said last night, she knows that.

"I made a decision when I had Noah. I'd met other single moms and saw what havoc dating could wreak on their lives. I know what it did to me when I was a kid." She swallows hard.

"Mom had relationships with three different guys before she married Nelson. Each of them serious enough that I thought they'd be in my life forever. I . . ." She searches my face as if she's looking for a sign that I understand. "I got attached, and when they left her, they were leaving me too. By the time she married Nelson, I'd started to feel desperate. Kids aren't stupid. They know they're part of the equation of a relationship. They hear the adults fighting about money and errands and who has to take the kid to dance. I thought it was my fault the other men had left."

"Molly . . ." My voice breaks on her name. Her eyes are locked on my headboard, as if it's too hard to say all this while looking at me.

"Don't give me your pity, okay? I don't like talking about it because I hate pity, but I want you to understand. Even if Nelson hadn't fucked me up, dating a single mom isn't like dating someone without kids. If I bring you home and then we don't work out, my son's affected too."

"Bring me home? We live together, Moll."

She rolls her eyes and almost—*almost*—smiles. "You know what I mean."

"Yeah." My voice is rough. "I think I do." And I already know that I don't like where this conversation is going.

"I decided that I wouldn't drag guys in and out of his life like that. That if I wanted to see men, it would never go any further than a few casual dates. I'll do whatever I have to do to save Noah from the screwed-up mindset I had. I never want my son to feel so desperate that he'd endure abuse for *my* sake."

Screwed-up mindset. The way she says it like that, it's almost like she blames herself for what her stepdad did to her. "It wasn't your job to stop him. It was his job to never violate you to begin with."

She waves a hand. "Yeah, I know all that."

But does she?

She bites her bottom lip. "Do you understand what I'm saying?"

My stomach sinks. I took a chance last night, crossed a line by telling her how I feel. "You're saying this can't happen."

She shakes her head then she rises to her knees and straddles my lap.

I draw in a ragged breath—because *fuck,* I like her here—but I keep my hands fisted at my sides. "Tell me what you want."

She flattens her hands against my chest and lowers her head to sweep her lips across mine. Lust surges down my spine.

"I'm saying," she whispers, "this is all I can give." She threads her fingers through my hair and nips at my lips. "But it's yours—if you want it. Just this, for as long as I'm staying here."

I grab her waist with one hand and thread the other through her hair. When I sweep my tongue across her lips, she moans and arches into me as I press my mouth to hers.

I can hardly think about what she's telling me. I can hardly think about anything more than her mouth on mine and the way she feels straddling my lap. She deepens the kiss, and I'm ready to flip her onto her back and peel off her clothes when I hear the front door open and close.

"Mommy!"

At the sound of Noah's voice, she scrambles off the bed, breathing hard. "You understand?"

"Mommy?"

I take a breath and try to direct the oxygen to my brain. I understand, but I don't like it. "I get it." I nod. I'm a guy, and Molly's a beautiful woman. I should feel like I've won the lottery. But we haven't even started, and I already know it's not enough. She's offering her body, and if that wasn't enough for me seven months ago when she lived in New York, it's not going to be enough now. Not now that she's here. Not now that I know her and *see* her.

She gives me one more once-over before backing out of the room to greet her son.

MOLLY

Noah and I spend Saturday morning together in the snow. I only have a few hours with him before Mom comes back to pick him up so I can go to work to set up for the local bank's Christmas party.

Noah and I built two snowpeople. His is a boy wearing a blue tie, and mine is a girl with a pink beret—both accessories were thrift-store finds I bought for Noah's dress-up box months ago. Noah giggles himself silly when Brayden comes out back to put sunglasses on both of our creations.

"What?" Brayden asks. "It's sunny, and snowman eyes are very sensitive."

"Excuse me, sir, but mine is a snow*girl*," I say, propping my hands on my hips. "She doesn't appreciate being called a man."

Brayden presses one hand against his chest and bows dramatically before my snowgirl. "My apologies, fair snow maiden. Please forgive my thoughtlessness and tell me how I can make it up to you."

"She can't *talk*," Noah says around a squeaky laugh. "She's made of *snow*."

Brayden covers her ears and gapes at Noah. "Now *you've* hurt her feelings too."

Noah frowns then walks slowly up to my snowgirl and kisses her cheek. "Sorry, snowgirl."

Brayden dips his head to put his ear next to the snowgirl's mouth. "What's that? Oh, really?" He turns to Noah. "She said that she forgives you, and because she wants to be friends, she's put some of her special magic hot chocolate on the table inside."

Noah perks up at the mention of hot chocolate, then looks to me. "Can I go see?"

"Of course, buddy. Go on in. I'm going to clean up a few things out here."

Noah races into the house, leaving Brayden and me alone in the backyard.

I swallow hard as I turn to him. My heart's just too full. "Thank you."

He brushes the falling snow from his dark hair. "For what?"

"For being so good with him. For never . . ." My gaze goes to the house, where I can see Noah at the counter with his mug of hot chocolate. "For never getting annoyed that he's around. Even if it means interrupting an important conversation."

Brayden's smile is gentle but full, and it sends a shower of snow flurries through my belly. "I like Noah, and I like when he's around. As for this morning's conversation . . ." He takes a breath, then tucks a lock of my hair behind my ear. "I think I was done talking by the time he came in anyway."

He skims his thumb along my jaw, and heat rushes through my blood as I imagine what might have happened if I'd found the courage to go to Brayden's room at five when I first heard him up. His gaze drops to my mouth, his pupils dilating. I know he's thinking the same thing I am. "You should go inside and drink your magical hot chocolate before it goes cold."

I want to kiss him so badly, but when I follow his gaze to the kitchen windows, I see Noah watching us. "Did my snowgirl leave any magic hot chocolate for you?"

"Yeah. And it's a good thing, too." Brayden heads toward the door but turns his head to drag his gaze over me. "I'm definitely craving something sweet."

BRAYDEN

*M*olly is trying to kill me. That's the only explanation for why she would walk into the kitchen in a fluffy white robe when her wet hair tells me there's a ninety percent chance she's naked beneath that terrycloth.

Jill arrived to pick up Noah shortly after we finished our hot cocoa, and Molly got in the shower as soon as they left. It was all I could do not to follow her. Since I don't want our first time back together to be a quick shower fuck, I made myself resist.

But now she's in my kitchen. In her robe. And probably naked underneath it.

"Why are you looking at me like that?" She leans against the pantry door and smiles at me over her steaming mug of coffee.

"I'm trying to decide what you are or aren't wearing beneath that robe, and if you're deliberately trying to make me lose my mind."

She sets her mug on the counter and tugs on the tie around her waist—but sadly, not hard enough to make it come undone. "You should come find out."

I stalk toward her, desperate to taste her again, to feel her skin under my hands. "When do you have to leave?"

"Too soon."

I swallow hard. Now that I've been given permission to touch her, I don't want her anywhere but my bed.

Permission to touch her but not to start a relationship.

It's an offer I know I should resist, but I can't. *Christ.* Maybe it'll be worth it—letting her go, watching her walk away—if it means for a short while I get to feel her in my arms again.

I press her against the wall, and her body arches into mine as I lower my mouth to hers—a sweep of lips and tongues, her hands on my chest, curling into my shirt.

I snake my hand between our bodies and untie her robe. The material parts, and I slip my hand beneath it and hiss when I feel the scrap of lace at her hip. Breaking the kiss, I step back and push the robe off her shoulders. Her lips part and her eyes go dark as it falls to the floor. I study her—the pert nipples under the black lace bra, the barely there V of lace between her thighs.

I don't know why, but the thought of her putting the robe on after her lace bra and panties makes this hotter. Maybe because it seems deliberate. Like she put on the lace, thinking of me, and came into the kitchen in her robe because she wanted to make sure I saw it.

I shake my head in wonder and drag a knuckle slowly down the side of her breast, the dip of her waist, and the curve of her hip. In the sunlight coming in the kitchen windows, I can make out faint stretchmarks across her belly I never noticed during our night together. The marks from carrying her son. "You're so beautiful. I can't imagine any way you could be more perfect."

She pulls me forward by the hem of my shirt and kisses me hard before stepping back to tug it off over my head. "I want to look too," she says, tossing my shirt to the floor.

I hold my breath as she runs her fingertips down my chest, past my waistband and over the fly of my jeans.

"We have fifteen minutes before I need to go," she says, her eyes eating me up. "Take me to bed."

I lean forward and nip at her neck. "That's not nearly enough time."

She whimpers and arches into me. "Sure it is."

Smiling, I step closer so I can position a thigh between her legs. She smells so damn good, a heady cocktail of her arousal and strawberry shampoo. I want to kiss every inch of her. "I won't be rushed," I murmur, but I cup her breast in my hand and pinch her nipple. I love the way she gasps. The way her hands dive into my hair and tug.

"Please, Brayden." She rocks against my thigh, circling her hips and moaning into my ear. "I want you so badly."

The front door clatters open. The sound of my brothers'

bickering comes to us from the foyer.

Molly's eyes go wide. Grinning, I grab her hand and guide her into the dark pantry with me, softly clicking the door closed behind us. My brothers storm their way into the kitchen, and I make a mental note to talk to them about *knocking*.

"We're here early," Jake says. "Let's get this party started."

"Brayden, where the fuck are you?" Carter calls.

Ignoring him, I step forward and skim my hands down Molly's sides. She shivers. I cup her ass as I lower my mouth to hers.

"Brayden?" Jake calls. "You here?"

"What are they doing here?" Molly whispers.

"Shh," I whisper, my lips brushing across hers as I speak. "They'll hear you."

She stiffens and shakes her head. "Can this be our secret? Are you okay with keeping it from your family?"

I still at her words. I meant I didn't think she wanted my brothers catching her naked in my arms, not that I didn't think she wanted them to know we were . . . involved.

She lifts her hands to my face. "I don't want to answer questions about what we are and aren't. You know?"

"This can be a secret. It can be whatever you want," I say, leaning my forehead against hers. I squeeze my eyes shut for a beat. Staying inside her lines might just be torture. "You make the rules, Moll."

She rakes a hand down my chest and unbuttons my jeans. She slips her hand into my pants and cups my cock through my boxers. "I want *you*. Now."

I lift her onto the counter and spread her legs so I can step between them. Her hands find my hair again, threading through and tugging as our mouths meet in the dark. She's intoxicating—her soft skin, the minty taste of her toothpaste, and the smell of her strawberry shampoo. She makes me feel like I'm sixteen again and sneaking strawberry wine and making out with my crush. But it's better. Because we're completely sober, and Molly McKinley is in my arms, trembling in response to my mouth running down her neck, to my lips skimming along her unbelievably soft skin.

I latch on to the tender spot right beneath her ear and roll her nipple through her bra. She makes a desperate sound that might be my name.

"Shh," I say, but I'm barely aware of my brothers' voices in the kitchen. They might as well be in Mexico for all their presence matters to me. I'm entirely focused on Molly—the feel of her, the way she reacts to me, and the things I want to do. We don't have nearly enough time, but I'm not about to send her away aching.

I slowly make my way down her body, teasing her nipples, circling her navel, grazing the waistband of her panties.

On the other side of the door, I hear someone clear his throat, then Jake says, "Yeah, we'll just come back later."

They've spotted her robe and my shirt, no doubt. They'll probably want an explanation for that and will see right through me when I tell them Molly and I aren't involved. That's tonight's problem. All that matters in this moment is bringing some satisfaction to the woman in my arms.

With one hand in her hair, I drop the other to her parted legs and lightly brush a knuckle against her, feeling how wet she is through the fabric of her panties. She jerks her hips, chasing the pressure of my hand.

I do another teasing pass and suck her earlobe between my teeth. "I want to play with you for hours," I whisper into her ear. I pull the lace to the side and circle her opening. She's so wet. I could lose my whole day touching her. "I want to taste you right here."

"Brayden." She shudders in my arms. "I think about this all the time. Your hands . . ."

I slide a finger into her, and she gasps. She's tight and slick, and the sounds she's making . . . "When I have more time, I'm going to kiss you here again." I bite her neck, her shoulder, sucking and scraping my teeth the way I know she likes. "I've thought about you coming under my mouth so many times. Have you thought about it, Molly? Thought about me sucking you? Licking you?" I thrust into her, pulling out and adding a second finger before giving her the pressure of my palm against her clit.

"Yes," she whispers. "So many times."

"I want you to think about it all night at work. About me and how I'm going to touch you when you get home."

She trembles in my arms. Her body winds tighter around my fingers then releases. She bites my shoulder hard as she comes, muffling her cry.

I rub her gently through the last waves of her climax. She clings to me in the dark. Tonight, I'll touch her with the lights on. I need to see her face, to watch the pleasure wash over her as she comes.

When I know she's spent, I kiss her—a long and thorough kiss meant to tell her what I'm not allowed to say in words. *This is more than touching. This is more than physical. You're worth more*

176

than you're letting me give you.

I hold her until her breathing slows. "Sorry about the interruption, but I'm pretty sure they left. I'll go out to get your robe and make sure they're gone."

She hops off the counter and strokes me through my unbuttoned jeans. I'm painfully hard, and the feel of her hand rips a groan from my chest. "What about you?"

"Later." I take her hand and bring it to my lips, kissing her fingers one at a time.

"But don't you want . . .?"

I kiss her palm, opening my mouth to suck lightly on the pad of her thumb. "If we're going to be lovers, you'll have to accept that sometimes it's going to be about you." I brush my mouth across hers. I want more. Deeper. Longer. I resist. "Sometimes the thing I want most is to feel you come."

With those words, I button my jeans and slip out of the pantry to get her robe.

"The coast is clear," I say, opening the door for her. "My brothers left."

She squints into the light, and I memorize her face. I love the way her cheeks are flushed and her lips are dark pink from my mouth. "Why were they here?"

I shrug. "My family doesn't need a reason. I'm guessing they wanted to talk about our plans for tonight."

"Oh, right. The bachelor party."

Nodding, I follow her gaze to the clock. "I didn't give you much time to get ready."

She grins. "Worth it."

"What time does the party end tonight?" I'll have to find a

way to distract myself so I'm not counting down the minutes until I can touch her again.

"They have the room until eleven, but we should be mostly done by the time they clear out. I'll be home by midnight."

"I can sneak away from the party early and come help you clean up if you want."

She shakes her head. "No. I'm pretty sure I'd end up locking us in my office so I could have my way with you."

"So that's a yes?"

Heat flares in her eyes. "I had no idea you had such a wild streak, Mr. Jackson."

I rub my thumb over her bottom lip. "I don't. Only a weakness for you."

She touches my shoulder. There's a small red mark on the spot where she bit me to quiet her moans. "Sorry."

I grin. "Worth it."

Seventeen

BRAYDEN

*E*than only had one request for his bachelor party, and it was simple: No strip clubs.

Since strip clubs make me want to bathe in rubbing alcohol—no offense to the lovely ladies working in them—I was more than happy to oblige. My brothers and I took the groom-to-be to the family cabin, where we played paintball in the snow; then, after we all showered and changed, we went to a restaurant in Grand Rapids known for its bourbon selection.

We finished dinner an hour ago and are lingering in our private room in the back of the restaurant. Everyone's having fun, and they're nice and loose from the bourbon samples—everyone but me, that is, since I'm taking it easy on the booze tonight. We have a driver taking us back to Jackson Harbor, but the last thing I want is to be too drunk to seduce my beautiful roommate.

Of course, I've been thinking about her since she left for work, and all of my brothers have noticed how distracted I am. Despite my efforts to be fully present for them, my mind is at least eighty percent in the pantry, calling up the feel of her breathy moans against my ear.

"Brayden?"

I spin around at the sound of that familiar voice and see Sara, her eyes bright, her hand pressed against her chest.

"It really is you. What are the chances?" She turns her head to take in each of my brothers at the table one at a time. "All of the Jackson boys are here."

I feel the irritation rolling off my brothers, but they all stay silent, letting me decide how this will go. "Bachelor party," I say, hoisting my barely touched bourbon.

She pales and stiffens. "Congratulations," she says to . . . *me.* She thinks I mean *my* bachelor party. She must be thinking of the way Molly slung her arm around my waist at the tasting room—a deceit I didn't like but didn't correct.

"Ethan's," I say gently.

"Oh!" I'd be a fool to miss the way her posture loosens. She shifts her attention to Ethan, and her face goes soft. "I heard about Elena. I'm so sorry. She was a good woman."

"Thank you," Ethan says. Once, he would have said more. Once, he would have shared his feelings with Sara as easily as he would with one of us, because once, Sara was as much a part of our family as Ava and Nic are today. But tonight, she gets two words and no more. I'm not the only one she hurt when she disappeared.

"I'll get out of your hair." Sara shifts awkwardly, clearly not wanting to leave us yet, then meets my eyes. "I hope we can get that meal together. I've been waiting for your call." With a tiny wave, she turns around and heads back to the restaurant's main dining room.

Ethan gives me a long, hard look, and I just shake my head, letting him know I don't want to talk about it. Then I'm saved by the buzz of his phone. He pulls it from his pocket and laughs at whatever he sees. "Lilly and Nic made a giant pillow fort—pardon me, *castle*—in the basement, and Lilly begged to sleep in it." He turns his phone to show us Lilly, her mouth hanging open in sleep. She's surrounded by a toppled pillow fort and has a tiara on her little head. "She didn't want to take off her crown because she's a princess tonight."

"Excuse me." Jake scoffs. "My niece is a princess *every* night, brother."

Ethan chuckles. "Of course she is. My mistake."

"Nic's home? Isn't the bachelorette party tonight?" Carter asks, his eyes a little glazed from the booze.

"Not until Thursday," Ethan says. "That's the only day the girls' schedules aligned."

Carter smirks. "I wonder what they're doing."

Ethan squeezes the back of his neck, as if just thinking about it stresses him out. "Veronica's planning it," Ethan says, referring to his fiancée's twin sister, "so Nic is preparing for the worst."

"The worst being mostly naked, oiled-up men rubbing on your fiancée and her friends?" Carter asks.

Levi laughs. "You volunteering to do the honors, Carter? I hear women love the firefighter fantasy."

"Screw you," Carter says, but there's no venom in his tone.

Ethan shrugs. "I don't know what the plans are, but I'm not worried about it. I just want her to have fun."

"Ellie said Veronica has been very tight-lipped about it," Levi says.

"Poor Nic," Ethan mutters.

"Speaking of Ellie," Jake says, swishing his bourbon in the bottom of his glass. "That all worked out? You two are good?"

Levi drags a hand through his hair and nods. "We're great. The last month . . ." He takes a sip of his drink, then studies the glass as if looking for the words. "It was hard, waiting for her to be ready, but it was good, you know? I jumped in too fast when she and Colton split, and then I was there again before Ellie could even remember everything. I think we both needed to know that we could wait and be okay. That this feeling between us isn't something we have to rush to hold on to. It's not going anywhere, and neither are we."

Ethan grins. "Did my little brother just drop a wisdom bomb on my bachelor party?"

"Shut the fuck up," Levi says. "I voted for the strip club."

"Of course you did," Jake mutters.

"Fuck, I think this means I'm about to be the last single Jackson brother," Carter says. "Lord help me."

Jake and Ethan laugh, but Levi frowns and points a thumb at me. "Are you forgetting about perpetually single Brayden here?" His gaze darts to the doorway where my ex just disappeared, and his eyes go wide. "Fuck, you didn't get back together with Sara, did you?"

Ethan coughs on his bourbon.

I shake my head. "No."

"He's still avoiding her," Carter says.

Jake grunts. "Can't blame him there."

"I'm not talking about Sara tonight." But, fuck, I do need to call her and set up a meeting. Maybe coffee or something. I've thought about it some, weighed the pros and cons of letting her say her piece, and then got distracted. Tonight was a rude reminder.

"So it's safe to say that wasn't *Sara's* robe on your kitchen floor this morning?" Carter asks.

Jake jabs an elbow in his side. "Hush. If he wanted us to know what he was doing, he wouldn't have been hiding in the pantry."

I scowl at my brothers. "You all need to learn to knock."

Jake puts his drink down and holds up both hands. "I promise, after what I think I almost walked in on, I'll be knocking in the future."

Levi frowns, and I could laugh at the confusion on his face if I found my situation with Molly remotely amusing. He's been so busy with the opening of the tasting room and his new Jackson Brews marketing responsibilities—never mind the distraction of getting back together with his girlfriend—that he seems to be the only one who's oblivious to my unrequited love for my roommate. "Molly?" he asks softly, almost as if he's afraid I'll be offended if he's wrong. "Shit. You and Molly? I thought that was a one-time thing. When did this happen?"

"It didn't," I say. "Don't listen to these idiots. Molly and I are roommates. That's it."

"Roommates who fuck in the pantry?" Carter asks.

I shoot him a glare, and he ducks his head and holds one hand up in surrender. He knows better than to say more, though

I can tell he's tempted.

"Your secret is safe with us, brother," Jake says.

I fold my arms and lean back in my chair. "Meaning you've already told Ava?"

He shrugs. "There was a woman's robe and one of your T-shirts in the middle of the kitchen floor and *sounds* coming from the pantry. Was I supposed to keep that to myself?"

I just glare at him, and this time it's Carter who elbows Jake. "I think that's a yes," he mutters.

Jake narrows his eyes. "Do you understand how easily heartbroken my pregnant wife is? I can't risk hurting her feelings by keeping secrets."

"Try," I mutter. "And don't make assumptions about what you saw."

"What about what we heard?" Carter says to Jake under his breath.

I glare.

"I'm empty," Levi says, pushing out of his chair.

"I can be," Carter says. He drains his glass, and Jake follows suit.

"Need anything?" Levi asks Ethan and me.

We shake our heads and watch our brothers head to the bar for more bourbon.

Next to me, Ethan clears his throat. "So, how *is* the roommate situation going?"

"The house is plenty big enough," I say. Not really an answer.

"You and Molly . . . get along okay?" He grimaces. "Alleged pantry encounter aside?"

I just stare at him. "Why don't you ask what you want to ask?"

"You haven't told her how you feel. The whole of it."

It's not a question, so I don't bother to respond.

Ethan's quiet for a long time, and I think he's going to drop the subject completely until he says, "I remember when Nic moved in after we'd, eh, *been together*." He smiles, though he certainly didn't find the situation amusing at the time. Ethan and Nic had met at Jackson Brews and ended up going back to her hotel room. The next day, he found out she was his new nanny. "I had no interest in a relationship, especially with someone Lilly might grow attached to. But I couldn't stay away from her."

"It worked out all right." Next weekend, three days before Christmas, Nic and Ethan will say their vows in front of the Jackson Harbor lighthouse, and Nic will officially be part of our family. Unofficially, she's been part of it since the first family dinner she attended. She just clicked into place. *Not so different than Molly and Noah.*

Ethan shakes his head. "I'm lucky I didn't lose her. I thought I needed to protect Lilly and almost screwed everything up in the process."

"If Molly ever gave me a chance—and trust me, despite what those assholes made it sound like, that's a big *if*—I won't screw it up. You don't have to worry about that."

"Maybe you won't. But *she's* the one with the kid. She's the one who has the most to lose. The most to protect."

I stare at him. "I would never hurt Noah."

"I know that. Hell, she probably knows that too, but parenthood makes us irrational." He takes a breath, as if weighing whether to say more.

"Say it."

"Whatever you do, you need to talk to Sara before you start something with Molly. You never got to close that door. Don't muddy your chances with Molly by missing an opportunity for closure."

I nod. "I've been thinking the same thing."

Standing from his chair, he stretches, then smacks me on the shoulder. "Why don't you come with me and see if we can talk our brothers into cutting out early tonight? My fiancée's at home, and if we leave now, I can have a drink with her before I sweet-talk her into getting naked."

"Careful. You two already act like an old married couple."

Ethan shrugs. "Bachelor parties are for celebrating your last night as a free man. I can't think of a better way to celebrate than with that hot chick I picked up in a bar once."

"Fair enough." I follow him to find our brothers. Truth be told, I'm as anxious to get home as Ethan is.

Eighteen

MOLLY

By the time I park my car in Brayden's garage, my feet are aching and every muscle in my body is crying.

Tonight went pretty well, but one of my servers got a stomach bug and had to leave in the middle of her shift, meaning the other servers and I had to run ourselves ragged to pick up the slack.

But when I open the door and see tealight candles and rose petals leading a path down the hall, all that exhaustion hanging on me floats away like fluffy snow on a winter breeze. Down the hall, music plays softly beyond Brayden's bedroom door, and every one of my aching muscles quiets as another part of me wakes up.

I hook my purse and coat on the rack in the hall and follow the candlelit path to the bedroom, my heart hammering.

Brayden meets me in the doorway and hands me a cold glass

of champagne. Our fingers brush as I take it from him. "The bath is hot and ready for you."

I smile over the rim of my glass. "Are you suggesting I might stink?"

His eyes roam over me. "I'm suggesting you might have had a long day and enjoy a soak. I didn't think you'd appreciate me ripping off your clothes the second you walk in the door."

I step closer. "Are you sure about that?"

His grin is unlike any smile he's ever given me before—mischievous and a little goofy. I might even say boyish. "I'm trying to be a considerate lover."

"That might be overrated," I murmur, but I do have the film of food service on my skin and know I'll feel a thousand percent sexier after a bath.

I saunter into the bedroom and turn to watch him while I drain my champagne. Placing my glass on the dresser, I meet his eyes. I slowly strip out of my dress then peel off my bra and panties. He watches every move and doesn't so much as blink. "Join me in the bath?"

His neck bobs as he swallows. "If you want."

I head toward the bathroom, swinging my hips and tossing him my most suggestive smile over my shoulder. "What do you think?"

The bathroom is more of the same—rose petals sprinkled around the tub, candles flickering on every surface—and the oversized, jetted tub is full of steaming, bubbling water that calls to me.

I pile my hair into a knot on top of my head and climb in. When Brayden walks into the bathroom, he's gloriously naked and *hard.* Lust sears through me. I reach out my hand, and he steps into the tub. He sinks into the water and leads me into his lap, wrapping his arms around me.

The bath is hot, and when Brayden kicks on the jets, it pulls the tension from my muscles. I moan and melt into him, aware of the strength of him behind me, the length of his cock against my ass.

"How was the bachelor party?" I ask, trying to hide how much I just want to turn in his arms and slide onto him.

"It went well." He presses his open mouth to my neck, and I tilt my head to the side, sighing into his kiss. "I think Ethan was happy, so that's all that matters."

"All of your brothers made it?"

His hands still their roaming across my stomach. "Do you really want to talk about my brothers right now?"

Chuckling, I turn in his embrace, wrapping my arms around his neck. "You're always thoughtful enough to ask me about my day." I straddle him, positioning my knees on either side of his hips. "I was just trying to return the courtesy."

He groans and buries his face in my neck, scraping the tender skin with his beard as he nips, sucks, kisses. I rock against him. Harder. Faster.

He slides his hands down my soapy back and grips my hips, stilling me. "You keep doing that, and I'm going to end up inside you without a condom."

My breath catches at the husky baritone of his voice and at the thought of feeling him like that. What would it be like, to be that close to him? To give myself to him without any barrier between us? I circle my hips despite his grip. "Would you mind?

I'm on the pill."

Cursing under his breath, he pulls back to meet my eyes. "Molly . . ."

I shift my hips slightly, changing the angle where our bodies touch, and he's there—positioned against my entrance. I'm so ready. I have been all day long. Ready for him. For this. "Is it okay?"

His throat bobs as he swallows. "Yeah." The word is breathless—more plea than permission—and I sink down onto him. My breath leaves me in a rush, because he feels amazing. Hard and strong, and I'm so full.

I tuck my face into the crook of his neck, hiding my face as emotion I don't understand surges through me. This is Brayden, and he's kind and tender and *amazing*. He's the kind of guy who thinks to buy rose petals and to light candles. To pour champagne. The kind of guy who wants to get me off more than himself.

His hands are all over me, sliding up and down my back and gripping my hips as he whispers in my ear. *So good. God, you're beautiful. I've thought about you all day.*

I keep my face buried in his neck, trying to hide, because I feel too exposed. Too vulnerable.

But when I'm close from his filling me so completely and pressing so impossibly deep, he slides his hands into my hair and draws me back to look into my eyes. "I want to see your face when you come," he murmurs, and the words are my undoing, making my whole body coil tighter and tighter before I shatter around him. I'm a thousand broken pieces somehow held together by the stroke of his hands on my back and the intensity of his eyes on my face. He's studying me like I'm a piece of fine art he wants imprinted on his memory.

I kiss him as I start moving again. I rub my tongue over his and tangle my hands in his hair, and I move faster as he swells inside me. When his orgasm hits, he rocks deeper and deeper until his climax barrels through him and he throws his head back and closes his eyes.

After, he gets a washcloth and washes every inch of me, smiling a bit as he takes extra care with my breasts and between my legs. When we finally climb out of the tub, my fingers are shriveled like raisins and the air is frigid. He wraps me in a blanket and leads me to the living room, where the lights of the Christmas tree twinkle in the dark room. When he flicks on the gas fireplace, I see he has another blanket spread out in front of the hearth.

There, he lays me down and kisses me gently, until we're both spent and falling asleep in front of the flickering fire.

BRAYDEN

The grandfather clock at the front of the house chimes three as I scoop Molly into my arms and carry her to my bed.

She's so beautiful—nude and flushed from the heat of the fire, her lips still swollen from my kisses. She clings to me in her sleep, only waking as I pull the blankets down and lower her to the mattress.

"Brayden?" Sitting up, she rubs her eyes and looks at the

clock. "I should go to my room. I don't want Noah to see me sleeping in here."

I frown. "He's at your mom's tonight."

"He'll be home early." She lifts her eyes to meet mine, and I see the apology there as clearly as a line drawn in the sand. "I can't risk it."

I ignore the pang in my chest and take her hand as she climbs out of my bed. I ignore the voice that says this is the least of the hurt I've signed up for, and take her to her room, watch as she pulls on pajamas, then tuck her into her bed and kiss her good night.

Nineteen

MOLLY

"Mommy, Mommy! Wake up!" Little hands grip my arm and shake me. "Hurry, you've gotta wake up or we'll miss it!"

I squint at the clock on my bedside table through one eye and groan. It's seven a.m. I didn't come to bed until after three, and the idea of pulling myself out now makes me want to sob with exhaustion. "Hey, baby." I pat the mattress beside me. "Why don't you climb into bed with Mommy and see if you can fall back to sleep?"

"No sleeping, Mommy! You need to wake up. Lilly's here. She's going Christmas tree hunting."

I push myself up, letting my blankets and their delicious warmth fall away as I try to figure out what Lilly and Christmas trees and hunting have to do with me waking up.

I blink at my son, who's practically bouncing he's so excited,

193

and then spot Brayden leaning in my bedroom doorway. "Sorry about this," Brayden says. "The guys told me the plan last night, and I meant to invite you when you got home from work, but it . . . slipped my mind."

I rub my eyes and look at the clock again to make sure I didn't read it wrong the first time. No, it really is seven a.m.

Brayden was up as late as I was. How the hell does he look so . . . *conscious*?

"What's going on again?" I do my best to infuse my voice with a little enthusiasm for Noah's sake, but . . . *tired*. "Lilly's going hunting?"

Noah climbs on the bed, his eyes alight with excitement. He takes my face in his little hands. "For Christmas trees, Mommy! Brayden says I can come help!"

"*If* it's okay with your mom," Brayden says gently.

"You already have a Christmas tree," I tell Brayden stupidly. I mean, obviously he knows that, but I'm tired and I'm going to need someone to explain this to me in short sentences. Preferably with caffeine.

"We all go together to pick out the tree for the family cabin every year. This is the first chance we've had to do it."

"Oh. That makes more sense. I guess." God, I'd kill for a cup of Shay's coffee right now, and I'm pretty sure I can smell it brewing downstairs.

"You don't have to come if you need to sleep, but we'd be happy to take Noah along."

"Please, Mommy?" He takes my hand and squeezes it between both of his, and his unadulterated enthusiasm tugs hard at my heart. This kid is *everything*. "*Please*?"

"Of course." I ruffle his hair with my free hand. Christmas tree hunting.

I always made a big deal of our traditions when we were in New York. We went to the Christmas tree lighting every year and ice skating in Central Park, and Noah has helped me decorate the tree since he was eighteen months old and barely had enough coordination to slide the ornaments onto the branches.

"And you'll come too?" Noah asks.

Exhausted or not, there's absolutely no way I could deny him such a simple pleasure. "I wouldn't miss it."

"Then hurry and get dressed. Lilly's already here!" He scrambles off the bed and past Brayden, no doubt rushing back down the stairs so he doesn't miss another moment with his beloved Lilly.

Brayden folds his arms and watches me climb from the bed. Closing my eyes, I stretch up onto my toes, reaching my arms high above my head. The little sleep I managed last night was definitely not enough. When I open my eyes, Brayden's are skimming over me in my sleep clothes—just a red tank and a pair of flannel pants, but one would think I was wearing red lace from the heat in his eyes.

"I'm sorry I forgot to tell you," he says. "I planned to, but I didn't remember until I was alone in my bed."

"You could have woken me up."

His lips curve into that sexy half-smile that could make me drop my panties in a heartbeat. "If I'd come in here and woken you up, something tells me I would have quickly forgotten again."

"How long has Noah been home?" I feel like a bit of a slacker mom this morning. I'm pretty sure I was sleeping like the dead.

"Your mom got here about fifteen minutes ago. She's still here, talking to Ava."

Downstairs, the front door opens, and I hear a familiar female voice call out good morning, and Levi grumbling about how early it is. "Is that Ellie?"

"Oh, yes, it is. Levi went to her art show in Indiana yesterday, and they're officially back together. Another piece of information I got last night and forgot to tell you."

Warmth floods my chest. "It was only a matter of time."

Brayden grunts. "Pretty sure it felt like forever for Levi."

"Probably."

He glances over his shoulder, maybe checking the hallway, and then steps into my bedroom. He closes the door behind him before prowling toward me. "Can you forgive me for being so irresponsible and forgetting to tell you about Jackson current events?"

I smirk. Sure, he could have remembered to tell me, but he wasn't the only one desperate to get naked when I got home last night. And with him looking at me like that now, I'm wishing his family weren't gathering downstairs.

He takes another step forward and slides his hands under my tank, his rough calluses scraping the sensitive skin on my belly as he looks down at me. "I'm glad you're coming, but keeping my hands off you all day might be a bigger challenge than getting Levi out of bed before eight." One thumb skims over my navel, and he lowers his mouth to my ear.

I arch into him, wanting his hands and mouth and . . . anything, anything he can give me in this little time we can steal before going downstairs.

But he steps back with a grin. "I'll see you downstairs. Dress warm." His gaze flicks to my breasts, so intense it's like a physical brush against my nipples. "It's cold out there."

He walks out of my bedroom and closes the door behind him. The thought of waiting until after Noah goes to bed before I touch Brayden again makes me whimper, and despite the chill waiting for me outside, I rush to the bathroom to take a *very* cold shower.

BRAYDEN

Noah is in heaven. He chases Lilly up and down row after row of pine trees as my siblings debate the merits of the shorter, fatter tree or the taller, thinner one.

Molly stands near Shay, delight all over her face as she watches her son race through the snow. She's barely looked my way once today, and I'm more than a little impressed with her poker face. I've always been a private person, so I didn't think keeping this secret would bother me, but it's been less than twenty-four hours since we agreed we were doing this, and I already hate it.

I want to stand behind her and wrap my arms around her as we watch the kids play. I want to kiss her in front of my family and make sure they understand how important Molly is to me.

"I think Lilly's found the first member of her entourage," Ethan says, coming up to stand beside me.

"Noah idolizes her."

"It goes both ways." Ethan's grin grows as Lilly doubles back and Noah turns so fast to follow that he falls on his face in the snow. Unfazed, he pushes himself up and resumes his chase. "She might not admit it, but she adores Noah. She's been desperate to have more kids around."

"She'll be thrilled when Ava and Jake's baby is born." I eye my sister-in-law, who's cradled in Jake's arms as he stands behind her. He lowers his head to whisper something in her ear, stroking her rounded belly, and she grins.

"She will," Ethan agrees. "You know how obsessed she is with babies. But it's not the same. She's already seven, and that age difference will mean that all the little cousins she has coming will be too young to be playmates."

"Lilly the cousin-slash-babysitter."

"Maybe in six or seven years." Sighing, he shrugs. "I'm glad Noah's around. He's a good kid, and I'm grateful Molly lets him be a part of all this."

As if sensing that we're talking about her, Molly meets my eyes from across the clearing and gives a tentative smile. She's gorgeous today. Every day. But there's something about seeing her a little unraveled—no makeup, save for a little gloss on her lips, her hair in a sloppy bun on top of her head. When she came downstairs in a pair of leggings and an oversized hoodie, I nearly tripped. Even my mom got quiet next to me. Molly couldn't know what her appearance means to us, how important it is to everyone in my family that the people we call our own feel comfortable enough to be casual when it suits them. It's something so minor that proves so much.

I return her smile and, while I have her attention, drag my

gaze over her with slow, meaningful intensity. When I bring it back to her face, those pink cheeks have flared bright red.

"Daddy!" Lilly screeches. She stomps toward Ethan in the snow, Noah hot on her heels with his arms wrapped around his chest and his lip stuck out in a pout. "Daddy, tell Noah that Santa does *not* give presents to naughty kids."

My gaze flicks to Molly, who's gone pale, even with the frigid nip of the wind on her cheeks. She covers her mouth and her eyes go wide.

"She's lying," Noah says.

"Am not!" Lilly says, spinning on the poor kid. "And if you throw snow at me again, Santa won't come."

Ethan looks between his daughter and Molly but keeps his mouth shut while Molly jogs over to us.

"Noah said Santa brings presents to kids even if they're naughty. Tell him that's wrong!"

Ethan cringes, and I recognize the face of a parent who feels stuck.

I stoop and crook my finger to Lilly until she stomps closer. I lower my voice so only she can hear. "You know Santa's going to bring you presents this year, right?"

She wrinkles her forehead, and I can see that stubborn calculation in her eyes. She doesn't like to be wrong. "I know."

"And be honest, kiddo, did you break the rules at all this year? Sneak an extra piece of candy from your Halloween bucket or run by the pool when your dad told you to walk?"

"Yeah, but I'm not *naughty!*"

I nod. "I know you're not. In fact, you're awesome, and I think you learn from your mistakes. I think Santa believes that too. I think Santa believes that about all kids." I turn to Noah and signal him to join us. His bottom lip quivers, and he and his mom come over together.

Molly squats so she's eye level with her son. "What do you have to say to Lilly?"

"Sorry I threw snow," he says. "I won't do it again."

Lilly lifts her chin and pats Noah's head, clearly seeing this as her moment to shine as the big kid. "I forgive you, Noah." She looks at me and then back to Noah. "And I'm sorry about what I said about Santa. I'm sure he'll still bring you presents."

I squeeze Lilly's shoulder. "I think Nana is waiting for you over by the car. She needs some help pouring the hot chocolate."

Lilly lights up. "Come on, Noah!" And they race away in a burst of flying snow and giggles.

Molly is staring at me.

"You handled that like a *pro*, Brayden," Ethan says, already heading after the kids to meet them and Mom at the car. "Well done."

I shrug, trying to read the look on Molly's face, to understand the caution in her eyes.

"Thank you," she says softly.

"Are you okay?"

She shifts that worried gaze to Noah, whose eyes are big as my mom fills his mug with hot chocolate from the canister she brought. "I'm fine."

I want to wrap my arms around her, to reassure her that whatever has her upset will be okay. But my family is watching. She doesn't want them to see us together like that, and I hate it.

MOLLY

"Why have you never been married?" I ask Brayden Sunday night in bed.

"Why have *you* never been married?"

I huff out a breath. "I think that's pretty obvious." I pull back so I can see his face, but he's completely serious.

I should be exhausted. I've been Christmas tree hunting on only a few hours of sleep, followed by meetings with three different couples interested in having receptions at the Jackson Brews Banquet Center, and then spent an evening decorating at the Jackson family cabin—because Noah was floating when we were invited and, honestly, I didn't *want* to say no. I got Noah in bed later than usual and should have fallen right into my own bed after, but instead, I found myself naked in Brayden's room.

"It's not obvious to me," he says, his eyes searching my face.

"Noah is my priority. I made a decision to put him first. But what about you? Are you a consummate bachelor, or what?"

He sighs heavily and rolls to his back, where he stares at the ceiling for several long beats of silence. "My siblings would tell you that I'm too closed off. That I haven't had a serious relationship since Sara, because I don't let people in."

"Interesting." *Sara.* I haven't heard anything about her since I saw her at the tasting room Thursday night. I wonder what ever happened with that. Did he call her? Did she leave town again?

"And what would *you* say?"

"I would say that you don't grow up in a house like mine, seeing the way my parents loved each other, without being really damn picky about who you're willing to share your life with."

I study his profile, and something heavy presses on my chest. "You deserve to be picky." Then, because I realize we're talking about the possibility of him finding someone else, I jump to change the subject. "Thank you for what you did today—at the tree farm." I sit up and lean back against the headboard. "You handled it perfectly."

"It was nothing."

It was everything. "Your family is pretty amazing." I stretch my legs out and flex my feet. "I was always so jealous of that."

Brayden rolls to face me. "Your mom's great. And you have Ava and Colton."

I huff out a breath. "Yeah, and Ava and I are great now, but she pretty much hated me the few years we lived together in high school, and Colton and I were never close."

"Because he wanted you?"

I cringe at the reminder. Colton hasn't felt that way about me in years, but his old crush combined with an instinctive protectiveness caused him a lot of trouble last summer. I shrug. "So he says, but I think he always liked the idea of me more than anything. I'm grateful for Ava and Colton, but if you walked into that stupid mansion when Nelson was alive, you would have understood why I envy your family."

He sits up and cups my face in his big hand. "I don't have to experience the chill of a house under Nelson's rule to understand that. I know my family is special—have always known, even when I was a selfish teenager who wanted to escape their constant presence."

"I'm grateful . . ." I swallow, measuring my words. "I'm grateful for your family. The way they include Noah. I want him to experience that. Even the fight with Lilly today—it's like they're cousins. My dad left when I was six, and every year after that until Mom married Nelson, I'd ask Santa for a family." Brayden's still watching me, so I drop my gaze to my lap and study my hands. "Maybe a ten-year-old is too big to believe in Santa Claus, but I did. I believed with the fierce passion of a child who needed to believe in magic to survive. Then Mom married Nelson, and I got a dad and stepbrother and stepsister in one fell swoop. I told everyone at school that Santa was real. They laughed at me, but I didn't care. I *knew*."

"But your new family wasn't much of a gift at all," he whispers.

I still can't look at him. I pick at my nails. "The first time Nelson touched me, it was Christmas Eve. He told me I had to be quiet or Santa would hear and he'd take my presents away."

The whole bed shifts as he tenses beside me. "That sonofabitch."

"I knew then that there was no such thing as Santa or magic. Just adults who used the story to manipulate little kids. But I also knew that my mom was *happy* for the first time in years, and if I told her . . . if I admitted what happened, I'd be taking that from her."

"Jesus," he says, and anger comes off him in waves.

"That's why I tell my son that Santa will come regardless of his behavior. Because Santa is love, and love is unconditional." I shake my head. Almost without exception, I don't talk about

Nelson. I'm not sure what made me do it tonight. I could have explained this to Brayden without the details. And yet ... "Maybe I shouldn't have done the Santa thing with Noah, but we all need a little magic in our lives."

"There's nothing wrong with letting your child believe in magic. In something better for the hard days," he says. His voice is so tight that I force myself to look at him and see his jaw is hard and those dark eyes are cold.

I don't know what to make of his expression, but I'm already wishing I hadn't shared so much, hadn't let him see more of my broken self. "Tell me what you're thinking."

His eyes flash to angry in a heartbeat. "I'm glad the sonofabitch is dead."

MOLLY

"Molly, there are a couple of women in the kitchen asking to see you."

I pull my attention from my spreadsheets to look at my chef. I'm not even supposed to be here today, so I have no idea who'd be looking for me. "Who?"

She shrugs. Justine is great with the cooking and planning the meals, but when it comes to giving messages or, you know, basic interpersonal communication skills, she definitely falls a bit short. Since potential catering clients talk to me and not her, I overlook it.

I push out of my chair and follow her back to the kitchen.

"Brayden's sister and that hot Indian chick," the sous chef says when he spots me. "They went to the tasting room."

"Thanks." I weave my way through the staff doing the prep

work for tomorrow's dinner and push into the tasting room side of the building. There, at the far table, are Teagan and Shay. "My sous chef called you 'that hot Indian chick,'" I tell Teagan.

She rubs her hands together and waggles her brows. "And is he single?"

"Single," I say with a nod, "but only twenty-one."

"Single, legal, and knows how to cook." She shrugs. "Please give him my number."

I laugh and then look between her and Shay. "What are you two doing here?"

"Rescuing you from yourself," Shay says. "All you do is work!"

I smile at my friends. "There's a lot to be done."

"But it's your day off!"

"I'm opening a new business. Days off will come later."

Teagan waves away my objection. "That doesn't mean you can't make time for your girls."

I gape in mock offense. "Hey, Nic's bachelorette party is Thursday night, and I promised I'd be there. It's on my *schedule*."

Shay grins. "Teagan and I wanted to steal you before then."

I cock a brow, waiting.

Teagan makes a show of looking around the empty room, as if she's about to spill state secrets. "The other girls are all too sweet to tell us no when we want to go out, but you know they'd rather be at home bumping uglies with their Jackson boys."

Shay cringes. "Those *boys* are my brothers. Can we not talk about what they're *bumping*?"

Teagan chortles shamelessly. "Anyway, we're starting some super-secret single ladies' dates."

I try to smile. I really, really do, but I'm pretty sure a mirror would confirm that I look more nauseated than happy. "That sounds . . . great."

"Liar," Shay says, standing and linking her arm with mine. "You hate the idea of getting stuck at the singles' table."

I laugh. "I have no objection to the singles' table. If anything, I'd like to reserve my spot, but the nights out . . ." I shrug. "I have a kid I already miss too many evenings with. I'm not sure I'm excited about missing more time with him."

"Understandable," Shay says, and the girls lead me through the kitchen and back to my office.

"Which is why we're the perfect friends," Teagan says. "Shay's schedule is flexible, and my twelve-hour shifts mean I only like to go out on my days off, but I'm not restricted to nights."

Shay grabs my coat off the hook inside my office. "What she's saying is we're taking you to breakfast. At least once a week, just to make sure you don't turn into a workaholic zombie like my brother."

"Oh." I grin. I can do breakfast. "I think that's actually a fabulous idea." Mornings are the best for me to get in some friend time without missing out with Noah, and I've pretty much wrapped up everything I wanted to do here this morning anyway. "Where are we going?"

"Jordan's Inn," Shay says.

Teagan nods. "They have a mimosa bar and the best omelets I've ever had in my life. Before my first brunch there, I didn't even know eggs could be orgasmic."

I arch a brow. "Champagne and orgasmic eggs, all before ten a.m. on a Monday? I'm afraid to ask what else you ladies have planned."

"Oh, just you wait," Shay says.

I head down the hall to let Brayden know I'm out for the day, but I find his office door shut and the lights off. That's not like him at all. Barring when he leaves for meetings, he's usually working at his desk all morning Monday through Friday—if not on weekends too.

"I think he had plans this morning," Shay says when she notices me staring at the closed door. "Come on, let's go do some day drinking."

Teagan flashes her a smile that looks suspiciously conspiratorial.

"What are you two up to?" I ask.

"Not a thing. Just taking our new bestie to breakfast."

BRAYDEN

"God, look at you!" Sara squeezes my biceps and pulls me into a hug. I swallow hard as she curls herself into my chest. I don't know what to do with my arms, my hands. I awkwardly pat her shoulders, but if she notices my reluctance to return her embrace, she doesn't let on. "You're still the most handsome guy in town."

I smirk at that little piece of flattery. "How would you know? You haven't been around in years."

She laughs. "Touché."

Yesterday afternoon, while Molly was meeting with clients,

I finally texted Sara and told her we could meet. The longer I thought about it, the more I realized I truly have already moved on, and if she needs to give me her explanation to move on with *her* life, I want to give her that. She hurt me, but for two years before that, she was everything. It's a gift to the Sara from those years that I agreed to this. It's a gift to myself that I chose breakfast and to get it over with as soon as possible.

The server leads us to our table and gives us menus. I already know my order, so I use the opportunity to study the woman I once believed I'd grow old with.

Sara Jeffers hasn't changed. It's been ten years since she tore my life apart, but she's the same bright-eyed, beautiful woman. She still wears her blond hair long and swept over her shoulder in a braid, still toys with the end when she's nervous. We're even meeting at our favorite breakfast place—just like we did every Friday morning while she was in law school.

Everything is the same. Except me. I don't feel the same at all. *Thank God.* When she left, I had to live with wreckage in my chest. I could hardly breathe through it, and I only survived by throwing myself even more into my work. Nine years ago, I wouldn't have been able to have this meeting in public. Hell, for a few months after she left, I couldn't even say her name without feeling like I was being ripped in two.

Sara puts down her menu and beams at me. "Tell me everything I've missed."

I arch a brow. "You've been gone nearly a decade. You've missed . . . " *Everything.* "A lot of things have changed." *Except you, apparently.* But I'm not sure I want to go there.

Something flashes over her face. If I didn't know better, I'd think it was regret. She unfolds her napkin and places it in her lap before toying with her silverware. "I wanted to call so many times, but I knew you wouldn't want to talk to me." When I don't answer, she meets my gaze again. "I'm so sorry, Brayden. You have no idea how many things I regret."

I swallow hard. She seems so sincere, but it's too late. "At least you had the choice to call, the choice to reach out. You disappeared and took that choice from me."

The server appears with coffee and saves me from having to immediately say more. She fills our mugs and takes our orders before walking away. A bowl of oatmeal and a side of egg whites for Sara, and the California omelet for me. "Would either of you care for the mimosa bar?" the server asks. "Or a bellini?"

"Not for me, thank you," I say, then look to Sara, who I've never known to skip an opportunity for champagne.

"Coffee is fine," she says with a smile. When the server walks away, she tugs on a lock of hair and says, "I'm twelve months sober."

I blink. *Sober.* "I didn't know . . ." I swallow back the rest of that ridiculous sentence and shake my head. "Congratulations."

"No one knew. Not back then, at least. Even when I checked myself in for treatment, only a couple of close friends knew." She drops her gaze to her silverware. "I didn't even tell my family."

I didn't know. But hell, in retrospect, *I should have.* "I'm sorry."

"What on earth do you think you need to apologize for?" she asks softly.

"Brayden!"

My attention is pulled away to the blonde strolling toward

us. *Molly.* I blink at her.

"Hey, bossman!" She grins at me and teeters slightly, pink-cheeked and grinning. *Tipsy Molly.* "You can't seem to escape me no matter where you go, can you?"

"What are you doing here?" I scan the room and get my answer when I spot Shay and Teagan in a booth against the wall. Carter, Jake, and Levi all knew I'd be here this morning. I told them at the gym. I'd bet good money they shared that information with our sister.

Sara looks back and forth between me and Molly, who goes still when she realizes who I'm with.

I clear my throat. "Molly, this is my friend Sara. Sara, this is Molly, my—"

"Roommate," Molly blurts, jabbing her hand in Sara's direction. "Just roommate, nothing more. Well, I guess more, because he's also my boss. My boss and roommate, but we're totally platonic. No worries there. Sorry about the other night."

Totally platonic. Is she lying because she doesn't want anyone to know about us or because she thinks that's what I want? I grimace and watch as Sara takes Molly's hand and gives it a tentative shake. "Nice to meet you, Molly."

"You too." Molly's gaze ping-pongs between me and Sara. She drags her bottom lip between her teeth like she's biting back a question. She steadies her attention on me and says, "Your sister and Teagan said I work too much, so I'm taking the rest of the day off."

"You're entitled."

"But I'll be there tomorrow." She holds up two fingers. "Totally sober, scout's honor."

I feel my lips twitch in amusement. There shouldn't be anything funny about this situation, but Molly's so nervous and awkward about this meeting, and she's adorable when she's nervous. Shay might have known I'd be here with Sara, but it's obvious Molly had no idea. "Enjoy your day off, Molly. You've earned it."

"You too." She waves between me and Sara and winces. "I mean, obviously you already are, but I hope you keep enjoying it."

In the next breath, Shay is behind her, giving Sara a smile so obviously fake I hope my sister never tries for a career in acting.

Sara brightens at the sight of her. "Shay! Oh my goodness, how are you?"

"Good. Just having some mimosas with my friend here," Shay says, smacking Molly on the shoulder. "We have to head out, but it's nice to see you."

Sara deflates a bit, recognizing the brush-off for what it is. "Yeah. Sure."

Shay gives me a hard look and mouths, *Team Molly.*

I'm not much of a mind reader, but I'm pretty sure the steel in Shay's eyes means she'll kick me in the balls if I'm thinking of getting back together with Sara.

Sara and I both watch in an awkward silence as Shay, Molly, and Teagan giggle their way out of the restaurant.

"I guess it was foolish not to expect your sister to hate me."

"She doesn't hate you." That might be a lie, so I try for truth. "She's never used those words, at least, only said that she's angry with you."

Sara takes a long sip of her coffee. "I always loved your family.

Sometimes it felt like losing them was as hard as losing you." She meets my eyes. "I always believed they'd be my family too one day."

I thought the same, but I don't bother saying so.

Sara blows out a breath. "So, that's your roommate? And she works for you?"

I grimace. Leave it to Molly to make something awkward in an attempt to make it less awkward. "She runs the new banquet center that's attached to the tasting room, and she's staying at my house temporarily."

"Sounds cozy."

"She and her son needed a place to stay for a couple of months."

Her eyes go sad. "That's just like you to swoop in and play the hero."

I shrug. "I have the room. Anyone would have done it."

She studies me, trying to read my expression. Sara was always good at reading me when no one else bothered. "She's pretty."

I nod. Denying it will just make me look and feel like a liar.

"And young."

I shrug. Again, no use denying it.

"Does she know you're in love with her?"

"Don't." The word is soft, but she hears the warning and straightens.

"It's not my business anyway, right?" She turns away from me and smiles at the waitress, who slides our food in front of us.

When we're alone again, I ask, "Why'd you ask me here, Sare?"

Her smile wobbles. "You called me Sare. No one's called

me that since . . ." She shakes her head and picks up her fork. "I wanted to apologize for . . . everything."

"It was a long time ago."

"I know you said you forgave me for what I did." She picks up her fork and pushes her egg whites around her plate. "I couldn't forgive myself, and I didn't want to admit that I needed help."

The reminder of those last days between us doesn't hurt as much as I anticipated. It's like going to debride a wound, only to find it's already healed. "I wish you had."

She nods, still not meeting my eyes. "Your whole world was tied to alcohol, Brayden. I couldn't . . . I needed to cut it out of my life completely, and I didn't see any way of doing that without asking you to do the same."

"I would have." It's true. I'd have walked away from the family business for her. My father was still healthy when she left, so it would have been easy. And everything would have been different.

"I know. That's why I couldn't tell you. I was so ashamed."

"Thank you for telling me now." I reach across the table and put my hand over hers. "I mean it."

"There's another reason I brought you here. I wanted to tell you in person that I'm moving back to Jackson Harbor." She takes a long, shaky breath. "And that I never stopped loving you, so if you ever find it in your heart to give me a second chance . . ." Her lip quivers. "I know it sounds crazy, but I'd never forgive myself if I didn't tell you."

Twenty-One

MOLLY

A blast of frigid air hits me in the face as we push out of the restaurant and race to Teagan's car. I climb into the back, letting Shay have the front seat.

"Did you know Brayden would be there?" I ask.

"I did," Shay says.

"Shay! What the hell? I just made an ass of myself." And now I have this awful feeling in my stomach. Like maybe I'm in the way and if I already know I can't be with Brayden, I have no right to keep him from someone who could plan a future with him.

Shay buckles up, then turns sideways in her seat to look at me. "It didn't go as planned, okay? I thought Brayden would notice you were there and come over to say hi."

I gape at her. "I see him every single day. I *live* with him. And you made me look like some sort of awful stalker because you were hoping he'd *say hi*?"

Shay and Teagan exchange a look, and Teagan says, "She was hoping Sara would see the way he looks at you and back off before trying to get him back."

The way he looks at me? I swallow the bubble of hope those words put in my throat. It doesn't matter how he looks at me. We are what we are, and nothing more. And anyway, she's probably mistaking lust for something else. "I feel like a pawn, and I don't like it."

"I'm sorry." Shay throws up her hands. "I swear I don't normally meddle so much in my brothers' love lives, but I've been protective of Brayden since Sara left, and Molly, the two of you are making me *crazy*. Can't you just jump him before he makes a big mistake and takes her back?"

If my interaction with Brayden hadn't cemented the second mimosa as a bad idea, I'm sure of it now as I try and fail to understand Shay's logic. She took me to brunch hoping Brayden would say hi, and she wants me to jump her brother? *Hello—been there, done that, plan to do it again tonight.* "You're not making any sense to me."

"Has Brayden told you anything about Sara?" Shay asks as Teagan starts the car.

I frown. The night I met Sara was weird. Brayden practically pinned me against the building, and for a minute I actually thought he was going to kiss me, but he kept his history with Sara a secret. "Not much. He was pretty upset that I interfered, so I didn't bring it up again after I got home. What happened between them?"

"I think he'd be irritated with me if I told you," Shay says.

I sag in my seat in disappointment. "Okay. I understand."

"So I'm going to do it," Teagan says. She pulls out of her parking space and onto the road. "Ten years ago, right before Brayden was going to propose, the bitch cheated on him with one of her law professors."

My stomach drops. "Oh, no." I shake my head. "Wait. Teagan, I didn't think you even lived here ten years ago."

"I didn't. I just know the story," Teagan says, meeting my eyes in the rearview mirror. "He didn't tell anyone what happened, but word got around. Brayden thought they could work through it."

"He loved her so much," Shay whispers.

"Then she ghosted him," Teagan says. "She skipped town, changed her number, blocked him on social media, and told her family she didn't want them to tell him where she was."

I know my jaw is hanging open, but all I can do is shake my head. "She ran away from *Brayden*? Did she leave with the professor?"

"Nope. He still teaches at JHU. No one knows exactly why she left," Teagan says, and Shay nods along in agreement, her lips sealed. "But it destroyed him. She was the love of his life."

"That sounds like someone running from an abusive relationship."

Shay turns up her palms. "I know, right?" She snaps her mouth shut again and looks at Teagan.

Teagan gives her a soft, sympathetic smile before continuing. "It killed him. He tore himself up trying to figure out what he did to make her feel like she needed to disappear like that."

Shay turns back in her seat to face the road, and I barely hear her when she says, "He's never been the same. Never moved on or wanted to . . ." Her eyes are sad when she slowly turns back to me. "Until you, Molly. Until you."

BRAYDEN

The stars shine so brightly tonight that I can almost forget about the bitter wind wrapping around me and threatening to seize my bones.

The back door clicks behind Molly as she joins me on the patio. After my breakfast with Sara, I spent the rest of the afternoon and most of my evening at the office. I wasn't ready to face Molly or to think about how easy it was for her to downplay our relationship, as if she'd be happy to help me reconnect with Sara, happy to step aside. *To leave.*

By the time I got home, Molly and Noah were in the middle of their bath-and-bedtime routine. I went for a run on the treadmill in the basement, and when that didn't clear my head, I came out here.

Molly offers me a tentative smile and hands me a beer. "I thought you might need this."

I take it and study the label as she settles into the seat beside me. "Thanks."

"Do you want to talk about Sara?"

I want to talk about you. I search her face for any indication that she might understand what's really gotten under my skin, but I see none. "Ten years ago, Sara up and left me, and I didn't know why. Today, she explained." I swallow. "So, now I finally know, and . . ." I squeeze the back of my neck, but it does nothing to release the tension knotting there.

Molly puts her beer down and stands behind my chair. Her hands settle on my shoulders, her thumbs rubbing circles on my neck. I close my eyes and feel the tension leak away. Not just because she's massaging my tight muscles, but because she's *here*.

I bow my head to give her better access to my tight spots. "I can almost understand why she did it. She knew I would've walked away from everything to be with her. Not just the family business, but Jackson Harbor. And she knew how important my family was—*is*—to me. She needed to get away from it, and I was so blind to her battle with alcoholism that I didn't even know."

"She hid it? The alcoholism?"

Shame washes over me. "I like to think I'd have seen it if we'd lived together, but we didn't. She didn't want to move in until after we were married, and I never questioned her wishes." I sigh as I see those days through a new lens. "I knew she could get out of hand when she drank. Sometimes it was hard to pull her away from the booze at parties and out at the bar, but we were young, and I told myself it was only sometimes. She was in law school, for Christ's sake, and at the top of her class. It was easy to write off any passing concerns I might have had, because other than those bad nights, her life seemed great. *Seemed* is the keyword, I guess."

"If you weren't living with her and she worked to hide it, I'm not sure how you could have known."

"I didn't want to know. That's on me. Until today, I had no idea how much she was struggling. I caught her sleeping with her law professor a few days before she left, and even that didn't clue me in. I thought they were having an affair, but she confessed this morning that she'd agreed to sleep with him if he'd change her grade. It's just one more piece of evidence proving I had no idea what was really going on with her when she left."

"Brayden," she says softly. "She hurt you. You couldn't have been expected to see through such a betrayal when you were in the middle of dealing with it."

"I saw what I wanted to see—the woman who made me relax, who helped me cut loose when I was stressed, and who dreamed of the same future I did."

Molly stills behind me, and her touch goes lighter. "What did you dream of?"

"The normal stuff. A family, kids, to stay in Jackson Harbor and turn my father's business into something so big the whole world could see how talented he was." I blow out a breath and watch it cloud in the cold air. "I can take responsibility for not looking closer at what I sometimes suspected might be a bigger problem for her, and I can understand why she thought leaving was the best thing for me."

"Then what's bothering you?"

I'm glad she's behind me. I'm glad I don't have to see her face when I admit, "I wanted to be enough for her to be selfish. I wanted to be so necessary to her happiness that she could have at least given the choice to *me*, let *me* decide if the sacrifice was worth giving us a chance."

"She . . . wants you back?" Was that a hitch in her voice or just wishful thinking on my part?

"Yeah. She does."

"Maybe you'd feel better if you talked about it."

I reach back and take her hand, squeezing her fingers in mine. "There's not much to talk about."

I swallow. The truth is, between the time Sara left until last spring when the job with Jackson Brews brought Molly into my life more regularly, I thought I wouldn't ever feel like that for someone again. I've avoided any relationship that would make me that vulnerable. I didn't want to give anyone the power to hurt me like Sara did. But I know without a doubt I'd happily hand that power over to Molly.

Hell, if I'm honest with myself, I already have.

MOLLY

Brayden fell asleep holding me, and I look at the clock by his bed and give myself ten minutes before I have to go up to my own bed. Any more, and I risk falling asleep myself.

I rest my cheek against his chest and close my eyes as I soak in his heat and the strength of him. He moans in his sleep, and his hands slide around to rest on the small of my back. Joy flutters to life in my stomach. Even with all the hustle of work and preparing for Christmas with Noah, I can't deny the last three days have been a bit of a dream. Honestly, my life was a dream before. I had an amazing job, great new friends, and Brayden's quiet but rock-solid support through every day—at work and at home. And now I have Brayden too. His hot eyes on me, his seductive whispers in my ear.

Soon, Christmas will be over, the New Year will be here, and it'll be time to move out. I won't have an excuse to have morning coffee with Brayden or evenings soaking with him in his hot tub. The plan was that we'd end this when I left, and if I don't want to end it—if I want us to try to *be* something—I'll have to do it without an excuse. I'd have to be willing to admit it's what I want, and be willing to risk it all falling apart.

Brayden's breathing is steady and deep, and I watch the clock tick through the minutes, feeling my allotted time coming to its inevitable end. I don't want it to. I want to stay here in his arms. I want so much I've never let myself imagine before this week. And because it scares me—the intensity with which I want it, and all I could lose if I make the leap and miss—I pull out of his embrace and climb off the bed.

"Molly?" He pushes himself to sitting.

"You don't need to get up." My thoughts sink into my stomach and twist into a knot. One end is yanked tight by everything I want—the fairytale, the unlikely happy ending—and the other by everything I know I've done and who I know I am.

Maybe we all make mistakes, and maybe I've had my reasons. Maybe I'm not to blame for being so fucked up and broken, but it doesn't change that I am. And Brayden deserves more than a broken mess who doesn't even know how love works.

I dip my head and press a kiss to his jaw, to the shadow of stubble there, and when I pull back and meet his eyes, I see his thinly veiled pain. He wants me to stay. To sleep with him.

I press a second kiss to his jaw, wondering if I could do it—if I could be brave enough to ask for more. I don't think he'd deny me. I think he'd try. Even if it's not what's best for him, if I wanted everything, he'd do his best to deliver.

Brayden doesn't do anything halfway. It's what makes him so successful. And maybe it's what scares me.

BRAYDEN

I didn't think seeing a woman at the stove could ever get me hard so fast, but I learn otherwise Wednesday morning when I find Molly in my kitchen. She's in fuzzy socks that come up to her knees, a T-shirt that barely covers her ass, and a thong. Her hair is wet, like she just got out of the shower. My mouth goes dry, and my cock strains against my fly.

I'd blame my reaction on the fact that this is still new between us—so new that I locked us in her office yesterday and spread her out on her desk because I couldn't wait to get home before tasting her. Or I could blame it on the fact that she left my room too soon again last night, that she still insists on waking up in her own bed in case Noah wakes before her. But the truth is I could have a month alone with her and never get enough.

Only when she shakes her ass to a song I can't hear do I realize she's wearing earbuds. I let myself stand there while she cooks her eggs, watching her dance from side to side, my thoughts torn between how much I want to touch her and how much I want . . . more. *This.* Her in my kitchen, in my shower, in my bed. Not just for now, and not just for sex.

But she's made it clear what she can offer and what she can't. I have to respect that, even if I don't like it. And that means I can touch her, taste her, take her to my bed and try not to hope for more, or I can take nothing at all . . . and still never know what it's like to wake up with her in my arms.

She must catch sight of me from the corner of her eye, because she startles and turns from her pan. "Oh, hey! I thought you had a meeting with an investor this morning."

I tuck my hands into my pockets. She switches off the stove and slides her eggs onto a plate. "It was canceled. Cute outfit."

She snorts. "My dress is in the dryer. I'm not planning on going to the banquet center like this. I promise."

"That's a shame."

She throws me a grin over her shoulder, completely unselfconscious about her clothes. Or lack thereof. "Want to have breakfast with me? I actually had my shit together this morning and ran on the treadmill right after dropping Noah at school. Now I can enjoy the rest of my morning instead of wasting it dreading exercise."

I laugh. "The guys asked after you at the gym."

She wrinkles her nose. "I'll come back after I get a full night's sleep."

I smirk. "I have no intention of letting that happen anytime soon."

She blushes. "Are you hungry?"

So hungry, but not for breakfast. "I already ate." I stalk toward her. I've watched long enough. Now I want to *touch.*

She braces her hands on the counter, her back to me as she watches the toaster. When I come up behind her, she stills and closes her eyes. I stop before our bodies touch, but I'm close enough that the smell of her strawberry shampoo fills my nose.

"I was hoping you'd be home," I admit, my voice rough as my hands drift to rest on her hips, on the satin strips of fabric over each one. "Noah's at school?"

She arches into me in invitation. "Yes."

"I threw the bolt on the front door in case we get any unexpected visitors." Sweeping her wet hair to the side, I press a kiss to the crook of her neck. She shivers as my fingertips skim her bare hips then circle around to sneak under her T-shirt and over her navel. Her eyes float closed, and she leans her head back against my shoulder, submitting to my touch and asking for more. "Too bad I didn't make it home sooner," I whisper into her ear. I inch my hands up and cup her breasts, growling in the back of my throat when I realize she's not wearing a bra. Her nipples are hard, and I roll them under my palms. "I think I'd have enjoyed meeting you in the shower."

She hums in approval, then circles her hips and rubs her ass against my cock. "What on earth would you have done with me in the shower?"

"Should I demonstrate?" I drop to my knees behind her and nip at the rounded cheek of her ass. She hisses out a curse, and I cup her between her legs, slipping forward to stroke her clit as I mark a path across her backside, nibbling and sucking across her lower back and over each hip.

Gasping, she rocks into my hand and grips the counter. "Brayden . . ."

She whimpers as I withdraw my hand, but wiggles to help me when I peel her panties down her legs. I grip her hips and pull her back, bending her at the hips to give my mouth better access to her sweet center. I dart out my tongue and stroke her. I revel in her gasps, the way she shifts into my mouth, unashamed to let me please her.

I love the taste of her. The sounds she makes. The feel of her skin under my roaming hands. I keep one hand on her clit and slide the other up her shirt again, rolling her nipple between two fingers until she cries out, arching her back and giving my mouth a better angle.

"Please," she gasps. "Brayden, please." She reaches behind her and tugs on my hair to pull me up.

I'm mindless as I obey her command. Standing, I unbuckle my jeans and shove them down my hips with my boxers. I grip her hips and drive into her, watching the way her arms brace against the counter and her back arches, listening to the desperate noises slipping from her throat.

When she looks over her shoulder, her blue eyes blaze as they meet mine, and pleasure is written all over her face. I wrap my arm around her waist to stroke her, and she clenches so tightly around my cock that I could come apart right there. I slow my thrusts, teasing her by nearly pulling out before driving deep again.

Her knuckles whiten where she grips the counter, and I draw tiny circles across her clit until she bucks in unbridled pleasure, crying out as her release rips through her. She reaches behind my neck and leans against me as I come.

Afterward, I run kisses down her neck and across her shoulder blades. We're half-dressed in the middle of my kitchen, and my chest is tight with tenderness I know she doesn't want to see, and my heart is clogged with words I know she doesn't want to hear.

Love. Somehow it's there, whether we're prepared for it or not. It grows whether it's wanted or not.

MOLLY

Brayden scoops me into his arms, and I yelp. He grins down at me and carries me to his bedroom, laying me out on his big bed. His eyes burn into me with so much lust that it's like we didn't just have sex. He looks at me like he's *starved.* Like he hasn't touched anyone in centuries and is desperate for the feel and taste of skin. *My* skin. *My* touch.

Five minutes ago, I was convinced he couldn't possibly wring another ounce of pleasure from my body, but now it flicks back to life one cell at a time under the heat of his gaze. I hold out a hand. "Are you going to get in bed with me or just stand there?"

He grins again. "I intend to spend most of my morning in bed with you." He pinches my ass hard enough to make me yelp. "But not yet. I'll be right back."

I watch him, my gaze on the way his unbuttoned jeans fall

low on his hips. He disappears down the hallway. I let my eyes float closed and nestle deeper into his blankets.

I don't know how much time has passed when I wake up to the smell of coffee and the sound of silverware clanking on a plate. I force my eyes open and see a steaming plate of eggs and toast as Brayden sets it on his bedside table.

"Fresh breakfast," he says, taking a seat on the edge of the bed. "Since the one you made went cold, thanks to me."

I smirk. "I didn't mind." I sit up in bed and take the coffee in my hands, inhaling deeply before taking a sip. "God, this is good."

"I'm glad you like it."

"So why did the investor cancel your meeting?"

"He didn't."

I frown. "But you said—"

"*I* canceled it."

"You canceled a meeting? You, *Brayden*?" I do my best to keep my jaw hinged. "Why?"

His nostrils flare, and his eyes darken. "Because I can't stop thinking about how it feels to be inside you. Or the sounds you make when you come."

My thighs clench, and heat pools in my belly and tugs lower, begging for a repeat performance of the magic show he worked on my body in the kitchen. I lick my lips and give him my best sultry grin. "Who would've guessed that quiet, all-business Brayden Jackson has such a dirty mouth?"

He arches a brow. "I don't remember you complaining about my mouth yesterday."

A shiver races through me at the reminder of being propped

on my desk, the sight of him lowering to his knees as he shoved my skirt up my hips and—as he promised that day in the pantry—kissing me through the lace of my panties until I was screaming his name. "Who said I was complaining?"

He smirks and opens his mouth to say something, but his phone rings from the bedside table. He closes his eyes and buries his face between my breasts. "Ignore it."

I grab it. "No. I won't be responsible for turning you into a delinquent." My grin falls away when I see the name on the screen. "It's Sara Jeffers."

He stiffens. "Just let it go to voicemail."

I should shove the phone in his hands and encourage him to take the call. Instead, I put it down on the bedside table and slip from his grasp to climb out of bed. "I need to get ready for work."

"Molly?"

"What?" I keep my face blank as I turn back to him.

"I don't know why she's calling."

I shrug. "It's fine."

The look in his eyes says he knows it's not fine at all, but he lets me walk out of his room, and the entire time I'm dressing for work, I'm thinking of our conversation Monday night.

He loved Sara because she wanted the same things he did—a family and kids. A future.

There's no doubt in my mind that he wants those things now. So why is he wasting time with me when I can't offer any of that?

MOLLY

"Do I want to know where we are?" Nic whispers.

I climb out of the limo Veronica rented for her twin sister's bachelorette party and cringe at the club in front of us. The marquee flashes promises in neon lights.

MALE DANCERS!

LIVE OUT YOUR WILDEST FANTASIES!

HALF-PRICE WELL DRINKS!

Veronica giggles, and Shay and I exchange a look. We all would have preferred a night in a big booth at Jackson Brews to a night with some stranger trying to rub his junk in our faces.

Nic's still blindfolded, at Veronica's insistence. I take her hand as we follow Veronica into the club. The guy on stage shakes his ass in nothing more than a G-string, a Santa hat, and a fluffy white beard. I cringe.

"Dear Lord," Shay whispers beside me. "I just threw up in my mouth a little."

"What?" Nic asks, reaching for her blindfold. "What is it?"

Veronica spins around and tugs off Nic's blindfold. "Surprise!"

Nic blinks as she surveys the club, her jaw dropping when she spots stripper Santa grinding his hips against a pole on the stage.

"The hottest Santa I've ever seen," Veronica says.

Teagan wrinkles her nose. "I can't disagree. And yet . . ."

Nic sends a pleading glance in my direction, and I shrug. She knows Veronica better than any of us. Surely she saw this coming.

A man in nothing but a pair of very tight leather shorts greets us with a grin. "Is this the bride-to-be?" He looks Nic up and down and then . . . *licks his lips.*

Nic's eyes widen, and she backs away a few feet.

"She is!" Veronica says. "We should have a table at the front reserved."

He grins and tilts his head toward the stage. "Right this way, ladies."

We follow him to our table in front of the stage. Our seats line one side of the table and face the stage—all the better to see stripper Santa, I suppose.

"What can I get you beauties?" our host asks as we sit.

"Booze," I say.

Teagan nods. "We're going to need a lot of booze."

Next to me, Shay whispers, "Amen."

"Shots of tequila," Veronica says. "For everyone but her." She points to Ava, who's still standing and looking at her chair like she might disinfect it before sitting.

"Oh, I like you already." The man flexes his pecs, making them dance up and down. Teagan snorts.

"I can't believe you're getting married this weekend," Veronica squeals, wrapping one arm around her twin sister. "I swear I'm not going to ruin this one."

"You'd better not," Teagan says. "Ethan would kill you."

Nic smiles softly. "I'm glad she ruined my first wedding. I'm loving the crazy turn my life took."

I reach down the table and squeeze her hand. "Are you nervous at all?"

Nic shakes her head. The woman is *glowing* with happiness, despite our surroundings. "I mean, maybe a little nervous about people staring at me, but not about the marriage part."

"Because my brother's a saint, blah-di-blah-blah," Shay says, but she's grinning. She can't hide how happy she is to see Nic marry her brother.

Our conversation is cut short when the G-string Santa spots us and walks to our side of the stage. Veronica screams and waves singles in the air, and the dancer pulls his beard off as he drops down and air-humps the floor.

I cut myself off after the second shot, but I have to admit that place was more entertaining with the tequila in my bloodstream. I didn't want a hangover tomorrow *or* to lose my wits when our server kept looking at me like he wanted me to be his midnight snack, so by the time we return to the little rental house Veronica got us for the night, I'm sober and wide awake while the bride and her twin are giggling drunk in their beds.

I pick up my phone to text Brayden.

> *Me: We're back at the house.*
> *Brayden: Dare I ask?*
> *Me: Santa in a G-string. Need I say more?*
> *Brayden: Please don't.*
> *Me: Everyone's drunk and passing out. I'm wide awake and jealous that they can sleep and I can't.*
> *Brayden: Wish you were here.*

His words send my heart racing, and I bite my bottom lip.

> *Me: Me too.*

"Sexting someone?" Teagan asks. She strolls into the kitchen and turns on the tap to fill a glass with water. "I saw the server give you his number."

I snort. "I might have accidentally thrown it away."

She grins, then chugs her water. "Everyone else is in bed. Grab your coat and come on." She waves me toward a set of stairs.

I follow her up past the second floor and to a narrower set of stairs and a little balcony off the attic. The bitterly cold air hits my face, and I pull up my hood and shove my hands into my pockets.

"Spill," she says, pulling the door shut behind me.

I frown. "What?"

"You've been walking around with this goofy smile on your

face for the last week. You're keeping secrets, and I think you've forgotten I adopted you as my BFF, so you don't get to keep secrets from me." She folds her arms, but there's no anger or disapproval on her face, just curiosity.

Swallowing, I slide down the wall and stare out into the frigid night. I can feel the smile tugging at my lips, and I realize I *want* to talk about it. I want to talk about *him*. "I'm seeing someone."

"I knew it!" she screeches, then smacks a hand over her mouth and says more softly, "I thought so. Tell me about him."

"He's . . ." Everything in me seems to vibrate at the thought of him. "I've never dated anyone who's so kind to me, and I don't mean that as a knock against the guys I've dated. I just . . ." I stare at my friend and wonder how vulnerable I'm willing to make myself. "He treats me like I'm something truly special. He's not a big talker, and he keeps his emotions close to the vest, but sometimes when we make love, I catch him smiling."

Teagan snorts. "A guy smiling during sex. I'm sure."

"No, not like that—like he can't help himself. Like he's trying to process the wonder of being with me. It would be easy to think I *am* special. With him, I could believe it."

Teagan squeezes my arm. "You are special, Molly. And I'm glad you found someone who can make you believe it."

My eyes flick to my lap and away from the stars. *Do you think someone like me could have something real?* I don't ask. Because she's my friend, and I know what her answer will be. It doesn't matter how much my friends believe in me; hearing them say it won't change how screwed up I am.

"Noah seems to really like him," she says.

I snap my eyes to hers. "What?"

Her expression is tender, and she adds, "I don't think anyone else knows. They suspect. Especially Shay. But . . ."

"Who . . . How?"

"We all see how you look at him. How he looks at you. I just thought it was a crush, though. I didn't realize the two of you were . . ."

"It's not a relationship. He knows I can't do that. I can't offer that." I attempt to smile. "So don't kick me out of your hot-singles club just yet."

Sadness pulls on her features. "Why can't you offer that? Because he's your boss?"

I sigh. "No, I don't really care about that. Not anymore, at least." I take a breath, searching for the words to explain something that's been less and less clear to me by the day. "I don't want anything serious. I just want to focus on Noah and work. Brayden knows all this, so stop looking at me like I'm kicking a puppy."

"Is that really what you want, Molly? I mean, when you think of your future, you truly want nothing more than a series of meaningless hookups? You don't want . . . more?"

"Girls like me don't get more."

Teagan bumps her shoulder against mine. "I didn't ask for your predictions, oracle. I asked what you *wanted*."

I wrap my arms around myself and tip my head up to study the cloudy night sky. "I want not to be so damn afraid."

"What's there to be afraid of? Falling for him?" She's staring at me and waits until I meet her eyes before adding, "Isn't it too late for that?"

Twenty-Four

BRAYDEN

"Uncle Levi said Molly can't keep her eyes off you, and you should be a man and stop ignoring her." My niece just grins up at me, as if she's completely oblivious to the pot she's stirring by delivering Levi's message.

I know better. That little pest is about to star in her second wedding in three months, and she's made it her personal mission to marry off all her uncles and her aunt Shay so she can wear more "princess dresses." Poor Levi and Ellie haven't even been back together a full week, and Lilly is already asking when they'll get married. A seven-year-old playing matchmaker is pretty hilarious when it's not you, but the last thing I need is her scaring away Molly.

Despite that, my gaze drifts to the woman in question, who's sitting in a booth at the back of Jackson Brews and having a beer with my sister. They're laughing and carrying on about something, and the sight of her here—laughing with Shay, hanging with my family, *one of us*—makes my chest ache. She worked all day, but tonight, for Ethan and Nic's rehearsal dinner, she gets to celebrate with us. I want to enjoy it, enjoy *her*, and pull her into my arms and kiss her until she knows just how much I love having her here, to let everyone else know she's mine. But those damn rules of hers keep my feet planted a good distance away, like they have been all night. I'm close enough to watch her but not so close that she's within reach. Because that might be too much temptation.

"Hey, stranger. A little birdie told me I might find you here tonight."

I pull my gaze off Molly and meet Sara's hazel eyes. I wait for that old hurt to hit. The feeling of my world being ripped out from under my feet when I never thought it was possible. That feeling lingered long after she left me. Every time I heard her name or smelled her perfume on my sheets. Every time I saw the professor she fucked.

That ache of betrayal and loneliness lasted too long. Until eventually I didn't trust the world beneath my feet. Until I let go of the idea of happily-ever-after for myself. For too long I thought that losing that with Sara meant losing it forever.

But the hurt doesn't come. The earth is steady beneath my feet, the air still filling my lungs, and I can only stare at her and marvel at how much I've changed. I guess time heals after all. But maybe I shouldn't give time all the credit. "What are you doing here, Sara?" Jackson Brews is open to the public tonight, but it's the last place I thought I'd run into her—she likely came here to seek me out.

"Not drinking, if that's what you're worried about." Her voice is thick, like she's talking around tears. "I was just hoping we might talk."

I search her face, see the sincerity in her eyes. "I thought we already did that."

"We did, and I should give you time to process everything, but . . ." She drops her gaze to her hands, twisted in front of her. "Do you think you'll ever be able to forgive me?"

I take them in mine. "It's been years. I've let go."

She cocks her head to the side, studying my face. "Let go, or moved on?"

Before I realize what I'm doing, I catch my gaze drifting back to Molly—her long blond hair and sparkling blue eyes. "I think the two may have gone hand in hand for me," I admit, to myself as much as her.

"I've missed you." She squeezes my shoulder. "I've never forgiven myself for losing you. You were the best thing that ever happened to me. I didn't realize how lucky I was." She steps closer and tilts her head back to hold my gaze. I can't help but compare it to how it feels to have Molly this close. How different this is. How *right* it feels to close the distance and pull Molly into my arms.

"Sara . . ." I'm not sure what to say, or if I should even say anything at all when I'm in such limbo with Molly. A year ago I'd have jumped on the chance to have Sara back. And ironically, a year ago I hadn't forgiven her. Maybe I needed to understand what she did in order to move on.

Sara takes advantage of my contemplative silence and lifts onto her toes to press her mouth to mine. I step away from the kiss, but not before her lips brush over mine.

"I'm sorry. I can't . . ." I don't get a chance to put my thoughts into words, because I spot Molly, standing ten feet away and staring at me like I've just torn out her heart.

When I meet her eyes, she turns on her heel and rushes through the kitchen door.

Sara grabs my arm before I even realize I'm chasing after Molly. "Brayden?"

I shake my head. "I can't do this right now, Sara." I look over my shoulder to where Molly disappeared into the kitchen. *Shit.*

MOLLY

The night is clear, and stars twinkle down from a cloudless winter sky as I push out into the lot behind Jackson Brews. I didn't take time to grab my coat, and the icy wind bites into my bare skin. I welcome the sting against my cheeks as I tilt my face to the stars. I won't cry. I have no right to cry.

They kissed.

I wish I could be angry about that, angry with Brayden for leading me on or for making me want so much more than I ever let myself believe I could have, but I'm cursed with enough rational thought that anger eludes me. This is my fault. Brayden is giving me what I asked for—no strings. No commitments. No future. None of the things I know he'll be so good at giving the right woman.

"Are you trying to catch pneumonia?"

I close my eyes at Brayden's voice. The deep rumble of it. The way it scrapes over my skin like a highly anticipated caress.

When I turn to him, he's pulling off his jacket and handing it to me. I shake my head. "Take it," he says, his voice hard enough that I decide it's not worth arguing.

I slip into it. It's still warm, and it smells like him—clean and spicy. The scent makes my head spin with memories that almost knock me off my feet.

He folds his arms and stares at me, his face hard. I expect a lecture or a speech about why my jealousy is unfair.

"Say it," I spit out when he says nothing.

He arches a brow. "What do you want me to say?" His eyes scan my face, snagging on my mouth for a beat before returning to meet my eyes. "Do you want me to apologize for what you saw in there?"

"No. You don't owe me an apology."

An emotion that I can't name passes across his face. "Then why are you looking at me like I just broke your heart?"

"Don't be ridiculous. You kissed her."

"*She* kissed *me*," he says.

"I'm sure it was a hardship," I mutter, hating the bitchy edge that laces every word. I shrug. "Relax. I don't have any claim to you, and I know it."

Those intense, dark eyes search my face. "You could, you know." His voice hitches, as if it's catching on something, stumbling over an emotion he's tried to hide and tripped on instead.

I scoff. I'm an idiot. This is stupid. But try as I might, I

241

can't ignore this *want* clawing at me. This wish that I could be someone else. This craving for more than a girl like me should expect. *Stupid, stupid, stupid.*

"What do you want, Molly?"

I frown at my feet. "Just fresh air. A minute alone."

He steps forward and takes my chin in his hand, tilting my face up until my eyes meet his. "Liar," he whispers.

"We're all liars," I whisper back.

"So tell me something true. Something real."

I open my mouth to say something snide and then close it again.

"Do you want me to go first?" he asks softly. When I don't answer, he goes on. "I like having you at the house." His hand slides into my hair, and his thumb traces the edge of my jaw. "I didn't realize how lonely it was there until I knew what it was like to have it filled with your laughter. I like sitting across from you with coffee in the mornings, and watching TV with you when we should both be in bed." He lowers his face to mine, but when I think he's going to kiss me, he simply brushes his nose against mine. "I like touching you, and I hate thinking about you leaving. Ever. Whether that's in January or February or in a year. I want you there. I want you with me."

I close my eyes, relishing his closeness, the heat of his breath on my lips, the rough strength of his hand along my jaw. And despite the harsh chill in the night air, I feel warm.

He pulls back. "Your turn."

I hesitate, unsure which of the thousand confessions swimming through my mind I should offer him, weighing the implications of each before finally circling back to what brought me out here to begin with. "I was jealous. Of her."

"Because she kissed me?"

"Yes." I shake my head. It's not that simple. "Because . . . despite everything, she's better for you than I am." I meet his eyes, my need to protect my heart at war with my need to offer myself to him. "Because she wanted—*wants*—the same things you do, and you could have a life with her. A family. A chance at happiness. And I . . ." I can't find the words, and draw in a ragged breath against the pain of the truth.

"You don't want to give me those things."

"It's not about what I want, Brayden. It's about who I am. I can't . . . I've never . . ." I tear my gaze away from those knowing eyes, from the tenderness and sympathy in them. I don't want sympathy. "I don't even know how to have a real relationship. A boyfriend. I've never had one." He's so silent that I don't have a choice but to meet his eyes again, to try to piece together his hidden thoughts from the shadows passing over his features. "Say something, you stubborn, silent ass."

He huffs out a laugh. "Do you want to be my girlfriend, Molly?"

My cheeks heat. "Don't mock me."

"Trust me, I wouldn't. Not about this." He wraps his arms around my back and draws me against his chest, leading me into a quiet dance to the music of the cars on the street and the icy breeze in the trees. He props his chin on the top of my head and rubs slow, lazy circles on my back. "She kissed me, but I didn't want her to. This time last year, I'd have given up everything to have her back—for better or worse—but I don't feel that way anymore."

"Why not?"

"Because I'm in love with someone else." My feet stop moving, but he continues. "This woman, the one I love? I'm not sure how she feels about me, but it doesn't matter. I can't turn off what I feel. I might be a stubborn ass, but I know what I want." He pulls back to look at me. "That's never been the problem."

"Then what's the problem?"

"I don't know what *you* want, Molly." His thumb is rough across my cheek as he sweeps away a tear I didn't realize I'd shed.

"I'm scared."

He nods. "Me too."

"Sara hurt you," I whisper.

He nods again. "She did."

"What if I hurt you too?"

"That's a risk I'm willing to take. Which is new for me, and completely unique to how I feel about you. I didn't think I wanted to risk that again, but for you it's not even a choice. It just is."

I swallow hard. "So what does this mean?"

"I guess that depends. Will you go out with me, Molly McKinley?"

"Like, go steady?" My words are as wobbly as my knees beneath my dress.

"Oh, yeah. With the dates and the kissing and . . . anything else you want."

"What if it doesn't work? What if I . . ." I'm not even sure what I'm afraid of, aside from this frazzled skittering of *don't fuck this up* running through my blood, not sure what question I can ask, aside from my secret whisper of *what if you realize you deserve better?*

"What if it does?" he asks. Then he lowers his mouth to mine and kisses me. His lips are warm, his kiss tender, his arms tightening around me.

When he breaks away, I'm breathless and shaking. "We should go back in. I need to say goodbye before I head to the banquet center and make sure everything's ready to go for tomorrow."

Smiling, he takes my hand and leads me inside, not releasing me until we reach the kitchen.

"You look smug, Brayden Jackson."

"I'm really your first boyfriend?"

My lips twitch. "Don't let it go to your head." Grinning, he turns away to leave me, but I grab his face in both hands. "You really love me?"

He doesn't try to hide the warmth in his smile, and lowers his mouth to my ear when he whispers, "Don't let it go to your head."

Twenty-Five

MOLLY

By the time I've finished checking everything for Nic and Ethan's reception, I'm exhausted, but I know my mind is buzzing too much to let me go right to bed when I get to Brayden's. I'm happy with how the banquet hall turned out with all the tables set for Nic and Ethan's reception and the decorations in place.

And then there's Brayden. Brayden, with his dark eyes and searching gazes. Brayden, who wants to be . . . who *is* my boyfriend.

The word fills me with schoolgirl giddiness as I lock my office door and head out to lock up the kitchen. I've never cared that I missed out on that. Sure, now that I'm older, I wish I'd handled things differently when I was a teenager, but though I could see the appeal of someone to call my own, I never actively longed for it outside of a practical standpoint. So many nights

I'd pick up Noah from daycare, and we'd get home and my other job was waiting for me. Not the caring for him—no, that never felt like work—but the household stuff. Making dinner, doing dishes, keeping up on laundry, paying bills. There were many nights I wished I had someone to share the burden of running a household. But until Brayden, I never dared wish for more.

I lock the walk-in coolers and freezers, and when I turn to hit the kitchen lights, there's Brayden, waiting for me in the hall with his arms crossed, that endlessly patient smirk on his face. My chest warms at his presence. *He came here for me.*

"I thought you were heading home from the bar." I approach slowly, suddenly feeling shy.

"I played DD for Levi and Ellie, but I thought I'd come for you next."

"I haven't been drinking," I say, smiling. I had a beer with Shay at dinner, but hardly enough to call for a designated driver.

His mouth splits into a grin. *Damn. That smile.* "I figured." He leans down and grabs the bottle of champagne and two glasses I hadn't noticed by his feet. "Shall we remedy that?" Before I can react, he pops the cork and fills the champagne flutes. The bubbles climb toward the rim of the glasses as he hands one to me and takes the other for himself.

"What are we toasting?" I ask quietly.

"Nic and Ethan, of course."

Clinking my glass to his, I nod. "Of course."

"He risked getting hurt again for that love."

I meet his eyes, and my heart aches a little as I see there what so many miss—the tenderness, the desperate need to be enough, the scarred pieces of a man who gave everything to the woman he loved and only got a broken heart in return. "Yes, he did."

"Here's to courage," he says softly, and I know he's not talking about Ethan and Nic anymore. He's talking about us. I say a silent prayer that, for him, I can be brave.

I clink my glass against his. "To courage."

He takes a sip and lowers his glass. "May I see it?"

I know what he means, and a swell of pride fills my chest and makes me smile. I turn toward the banquet hall and crook a finger over my shoulder for him to follow. I hold my breath as I open the door and turn on the lights.

This space has never looked so beautiful, and I couldn't be happier about how it turned out. The white chair covers are wrapped in red cloth bows, and the crystal centerpieces sit nestled in a nest of red and white roses, sprigs of holly, and pinecones. The artificial arrangements look fresh, and I know I'll get a ton of use out of them.

My staff spent the afternoon draping tulle across the exposed beams on the ceiling and carefully framing the dancefloor with pots of red poinsettias and stark white hydrangeas. Tomorrow, we'll light the candles in the centerpieces and turn off the overhead lights for the dimmer, softer light of the wall sconces, but it looks romantic even now, with the moonlight flooding in through the wall of windows at the far end of the space.

"Wow," Brayden says softly behind me. I hear the awe in his tone before I turn to see it on his face. "I knew your ideas would come together, but this is . . . magnificent."

I smile. "Nic and Ethan deserve the best."

He nods, his throat bobbing as he swallows and scans the room again. Is he thinking of the long journey his brother had to take to get here? Of the man's grief after losing his wife? Of the joy I'm told Nic brought back to his eyes? "They really do."

"The band will be on the stage," I say, motioning toward the elevated platform on the dance floor. "And we have bars set up on either side of the room. We have high-top cocktail tables set up around them so people will move toward the dance floor after the meal is over."

He shakes his head, taking it all in. "No one will ever know this is your first wedding."

"I wouldn't be happy with my work if they did." I scan the space, looking for missed details and finding none. "Thank you." I turn to him. "For giving me this opportunity."

He looks into my eyes, but I'm not sure what he's looking for. "You're welcome. It's a shame you did all this work and you'll be too busy managing the staff to enjoy the party with us."

I shrug. "I don't mind."

"There's no chance I can talk you into letting someone else take the reins tomorrow, is there?"

I snort and press my hand to his chest. "Hi, Pot, I'm Kettle."

He grins and grabs my hand before I can pull it away. "If I don't get to dance with you tomorrow, I'll just have to do it tonight."

Before I can protest, he takes my champagne glass and puts it on the floor with his.

He taps the screen of his phone until the opening chords of Prince's "I Would Die 4 U" fill the room. I laugh, a sound that's half joy and half disbelief. *He remembered.*

Grinning, I let him pull me into his arms. I drape my arms around his neck. "You're crazy. No one slow-dances to this song."

"Says who?" His gaze drops to my mouth and his smile falls away. "You've really never had a boyfriend?"

I shake my head and swallow. "I'm the girl guys take home for some fun, not the one they take home to Mom."

Something dark passes over his face, but he exhales and it's gone. "Strange, because my mom thinks you're the best thing ever."

My heart squeezes. "Your mom is awesome."

"Next time one of my siblings gets married, let's make sure you have a reliable number two who can run things so I can keep you in my arms all night."

The next time . . . "Who else is engaged?" Levi and Ellie are barely back together, and last I knew, they weren't rushing things.

He shrugs. "Nobody at the moment, but I'm sure someone will be hitting us up for the family discount in the next year or two."

I lean my head against his chest to hide my face and swallow hard. *Year or two.* He still expects me to be around then.

"You okay?" he whispers, so soft I can barely hear him over the music.

I'm afraid to speak, so I just nod. *I'm so good.*

BRAYDEN

*M*olly fell asleep on my lap, and I can't stop staring at her. She mumbles incoherent words for the third time since she drifted off, and I smile. She's a sleep talker. I shouldn't be surprised. She always has so much to say, so why should it be any different in sleep?

I turn off the TV—I've barely looked at it all night—and brush her blond hair from her face. When we got home, I told her to change into pajamas and meet me out here.

"Is pajamas code for slinky lingerie?" she asked. "Because all of mine's in storage."

I recommended flannel pants and a T-shirt, and she laughed like I'd lost my mind. Maybe she doesn't understand what I see when I look at her. That I was never drawn to her because of her cleavage or flirtatious smiles. She's beautiful, but beautiful is easy to resist. It's everything beneath the gloss and curves that made me fall in love.

If we didn't both have such a big day tomorrow, I probably would have danced with her until sunrise. We've danced around what we want for so long, and tonight we both found the courage to say we wanted more. Truthfully, I didn't want to come home. I'm afraid she'll wake up tomorrow and panic about our relationship, about what this change means.

Molly shifts in my lap then opens her eyes, stretching her arms over her head. "Shit. I fell asleep." She rubs her eyes, leaving a streak of mascara across her cheek. "I guess your masterful efforts at seduction failed."

I laugh. "Who said I was trying to seduce you?"

She pushes up on the couch and shakes her head, yawning. "The champagne, the dancing . . ." She cocks a brow at me. "The snuggling on the couch with your fingers stroking across my stomach?"

I grin. I've never smiled as much as I do around her. "Nope. Not a seduction. Just spending time with you."

She stands and stretches her arms over her head. "If you say so. Good night."

When she heads toward her bedroom, I follow and catch her before she hits the stairs. I turn her around, trapping her between the wall and my body and putting a hand on either side of her head. "Sleep with me."

Her gaze drops to my mouth, and she groans. "You're so painfully tempting, but I'm dead on my feet. I'm afraid I'd fall asleep in the middle and shatter that fragile male ego of yours."

I laugh. She can hardly keep her eyes open, and she thinks I'm asking for sex. "Not sex. *Sleep.*" I lower my mouth but give her only the faintest brush of my lips against hers. "I want you in my bed."

She searches my face for so long that I'm convinced she's trying to come up with a polite way to refuse me. "Are you real, Brayden Jackson?"

I chuckle and kiss the tip of her nose before sweeping her into my arms. "I could be a dream. Better sleep next to me to make sure I'm still here when you wake up."

Twenty-Six

MOLLY

*B*rayden Jackson was, indeed, still there when I woke up, as real as the heat in my blood and the flutter in my stomach when he rolled me onto my back and trailed kisses down my body, wishing me good morning in a way I could certainly get used to.

I had breakfast with Noah and Mom then headed to the banquet center to get my employees started on the setup.

Within the first hour of arriving there, I found out that Bella's stomach flu had spread to two other servers. I spent my morning making calls to employees who had the day off, but most had other plans or couldn't get childcare at the last minute. By the time we're on break and I'm preparing to run over to the ceremony site, I'm still short a server. That I can manage, but as I change into my dress for the ceremony, I say a prayer that the stomach flu won't spread to any more of my staff before the night is through.

I adjust my dress and head to the locker room mirror to check my makeup. I have other staff members taking care of the less labor-intensive reception setup, and I want to be there to see Nic walk down the aisle.

I'm checking my lipstick when Austin pushes through the door and flips the lock behind him.

Frowning, I meet his gaze in the mirror. "We keep that door unlocked. The restroom and shower stalls have their own locks."

He folds his arms and heads toward me. "I was hoping we could talk."

I slide my lipstick back into my purse and turn to him. "Is everything okay?"

His face goes serious, and he shakes his head. "I'm really hurting."

Oh, no. "Are you sick?" I cross the room and put a hand to his forehead, but before I can even register the temperature of his skin, he grabs my other hand and presses it against his crotch. I yank away and stumble back, and he unzips his pants and prowls toward me. His hand slides into his black briefs.

"Come on, Molly. I know what kind of slut you are. I know what you like. *Everyone* does. And I see how you look at me."

"Fuck you." I'm backed into a stall door, my gaze darting between him and the exit as he steps closer.

"Fuck *me*? It's your lucky day. You can. And I know you want to." He smiles, his eyes bright, as if this is some sort of game. As if we're having *fun* here. "Nobody will know."

"Don't come a single step closer." The old, sick terror claws at me, and I want to close my eyes and pretend this isn't happening.

"Or what? You'll tell my mommy? I think we both know

what she thinks of you after she caught you and Gabe together. I'm just an innocent, curious kid. And you're a slut who can't get enough dick. Just ask Jason Ralston and Brayden Jackson and all the other guys you've fucked in your office." He closes the distance between us with a final step, and I move fast, driving my knee up into his crotch. He shouts and crumples to the floor.

I dart around him, unlock the door with shaking hands, and run upstairs.

His shouts echo in the stairwell behind me. "We all see how easy you are. You aren't fooling anyone!"

I have to fight back the sting of tears and this burning ache in my chest. I'm a stupid fool. A stupid fool who thought she could return to Jackson Harbor without consequences. A fool who thought maybe she might be good enough for a man like Brayden Jackson.

I swing around the corner into my office and stumble into Brayden, already dressed in his suit for the ceremony.

"Are you okay?" He takes my shoulders in his hands and ducks his head to study my face. "What happened?"

"Nothing." The lie feels like a betrayal to my new life, to the woman I spent those long, lonely years in New York becoming. One word, and I've taken a thousand steps back toward the girl I used to be. *Everything's fine. It's nothing. It doesn't matter.* My eyes burn, and my skin feels too tight. "Don't you need to be at the ceremony site?" I'm shaking, and I know he can see it.

"Hey, tell me what happened." His voice is gentle but firm.

I swallow. "Not now," I whisper. Because I know if I explain, I'll lose it, and I need to keep it together until we get through this day.

"Is that Austin?"

I follow Brayden's gaze out my office window and to the parking lot nestled in the trees beyond, where Austin is tearing out of the lot in his fancy red sports car. His mom bought one of those for Gabe, too. I have vivid memories of sitting in the back seat with him and having him shove my head into his lap.

I swallow hard and lock away that memory. *Not now.* "We'll be short two servers," I say, the words too tight, but my eyes are dry and my head is up. I'm not the girl I used to be. Just ask Austin's balls.

Brayden meets my steely gaze and seems to understand that I'm not going to talk about it right now. "Okay," he says softly. "We'll make it work. Tell me what I can do."

BRAYDEN

"**H**as anyone ever told you that you shouldn't try to do everything yourself?"

Groaning, Molly opens her eyes. She's lying on the couch in the break room, her head at one end and her feet stretched to the other. "It's been mentioned a few times. By bosses before you."

"But you do it anyway." I slide onto the end of the couch, put her feet in my lap, and slip off her shoes. Upstairs, her staff is serving hors d'oeuvres at Ethan and Nic's cocktail hour, and in less than an hour, the bride and groom will be here. "Let me help."

"You're the best man. There's no way I'm letting you serve at this dinner," she whispers. I can hear the anguish in her voice. She wants to make tonight perfect, to make every event perfect. To prove herself to me—as if she needs to. "This is a disaster."

"It's not." I gently massage her arches.

She snorts. "Tell that to Nic and Ethan."

I'm silent for a long time, weighing my words against her disappointment and frustration before speaking. I know I can come off as condescending—my siblings remind me frequently— and that's the last thing I want right now. Molly is more than competent in her position. She's motivated, organized, and passionate. If anything, her expectations are too high. As her boss, I'm pretty sure I'm not ever supposed to think that. As the man who loves her, I just want her to give herself a break.

"I'll make adjustments," she says. "To the staff. To the way we serve and the way I train them. I won't let something like tonight happen again."

"It probably will," I say gently, and she winces. "And when it does, it won't be a reflection of your efforts or abilities. It'll simply be the nature of the beast. And if you always hustle to make it work like you have today and every day before, then our clients should consider themselves lucky."

She blinks at me, then swallows. "Thank you, Brayden."

"You're welcome." The words come out gruff, like they have to pass over the rough terrain of my raw emotions before making it past my lips. "Do you want to talk about what happened with the little shit who walked out?"

She's silent for a long time, and for a minute, I think she won't tell me. "I went to high school with his brother. Apparently,

Gabe hasn't grown up much in the last eight years and decided to share the escapades of his youth with his little brother." She takes a deep breath, and I wait, knowing she needs to get through this without me interrupting. "Austin cornered me down here on our break. He suggested I supply him with the same . . . *favors* I once gave his brother."

My whole body stiffens, but I try to keep the magnitude of my rage out of my voice when I say, "I hope you didn't—"

She flies upright. "I would *never*. Not at work, and certainly not with some *child*."

"That's not what I was going to say." But I see it on her face. That defensiveness. The shields she's honed after a lifetime of people assuming she would. The little teenage punk believing she would. Even though she's his boss, eight years older than him, and light-years better than him. "I was going to say that I hope you didn't feel like your position as his boss meant you shouldn't kick him in the nuts."

She swallows. "Obviously, I tried to handle it professionally, but he was persistent, and it got a little . . . ugly." She turns her head, her gaze shifting to the lockers, the shower stalls, anywhere but my eyes. "There are some moments when I'm not sure why I thought coming back to Jackson Harbor was a good idea."

The pain on her face does something to me—a tug in my chest somewhere between an ache and a need to act. It's the way I felt when I watched my father die, when I watched my mother fight cancer. The way I felt when Sara disappeared and cut herself out of my life so completely that I had no way of knowing if she was okay.

I exhale slowly and return my focus to her foot, digging my

thumbs into her heel before taking her other foot into my hand and giving it the same treatment as the first. "For what it's worth, I'm glad you came back. And not just because you're my girlfriend or because there's no one else I'd want in your position." I swallow hard. "You make me happy, Molly, and despite the assholes, I think you're blossoming here, and so is Noah."

She turns back to me. "Why are you so nice to me, Brayden?"

I hate that she even feels like she needs to ask. As if she doesn't deserve the same kindness as everyone else. "Would you rather I be cruel?"

She pulls her feet from my lap and scoots around to the seat next to me, never taking her eyes from my face. "I don't know what to do with kindness." A smile—wobbly and unsure, but a smile nevertheless. "Typical fucked-up girl with daddy issues."

"Don't." The word comes out harder than I intended, but I don't rush to soften it. I let it sit in the air between us, simmering with all the frustration I feel. When I speak again, my words are quieter, but the same steel is behind them. "Don't talk about yourself as if you're unremarkable, like you let them believe you were in high school. As if you're worth nothing more than the cheap pleasure you can give the nearest asshole."

"Why not? I earned it—my reputation. I earned it by blowing dozens of guys before I could vote. Austin didn't do anything most of the men in this town wouldn't do."

"That's bullshit." Anger simmers in my words.

"Wanna bet? Follow me around someday and see how they treat me."

"That's not what I mean. I mean it's bullshit to think that you *deserve* to be treated like that. How many guys in your high school fucked every girl who spread her legs? How many would take action from the easiest target?" She blinks then lifts a shoulder in a careless shrug that I don't buy for a second. "And if you walked up to them now and demanded sex just because they handed it over so willingly before, would that be okay?"

"Of course not," she whispers.

"You don't owe anyone any explanations for the decisions you made, and you sure as fuck don't owe me an apology for firing an asshole kid who dropped his pants and expected you to—"

She leans forward in a flash and presses her fingers to my lips. "Don't say it, okay?"

I exhale, letting go of the words I know she doesn't want me to say. I focus on the feel of her skin against my lips, her taste a breath away. I dream about this skin. About these fingers. I constantly think about this amazing woman I love, and sometimes I'm not sure love is going to be enough to make her understand what I see when I look at her.

I knew about Molly's reputation that night we were together in New York. We weren't in high school at the same time, but my brothers talked. Hell, guys my age talked. I didn't care about her reputation or about the choices she made back then. Some guys sleep around, and some girls sleep around. It doesn't matter to me.

But all that time, I thought Molly gave herself to those guys because she enjoyed it. Until she moved back to Jackson Harbor, I never knew the truth of what drove her—her history with her stepfather. If I'd known, I would have understood why she begged me not to take her home that night eight years ago, and I would have done everything in my power to put a stop to it then. If I'd known, I'd have made different decisions during my visit to the city last spring. Maybe I'd have wooed her and seduced her slowly instead of taking her to bed and making her think I was just another asshole who wanted to get her naked and nothing more.

I wish I *had* known. Because then I'd have understood that there were reasons she offered herself so easily and freely that night—reasons that had nothing to do with me or the connection between us. I'd have understood that Molly McKinley is a woman who needs to be taught her value, and that if I ever want her to see herself the way I see her, those lessons need to come from me.

She pulls her hand away and blinks at me. "I need to get upstairs."

"I love you," I say softly.

She tries to hide her wince, but I see it before she climbs off the couch and slides back into her shoes. "Brayden, I—"

"Miss McKinley!" Bella says, flying into the break room in a rush. "You said to come get you when the bride and groom got here."

"Thanks, Bella," she says.

"Are you sure you don't need me?" I ask again.

She shakes her head. "I'm beginning to think you're just trying to get out of your speech, Brayden."

Twenty-Seven

MOLLY

"Miss McKinley," Bella says softly after dinner's been served. "I think you need to see this." She holds out her phone.

I shake my head. "Not now, Bella." I nod toward the head table, where Brayden is about to give his speech as best man.

She bites her lip and looks anxiously between me and Brayden taking the microphone across the room. "Just look on Instagram as soon as you have a chance."

I nod then press a finger to my lips, indicating she should be quiet now. She rushes back to the kitchen to help the other servers clean up.

Dinner service went well, considering we were short-handed, but I haven't been able to chase away this gnawing feeling that's been eating at my stomach and whispering ugliness in my ear since the incident with Austin.

Austin's assumptions and presumptions about me brought all my old fears to the surface, and with every word Brayden said to try to make me feel better, I just kept thinking that what happened with Austin is more of the same. I got kicked out of my house because my landlord thought he was entitled to a piece of me, and when I didn't hand it over, he got pissed. Brayden lost an investor when I got drunk and careless and forgot I wasn't that girl anymore.

Tonight could have been worse, but it was a reminder that I can't leave my past mistakes behind. They will follow me, and I have no idea why Brayden would want to put up with it.

Behind the head table, he straightens his suit jacket and smiles at the room. He's gorgeous and kind, and the sight of him makes my throat go thick. "Good evening, everyone. I'm Brayden Jackson, Ethan's brother, which means I've had the absolute pleasure of being his best man, and it means now you get the dubious pleasure of listening to me speak. Anyone in my family can tell you that's not something I choose to do often." He pauses a beat while everyone laughs. "Tonight, however, I'm proud to say a few words." He turns toward the newlyweds. "I'm not someone who believes everything happens for a reason—at least not in the sense that there's some cosmic plan unrolling outside of our control. We lost our father too soon. I watched my mother lose the love of her life too soon and watched my siblings each struggle with their grief. And I guess that just hurt too much to accept as some cosmic plan." His gaze lands on Ethan. "When Ethan lost his first wife and was left to raise his daughter while ravaged by his grief, I knew I'd never believe such a thing."

The last of the guests' whispers quiet at the mention of Ethan's late wife, and all eyes settle on the best man.

"And now that I've convinced a room full of people that I should never be allowed to speak at a wedding again"—laughter—"I'll get to my point. Regardless of how good or bad the things in our life are, we get to choose. It's the choice that's the gift. Ethan and Nic chose love. Despite their individual heartaches. Despite their own fears of getting hurt. They could have declared their love just wasn't meant to be. Instead, they fought for something better than the heartache they'd both endured before. And because they made that choice, they found something that inspired even my old, jaded heart to believe in the power of love." He raises his glass. "To Nic and Ethan."

"To Nic and Ethan," the crowd calls in return, and they all drink. Even Brayden, who meets my eyes over his glass and holds my gaze. And because I'm a coward, because I'm not sure I can believe in the same things he does, I turn around and head for the kitchen, where my staff is working to clean up.

They have it under control, but Bella meets my eyes and pulls her phone from her pocket. A reminder.

I head to my office and pull my own phone from my purse, wondering if I'll even be able to find what she's talking about.

But I don't have to search, because my phone has blown up with notifications all leading back to Austin's last Instagram post.

Blowjob Molly, doing her thing. Thanks for everything, @MollyMcKinleyJB #happeningatJacksonBrews

With shaking hands, I press play on the video. It's only thirty seconds long, but by the time it's over, I feel my world in pieces around me. I close my office door and shut off the lights. Then I curl into the corner and I cry.

BRAYDEN

I was hoping Molly would have a chance to step away from the staff after dinner was cleared, but I haven't spotted her since my speech. Though I've left the majority of the details of running this place to her, I do know enough to understand that there's a lot to be done. Tonight, the staff doesn't just need to clean up from this plated dinner for one hundred and fifty; they'll need to do the prep work for the tasting room's lunch menu for tomorrow, and prepare for the catering events in the week ahead too.

I understand she's legitimately busy, and yet as the guests spill onto the dance floor and I'm left to contemplate my beer alone, I still feel like she's avoiding me.

Shay takes the seat beside me and crosses her legs. "Are you okay?"

"Sure. I'm fine. Wishing my girlfriend were out here, I guess, but good."

Shay flinches and looks away.

"What is it?"

She pulls her phone from her lap and puts it on the table, nudging it until it's in front of me. "I'm sorry," she whispers.

I unlock her phone and see she has Instagram pulled up and

a post from Austin on her screen.

The caption makes my blood boil, and I want to find the little punk and knock him out for using that horrible nickname. Hell, I already wanted to do worse for what he did to her this afternoon.

The first time I watch, I don't really know what I'm seeing—Molly, standing just inside her office, talking to Jason Ralston, who's in her doorway. Molly looks at the camera or whoever's holding the phone, then pulls Jason inside her office and shuts her door. Then it's just . . . the door.

I frown at my sister, and she swallows. "It has more . . . *effect* if you can hear them." There's an apology all over her face, and she shakes her head. "We don't know when he took this video."

I hand Shay's phone to her and push my chair back, heading outside to be alone. If this dread gnawing at me is any indication, I want to be alone in the cold when I watch—*listen*—to this.

The first time I do, my stomach plummets to my feet . . . lower. Molly pulls Jason Ralston in her office, and then she's *moaning*. I can hear the sounds she makes until they're interrupted by Austin's snicker on the other side of the camera.

I don't want to believe it. He could have added those sounds into the video. But I know Molly. I know her moans and her pleas. I know the sounds she makes when she's turned on and nearing climax, and I recognize her noises as clearly as I recognize her voice.

I knew she was seeing Jason. Maybe I didn't know they were sleeping together, and maybe the idea of her letting him touch her *here* makes me insane, but I knew they were on a date just last week. This video could have been—

Tuesday. For just a beat in the middle of her moans, the

camera pans to the daily schedule on the white erase board outside her office, and I know this video is from Tuesday. But which Tuesday? On Tuesday four days ago, I had her alone in her office—kissing her between her legs, making her writhe until she came against my face. Did she pull Jason in there before or after me?

I close my eyes, thinking about how she acted in front of Sara at the restaurant Monday morning—about how happy she was to pretend there was nothing between us *just in case* I wanted my old girlfriend back. I agreed to her boundaries. Her rules and restrictions on what we could be, but I never imagined . . .

I'm thrown back ten years to Sara and her professor, to finding out in the most embarrassing way that she was sleeping with him behind my back.

"I'm so sorry."

My head snaps up to Molly, standing coatless in the cold again, her arms wrapped around herself. Her eyes are bloodshot and her cheeks are mottled pink. In the streetlight illuminating the parking lot, I can see a streak of dried tears running through her makeup.

She chews on her bottom lip and looks everywhere but at me. "I'm so sorry. I don't know how he did this." She presses her hand to her mouth and whispers, "Or . . . why anyone would hate me so much."

She never wanted a relationship. She never wanted more.

But it doesn't matter if we were officially a couple when Austin took this video. It doesn't matter to me that she told me she can't do relationships. None of that matters when this awful betrayal is roaring in my ears that I'm an idiot. That I'm blind.

That Jason has something to offer her that had her pulling him into her office the same day I—

"I deserved to know." I swallow hard and look away—toward the building, the place we built *together*. She let him touch her there. "If you were fucking him and me at the same time, I deserved to know."

She gasps. "What?"

"We weren't using protection, Molly. I fucking *deserved* to know." I can't look at her. It hurts too much. And this feeling like maybe I don't have a right to be angry? That just makes my rage worse.

"You should get back inside." She swipes at her cheeks. "They're cutting the cake soon."

"That's all you have to say?"

She laughs, a hollow, empty sound. Her long inhale is so jagged that it sounds like it's running over a hundred razor blades on the way to her lungs. "Do you want me to say it's a lie? Would you even believe me? Go celebrate with your family."

I don't move. I'm not going to walk away from this conversation—I have no business being in that reception while I'm this angry anyway.

But she walks away from me, and I know this conversation is over.

BRAYDEN

The rest of Ethan and Nic's reception passes in a blur. I smile when I'm expected to, dance with whom I'm expected to, and generally give the performance of a lifetime. Only Shay knows what's going on. I suppose everyone else will soon enough.

Molly is scarce through the end of the party, though if I'm honest, I've avoided any moments when I thought she might show up.

When it's over, I can't get home fast enough, and I don't bother changing out of my suit before pouring myself some of Dad's bourbon.

How am I supposed to be okay with this? Do I just swallow my pride and pretend it doesn't tear me apart? What am I supposed to do when she gets home?

I must be a masochist, because I play the video again. And

again. I listen, as if the sounds she makes might tell me why she was with him when she had me. The useless clunking thing in my chest fractures more and more each time I watch that door close. Each time I hear those moans.

But the third time—the fourth?—I notice a glitch in the video between the moment the door closes and the moment the sounds start.

Maybe Austin trimmed the middle out to give the full effect in the short clip . . . but I listen again, turning the volume as loud as it'll go until I can almost make out the murmurs on the other side of the door. I know those sounds and those whispered pleas. I have them imprinted on my brain.

And then I hear it. *My name.*

"Brayden," she says. "Brayden, *please.* Oh my God . . ."

This isn't audio from her and Jason at all. It's audio from when I sat Molly on her desk, spread her thighs, and made her come through her panties. We were supposed to be alone, everyone done for the day, but when we came out of the office, Austin was in the hall playing on his phone. Or so I thought.

The sonofabitch was recording us.

He spliced together two different videos to hurt her, and it worked. He used her old reputation against her, against *us*, and I bought it. She believes she's not good enough for a real relationship, and tonight I let her think I believe that too.

MOLLY

I sit in my car for fifteen minutes after parking in Brayden's driveway.

I don't want to go inside. I don't want to see Brayden, because I'm sure if I do, I'll fall apart. And I don't want to see that he never came home, because I know if he went somewhere else to avoid me, that'll kill me too.

I'm going to stay at my mom's—Noah has the couch, so I can handle the floor for a night—but I need to get a few things first. Maybe even find the courage to tell Brayden the video is fake. Not that it matters.

Taking a deep breath, I climb out of my car and head inside.

Brayden's sitting in the living room with a glass of amber liquid—bourbon, if I know him like I think I do.

I want to rush past him. If I could get my things and go without talking to him, maybe I could survive this crushing in my chest, this awful pain that's so bad it steals my breath.

I make myself stop.

"I wasn't sure you'd come home," he says softly, standing.

Home. This isn't my home. It can't be. Even if I'd begun to imagine . . .

"We should talk."

I nod and take a breath. "I know you have no reason to believe me, but I didn't do anything with Jason that day I took him in my office."

"I know."

I jerk my head up, meeting his eyes. "You do?"

"The video looks bad." He drags a hand through his hair, his frustration evident in every jerky moment. "But I watched it, and now I can see he spliced two clips together."

I nod. I knew that the moment I saw it, and I planned to tell Brayden, but when he just accepted it as it was and assumed I'd let Jason touch me . . . Well, given what happened at the Christmas party, I couldn't blame him for assuming anything. "I know."

He lifts his hand to my face but drops it before he touches me. "Then why are you looking at me like this is over?"

"It was just a matter of time before something like this happened," I say, reciting the speech I planned on my drive home. "I try to teach Noah that we have to be held accountable for our actions, and that's all this is . . . me being held accountable for who I was."

"Don't let Austin off the hook like that. This was wrong and conniving and deceitful. You didn't *deserve* any of this."

I shrug. "But that doesn't change anything. And you and I . . ." My whole body is shaking with the words I have to say. I don't want to, but I don't see an alternative. "This was a bad idea anyway." I hardly recognize my own voice. The words come out too tight; I'm trying to push past the lump in my throat. "I really have to think of Noah first, and—"

"Cut the shit, Molly."

I blink at him. "What?"

"I know you believe it—this line you feed me and everybody else about trying to protect your son—but it's such bullshit. Noah and I are going to have a relationship no matter what happens to us. If you never give us a chance—if you walk away tonight and never speak another word to me—that won't change the way I feel about that kid. He's already part of my family, and if someday I fuck something up and hurt his feelings, I'll *hate* it. But you and I both know that's life. Sometimes the people we love make mistakes. But I'd never, *never* hurt him on purpose, no matter how much you hurt me. So please stop insulting me by pretending otherwise."

I straighten my spine and wrap my arms around myself. "You have no idea what it's like—"

"Don't I?"

My eyes go wide. "To be a single mom? To scrape by, paycheck to paycheck? To not know if your decisions are going to hurt the most precious gift that's ever been put into your care?" My heart races just thinking about it. *Christmas. Our promises to Noah. How excited he is to spend Christmas morning with Brayden.* I've already messed up. "With all due respect, Brayden, you don't know."

"I know what it's like to be terrified of being hurt again. I know what it's like to worry—*deep down*—that every fucked-up thing that's happened in your life is your fault, that if you'd just been *better*, if you'd just been *worthy*, then maybe things wouldn't have unfolded the way they did." He takes a step closer, and this time I stay still. I let him press against me, let him lower his mouth to my ear when he whispers, "And I know you. I *see* you. You're even more scared than I am, because he hurt you—*betrayed you*—in the worst way possible."

That's when I stumble back. At the *he* Brayden doesn't need to name. At that ugly, secret history I wish Brayden had never known. "You don't see me. You look at me and see a girl who was raped by her stepfather. You think you want me, but you really just want to save me." The words are so *raw* that bile rises in my throat. "I already know you think I'm *broken*, and I'll never be able to change what happened to me. I'll never know what it's like to have you look at me and see . . ." I turn my head and stare at the window and into the darkness, wishing I didn't have to say more, wishing I could hide from him—from today and all of this.

"See what?" he asks softly. "What do you want me to see when I look at you?"

"*Me*," I whisper, my attention still on the night beyond the window, because I might break if I look at him. "I just want you to see *me*."

He takes a step closer and takes my hand. I let him, and watch as he toys with our fingers. "You think I want to save you because you're broken?" Gently, he nudges my chin with his thumb until I lift my eyes to meet his.

"I heard you say it. I heard you tell Ethan."

"I know you did. And I'm sorry I used that word."

"Don't pretend. Don't take it back and pretend you didn't mean it." I can take a lot, can survive a lot, but I don't know if I can handle lies from Brayden. "I know I'm damaged goods. I'm ruined, and that's why I can't do this."

He opens his mouth, but I race for the door. There's nothing I need as much as I need to get away from this conversation and those beautiful, dark eyes so full of pity.

BRAYDEN

I flinch as I listen to the door click shut behind her. Each one of her words was another twist of the knife in my gut. *Damaged goods. Ruined. Broken.* To her, it's all the same.

And now she's gone, and I feel like something inside me is indeed broken beyond repair.

Twenty-Nine

MOLLY

Two days until Christmas, and who's sleep-deprived, heartbroken, and dragging her ass through the mall to finish her shopping? *This girl.*

Luckily, I have two friends who called me bright and early and asked to join me.

"How's the situation with Brayden?" Shay asks.

I groan. Unluckily, one of them shares blood with the guy I broke up with last night.

Teagan elbows her. "We agreed we weren't going to talk about it."

Shay scowls at Teagan. "It's almost Christmas. We can't very well give them time to figure it out on their own if we want a happy ending before Santa comes."

The words *happy ending* remind me of Brayden's flirting, and

I bite my lip. Until heartache lances through me, and I have to close my eyes.

"See?" Teagan waves a hand in my direction. "See what you've done?"

I take the girls by the wrists and lead them into the chain restaurant off the hall to our left. "If you two are going to bicker, I need a drink." And maybe lunch. I haven't eaten since breakfast yesterday. I wasn't up for risking it on my stressed belly this morning.

Teagan lights up. "Ooh! I like that plan."

After we're seated and give our drink and lunch orders to the waitress, Shay says, "We missed you and Noah at brunch this morning."

I frown. "Sorry. I guess my Jackson family brunch days are behind me."

"You don't think you're going to get out of it just because you move out, do you?" Shay asks. "Mom would never hear of it. She's already attached to you and Noah."

Teagan nods. She may not be a Jackson, but she's around them enough to be an authority on the family.

"But Brayden and I aren't—"

Shay waves a hand. "Doesn't matter. Mom's like a bad mob boss. Once you're in, there's no escaping."

"That's . . . weirdly comforting." I smile at the thought of sweet Kathleen as a mob boss and *almost* laugh. "I'm sorry about this mess, though. I knew better than to get involved with Brayden, and I did it anyway."

Teagan and Shay exchange a look, then Teagan clears her throat and says, "I need to step out and make a call." She slides out of the booth and heads for the door.

I cringe in Shay's direction. "Did she just leave so Brayden's overprotective sister can beat me up?"

Shay shrugs, but her face lights up as the waitress returns with our drinks. "You're my personal savior today," she says.

The waitress grins. "I get that a lot. Your food should be up soon."

Shay takes a sip of her beer and sighs happily.

"Thanks," I tell the waitress, but I wait until she goes before turning to Shay. "If you're going to give me a speech about how amazing your brother is, you can save yourself the trouble. I already know that. I've seen it for myself. This isn't about him."

"Are you sure about that?"

Nodding, I drag my finger down the condensation on the side of my pint glass. The beer snob in me wants to point out they're serving this stout way too cold, but judging by the way my stomach keeps flip-flopping, I won't be drinking it anyway. *I already miss him so much it hurts.* "I've always been the problem. Not him. If anything, I wish he weren't so great. Because then maybe . . ." I sigh. I can't even imagine a Brayden I'd be worthy of.

"I was in love once." Shay turns to the window and the busy parking lot beyond. "He took my breath away and made me smile, and I never believed I was worthy of him. As long as I believed I didn't deserve him, it was easy to walk away. Then one day I did, and my excuses were so convincing that he didn't come after me."

I swallow. "I'm sorry."

"It was no one's fault but mine. I thought I was so noble to walk away, and all I did was hurt us both." She squeezes her bare ring finger in a way that makes me wonder if she once wore a piece of jewelry there. Or if she only wanted to. "I can't take that back."

"That video is an embarrassment to the whole family," I say softly. "You're all so important to this community and so rock solid, but I've come along and tarnished that. I'm not being petty. This stuff is awful, and I don't want it to affect you guys."

She shrugs. "What about letting us decide if we're embarrassed?"

"Aren't you?"

Her grin stretches across her beautiful face and shows all her straight white teeth. "Nah. But I work out with Austin's mom sometimes, so I gave her a call this morning. She was so pissed at him—embarrassed that he'd post such a thing—that she shut down his social media and took away his phone *and* car. He deserves worse, but it's a start."

"Thank you, Shay." I pick up my beer, then put it back down before I take a drink. I'm not foolish enough to think that means the video is gone forever, but it feels good to know Austin's not getting away with it.

"Are you still doing Christmas morning at Brayden's?"

This time I do take a drink. "If he'll let me, I'd like to." I take another sip and sigh. "For Noah, and because Brayden made him a promise that's important to them both."

"Then Christmas at the family cabin after?" she asks. "It's a blast. We do a Nerf gun fight and stuff ourselves. Between Nic and Jake's cooking, it's the culinary event of the year."

"I have no doubt." I look up from my beer, search my friend's eyes, and only see sincerity there. "It feels selfish to show up to your family Christmas."

She shrugs. "So be selfish."

The waitress returns with our food, and Teagan emerges from the hallway and slides into her spot next to Shay.

I poke at my salad and recall what Brayden told me about Sara. She left because she thought it was the best thing for him, but he said he wanted to be loved enough that she'd dare to be selfish. Isn't that what he said about his feelings for me, too? That he was selfish when it came to me? I wonder if he might ever wish I was selfish enough to hold on to him.

When I think of the Instagram video, I know I don't deserve to ask any such thing, but the selfish devil on my shoulder folds her arms and tells me I should ask anyway.

BRAYDEN

Molly: Are you okay with Noah and I coming back to the house tonight and staying until after Christmas? I understand if you'd rather we didn't, but I want to leave that choice to you.

The text is a kick in the nuts. On the one hand, she's going to let me fulfill my promise to her son. On the other hand, there's nothing in that text that makes me believe she didn't mean it when she broke things off last night. But at least if she's here, I'll have a chance to speak to her.

Me: You and Noah are always welcome here. Thank you for letting me make good on my promise.

I have to run around town finishing my Christmas shopping Sunday evening, but when I get home, Molly and Noah are back, and it looks like a bag of flour has exploded in my kitchen.

"You have to roll it flat, remember?" Molly tells Noah. She has flour on her nose, her cheeks, and even smeared across her red Rudolph T-shirt. My steps falter. She looks like she belongs here, like she's *home*, and today is only one of many days she'll spend making cookies with Noah in this kitchen.

This is happiness for her—spending time with her son, making a mess and laughing—and the joy it brings her is so bright that it outshines the lights on the tree in the family room and fills the room more than the Christmas music playing on the stereo.

I swallow back the lump of emotion in my throat. "It smells amazing in here."

When she lifts her eyes to meet mine, the smile she was giving Noah is replaced by a cautious one. "Sorry about the mess."

I shake my head, surveying their progress. A dozen sugar cookies cut in various Christmas shapes fill the cooling rack, and a fresh cookie sheet is half filled with another batch. "It smells delicious. Noah must be making me dinner."

Noah's eyes flash to mine, and he releases a delighted screech. "You can't eat cookies for dinner!" His eyes widen as he turns to his mom and lowers his voice. "Can we?"

Molly shakes her head. "Nope. Even Brayden needs to have real food for dinner." She points to me over Noah's shoulder. "His muscles will shrivel up and disappear if he doesn't eat healthy foods."

Noah curls his arm to flex his bicep. "I have muscles too, Rayden."

I grin. "I see that. You must be really strong."

Noah nods solemnly and offers me a candy-cane-shaped cookie cutter. "You want a turn?"

I arch a brow. "Are you sure?"

Noah nods. "I got to make the rest. You can help."

Rolling up my sleeves, I go to the sink and wash my hands, and when I turn back to the mother and son, there's a look on Molly's face I can't read. I'm aware of her eyes on me with every move—as Noah gives me the cookie cutter and shows me how to press it into the dough, and as we work together to put the cookie on the sheet with the others.

"I used to make cookies with my mom every Christmas," I tell Noah. "She'd make dozens and dozens of cookies of all kinds."

Noah's jaw drops. "Did you get to eat them all?"

"Not too many. Mom made them as gifts for every family we knew, so my brothers and Shay and I had to fight over what was left. My favorites were the thumbprint cookies with the jam in the middle." I hand Noah the cookie cutter and watch him cut several more candy canes. I'm impressed with his fine motor skills. When Lilly was his age, she'd tear up the dough trying to move it onto the cookie sheet, and she'd always get frustrated. Now, however, she's become quite the little chef. She and Noah would probably have a blast making cookies together, if Noah could deal with her bossing him around.

"My favorite is the frosting kind," he says, transferring the cookies carefully. "Mom said we can't frost these till tomorrow, but then I can eat one."

"After dinner," she says.

Noah scowls and mumbles, "After dinner," like he was hoping she'd forget that part.

"Speaking of dinner," she says. I almost expected her to avoid me, so I'm surprised when her eyes lock on mine. "I'm going to slide these into the oven and clean up our mess so we can make tonight's meal. How does spaghetti sound?"

"Yes!" Noah pumps his fist in the air before looking at me. "You like basketti?"

"I do," I say cautiously, my gaze flicking to Molly's. After last night, I don't want to overstep and interrupt their family time.

"Good," she says. "You can make the salad while I cook the rest." She brushes a lock of hair out of her face and leaves a streak of flour behind. "Noah, if you get cleaned up, you can watch cartoons until dinner."

The kid races from the kitchen and up the stairs like she just told him the entire cast of *Paw Patrol* was waiting in his room.

Molly pops the cookies into the oven and takes a deep breath as she surveys the mess. Without a word, she rolls her shoulders back and gets to work, packing up ingredients to return to the pantry, stacking mixing bowls and measuring cups, and wiping down the counter.

I go to the sink while she cleans, filling it with hot, soapy water to take care of the bigger mixing bowls.

"You don't have to do that."

I shoot her a glance over my shoulder and have to bite back a laugh. The kitchen might be cleaner, but she's not. "You look like you've been attacked by a bag of flour."

She props her hands on her hips. "I want to see you make cookies with a four-year-old without turning into a hot mess."

I turn off the water and turn to her. "I didn't say I didn't like it." I resist the urge to drag my focus down her body slowly, but it takes all my self-control. *Molly undone.* That's how I think of her when she's like this. I don't need an advanced psych degree to understand why I find this version of her even more irresistible than the perfectly pressed and put-together businesswoman who runs my banquet center. "I'm glad you're here."

"Really?"

Nodding, I step closer, aware of her eyes on me and the way her body tenses and then relaxes as I step into her personal space—like she's fighting an internal battle between the part of her that wants me to keep that distance and the part that wants me to close it.

"Careful, or I'll get flour on your fancy shirt." Her gaze darts over my shoulder—checking that we're still alone, no doubt—before returning to my face.

"I'll risk it." I brace my arms on the counter on either side of her and lean forward. "I never got the chance to apologize last night."

"Apologize?"

She's close enough to kiss. I don't. "I'm sorry I believed that video even for a minute."

"Who can blame you for that?"

"You deserved more. Better. I proved everything you were afraid of by believing the picture he was trying to paint."

"I forgive you, Brayden." She studies me. "Anyone would have believed it."

"Thank you." I lean an inch closer. "And I'm also glad you're here, because you said some pretty awful things and then left before I could defend myself."

Her eyes go guarded. "It was a bad day. I apologize if I insulted you somehow."

"Oh, you really did."

She swallows, and I can tell she wants to push this aside and be done with this conversation, but her pride won't let her. "How?"

"You said I only want you because I want to save you."

"I—"

I press two fingers over her lips. "And you said I thought you were ruined and damaged goods."

She swallows, and her eyes search my face, but she doesn't shy away from my touch or try to move my fingers.

"I don't think you're ruined. I think you're amazing, but that doesn't change that I wish I'd taken things more slowly with you. Nelson hurt you, and you spent so long hiding it that you were never able to heal."

She swallows, and tears well in her eyes. "I'm fine," she whispers against my fingers.

"You're strong as hell, and you've carried on impressively despite the pain, proving to everyone that he didn't—*couldn't*—ruin you."

She takes my wrist and pulls my hand away. "Thank you."

She's uncomfortable talking about this, but I'm not done. "I'm not going to pretend you're not broken, not when I can see your broken pieces in the way you push me away, the way you refuse to give us a chance."

"I tried and—"

"One day isn't trying. It's not even a toe in the water." I take a deep breath, reining in my frustration. "Jason Ralston accused me of wanting to pretend you don't have a reputation and only seeing the new Molly. You accused me as only seeing you as broken. You're both wrong. I see *all* of you—broken bits, scars, and beautiful, breathtaking strength. I see all of you, and I want all of you. I'm not interested in picking you apart or only taking the shiny bits. I'm in love with the woman who's all of those things."

"You're the first person who's ever made me think I might be worth that." Slowly, she lifts her hand to my face, and her touch is such a profound relief that I think I might shudder at the contact. "I keep thinking about the speech you gave at the wedding. I think you're right."

"About what?"

"We have a choice. About how we respond to our situations—both our mistakes and our misfortunes." She runs her thumb down my jaw. "I don't have to let those things convince me I'm not worthy of happiness. I can choose to be brave." She lifts onto her toes and brushes her lips against mine. "I want to be brave for you. To be selfish enough about my own joy to be with you even before I'm convinced I deserve you."

The single brush of her lips wasn't enough, but the air fills with the sound of little feet racing down the stairs, so I steal my kiss fast, sweeping my mouth across hers before tugging her bottom lip between my teeth. Her answering moan unravels something inside me, but she steps away fast—just as Noah skids to a halt in the living room beyond the kitchen, the remote already clutched in his little hand.

Molly's blue eyes are still on me, and I wink at her. She smiles and damn near knocks me over with shock when she grabs me by the shirt and kisses me hard on the mouth right in front of her son.

"Mommy, did you just kiss Rayden?" Noah asks.

Pulling back, she looks at me from under her lashes and licks her lips. "I did."

"Why?" he asks, though his attention is more on the TV than on us as he waits for his show to load.

"Because I love him," she says softly.

"Oh," Noah says. "I love him too."

I can only stare at her and try to remember how to breathe.

She grins. "Dinner?"

I blink and finally draw in a breath. "I think Christmas just came early."

"Rayden!" Noah shouts from the family room, annoyance lacing his tone. "I said I love you!"

Molly ducks her head and bites her lip.

I pinch her butt before going to work on the dishes. "I love you too, buddy."

thirty

MOLLY

Christmas Eve and Christmas morning with Brayden and Noah was an endless whirlwind of activity, smiles, long looks across the room (between Brayden and me), occasional pouting (from my overexcited preschooler), and joy. But, in typical excited-child fashion, Noah had Brayden and I out of bed before six, and now, just before seven a.m., all his presents are already unwrapped and he's happily playing with new toys in the middle of the family room floor.

Brayden sits next to me on the couch and hands me a fresh cup of coffee. We didn't sleep much last night, and I can't even blame Santa for that. Every time I look at him, I want to kiss and touch him, to remind myself this is real.

"You're my hero," I say, then take a sip. "Remind me I owe you later."

His eyes dance with mischief. "Trust me, I won't forget."

I bite back a grin and lean over to press a kiss to his shoulder. "Thank you," I whisper. "For this morning and . . . everything else. This is the best Christmas we've ever had."

He reaches between the couch cushions and pulls out a small, wrapped box. "You haven't opened your present yet."

I don't know what's going on inside me, but it feels like my heart and stomach just joined hands and did a somersault. "Brayden . . ."

"Just open it," he says gently.

Swallowing hard, I rip the wrapping off the box and lift off the top. Inside on the most delicate silver chain is a beautiful, diamond-encrusted key. It sparkles in the firelight. "It's beautiful."

"There's something else underneath." He lifts the jewelry's insert and reveals a bronze door key.

"I already have a key to your house."

"This isn't to my house."

"What's it to?"

He grins. "You'll find out later. This goes with it." He hands me a . . .

"Is that a *blindfold*?" I say, my eyes darting to Noah before going back to Brayden.

He chuckles. "That's not what it's for." He rakes his gaze over my flannel Christmas PJs and matching fuzzy socks, and his eyes glaze like I'm wearing nothing but the necklace he just gave me. "But now that you mention it, I do love a multipurpose gift."

A thrill runs through me at the thought. *Later.* "So what *is* it for, then?"

"You'll find out soon enough."

Luckily for me, *soon enough* comes in less than two hours when Brayden tells us to climb into his car for Jackson Christmas at the family cabin. I'm a little nervous to go after the Instagram video incident, but Noah's delight is enough to make me forget my selfish fears and put on my new necklace and a brave face.

"We have to give your mom her last Christmas gift," Brayden announces to Noah on the highway. He hands me the blindfold I thought was tucked into my drawer at home. "If you will."

I frown at him. "Is this necessary?"

"Absolutely. Christmas is about surprises, and I want this to be a surprise."

"Come on, Mama!" Noah says.

I give what I hope comes off as a carefree shrug, pull the blindfold down over my eyes, and sit in darkness, listening to Christmas carols for twenty minutes.

I feel the rumble of gravel beneath the car when Brayden pulls off the highway. "Where are we?"

"Don't tell her, Noah," Brayden says.

"I *won't!*" Noah says from the back, clearly indignant that Brayden thinks he might ruin the surprise.

The car jerks to a stop, and I wait as I listen to the sounds of Brayden's opening and closing door, then his feet and Noah's on gravel before my door opens and big hands guide me out of the car and . . . somewhere. Brayden holds both of my hands, and I take one blind step after another.

"Brayden?" All I can hear are birds and wind and . . . is that Christmas music in the distance?

"Be patient. We're almost there."

Noah snickers behind me—the little pest loves being in on the secret.

"Since you're blindfolded," Brayden says, "I'll do the honors of using your key for you, but just so you know, this is where it goes."

"And where might *this* be?"

He slips off my blindfold as he opens the big wooden door to his family's cabin. Just inside the door, everyone is gathered—his brothers, Ava, Nic, Ellie, Shay, his mom, Lilly, and even Teagan are here.

"Merry Christmas!" they shout in unison.

"The key," Brayden says softly into my ear, "because this is your cabin now too." I hear him swallow as I stare at his grinning family. "And them, because you asked for a family for Christmas. I wanted to give you mine."

I spin to face him. I don't even care that everyone's watching us or what they'll think of me as I throw my arms around his neck and kiss him for all I'm worth.

BRAYDEN

Eight months later . . .

I haven't been this nervous since high school when I took Penny Halcomb to the movies for the first time. I spent thirty minutes trying to decide whether to hold her hand, and by the time she reached over to grab mine, my palms were so sweaty that she pulled away. Not my proudest moment.

Ooh La La! is packed today. School might be back in session in Jackson Harbor, but tourist season doesn't die down until well after Labor Day. Regardless, I couldn't think of a better place to have to ask the most important question I've asked in my entire life. And I'm not above a little hot chocolate and cupcake bribery to get the answer I'm hoping for.

"I brought you here because I need to ask you something," I say, nudging the blue box across the table. My niece informed me that if it wasn't Tiffany's, it wasn't good enough, and while I don't believe Molly would care if I shopped at Tiffany's or Walmart, I wanted to get the very best. "Do you know what that is?"

Noah McKinley has chocolate all over his mouth and cupcake frosting on his fingers. He licks his lips, his eyes wide as he peers at the diamond ring inside the box. "A ring," he says.

I nod. "It's a special ring, and I want to give it to your mom." "Okay."

"The thing is, I wanted to make sure it was okay with you first. If your mom wears this ring, it means we're going to be a family forever. You, me, and her."

Noah licks the frosting off the top of his half-demolished cupcake and gets chocolate frosting on his nose. "We're already a family. Aren't we?"

God, I love this kid. He's right. Molly and Noah have lived with me since before Christmas, and the only thing this ring would change is their last name. It's a change I want badly. "Yeah, we are. But if your mom marries me, I'll be her husband and she'll be my wife." I wish I could read his thoughts, because suddenly his expression turns solemn. He puts down his cupcake and pokes at it with his finger. "What is it, buddy?"

His forehead wrinkles as he stares at the ring. "You'd be Mommy's husband?"

I nod, and my stomach knots as his expression grows more unsure. "If she wants me, yeah."

He returns to his cupcake, poking at the frosting and avoiding my eyes. "Then could you be my dad?"

It's hard to get the damn words out, but I nod. "If you let me, then I'd like that a lot."

His head snaps up, and his smile stretches all the way up to his dark eyes. "I'd let you!"

The sound of a shuddering sob pulls my attention from Noah and to the crowded restaurant beyond our table.

"Mommy!" Noah shouts, jumping out of the booth and rushing to wrap his chocolatey hands around her legs.

She stoops to hug her son, but her big blue eyes stay on me. Her flushed cheeks are stained with tears. "I think I ruined the surprise," she whispers. She scoops Noah into her arms and slides into the booth across from me. "I left the office early and saw your car here, so I thought I'd stop and . . ." She swallows. I can tell she's trying, but she can't stop smiling. "Sorry."

My heart races so fast that I'm surprised I'm not out of breath. "Are you? Sorry?"

She shakes her head and draws in a ragged breath. "No. Not at all."

Tears stream down her face, and Noah puts his hands on her cheeks, leaving chocolate fingerprints behind. "Will you wear Brayden's special ring so we can be a family?"

She meets my eyes across the table and reaches for my hand. "We're already a family."

"But can he be my *dad*?" Noah says, bouncing in her lap. "*Please*?"

She chokes on a sob and kisses the top of her son's head. "I'd love that." When she turns her attention back to me, I've moved to a knee on the floor by her seat, the ring in my hand.

"I wasn't supposed to do this here," I whisper, feeling all the crowd's attention as it turns to me.

"Do it anyway," she says.

I drag in a long breath. I was going to prepare a speech and give her the perfect romantic night. But maybe this is better. Because we aren't perfect. Our love is like our life: intense and unexpected and messy, and I wouldn't trade it for perfect, even if I could. "I want all the Prince dance parties in my kitchen and movie nights in the family room. I want a thousand more workouts where you yell at my brothers for trying to kill you and . . ." I scan the room and lower my voice. "A lot of other things I'd rather not detail with an audience."

She laughs.

"You and Noah are already Jacksons. Now I just want to hear it when people say your name. Marry me? Be my wife?"

She offers me her chocolate-smeared left hand. "You had me at Prince."

I slide on the ring and then rise to pick up Noah. "Sorry, buddy, but I'm going to need you to slide over here for a minute." I plop him into the booth across from his mom. "I want to kiss my fiancée." I cup Molly's face in my hands and lower my mouth to hers.

"Ew!" Noah says. "Enough kisses."

"Never," Molly whispers against my mouth, and I smile and kiss her again.

THE END

Thank you for reading *Wrapped in Love*, book four in The Boys of Jackson Harbor series. I hope you'll check out Carter Jackson's happily-ever-after in *Crazy for Your Love*, coming spring of 2019! If you'd like to receive an email when I release a new book, please sign up for my newsletter on my website. I hope you enjoyed this book and will consider leaving a review. Thank you for reading. It's an honor!

Acknowledgments

A huge thank-you goes out to everyone who helped make this book a reality. Most of all, a big thanks to my family. Brian, I couldn't have written Molly's story without your understanding and support. It came at one of the hardest times in my life, and you held my hand and told me I didn't have to be *okay*. Thank you for letting me break when I needed to. You're better than any hero I've ever written. To my kids, Jack and Mary, you are awesome and fun and smart. I'm the luckiest mama ever! Thank you for inspiring me to be my very best. To my mom and sisters, thank you for letting me turn the girls' beach vacation into my own writing retreat. Best deadline week ever. Of course, to my dad, brothers, sisters, in-laws, aunts, uncles, various cousins, and cousins-in-law, thank you for cheering me on—each in your own way.

I'm lucky enough to have a life full of amazing friends. Thanks to my writing friends who sprint with me and talk me off the ledge when the book looks like a disaster. To my BFF, Mira Lyn Kelly, who does more than her fair share of hand-holding, hair-stroking, and pep-talking, my eternal gratitude.

To everyone who provided me feedback on this story along the way—especially Heather Carver, Samantha Leighton, Tina Allen, Nancy Miller, Lisa Kuhne, Dina Littner, and Janice Owen—you're all awesome. Lauren Clarke, thank you for the insightful line and content edits. You push me to be a better writer and make my stories the best they can be. Thanks to Arran McNicol at Editing720 for proofreading. I've worked hard to put together this team, and I'm proud of it!

Thank you to the people who helped me package this book and promote it. Sarah Eirew took the gorgeous cover photo and did the design and branding for the whole series. A shout-out to Lisa Kuhne for trying to keep me in line and for putting in random extra hours when I need her most. Nina and Social Butterfly PR, I can't believe we're coming to the close of a full year together! It's been better than I could have asked. I've loved working with you and your awesome assistants, especially Chanpreet and Hilary! To all of the bloggers, bookstagrammers, readers, and reviewers who help spread the word about my books, I am humbled by the time you take out of your busy lives for my stories. My thank you isn't enough, but it is sincere. You're the best.

To my agent, Dan Mandel, for believing in me and always believing the best is yet to come. Thanks to you and Stefanie Diaz for getting my books into the hands of readers all over the world. Thank you for being part of my team.

Finally, a big thank-you to my fans. Because of you, I'm living my dream. I couldn't do it without you. You're the coolest, smartest, best readers in the world. I appreciate each and every one of you!

XOXO,
Lexi